"I insist you atten̶d̶ ̶t̶h̶e̶ ̶w̶e̶d̶d̶i̶n̶g̶. It's the least I can d̶o̶.̶ ̶I̶t̶ ̶won't be any trouble adding an extra seat. Elizabeth's not bringing anyone to the wedding. You can be my personal guest."

Elizabeth blanched at her father's observation, while her brother burst out laughing.

Lucky tugged at his T-shirt. It was getting harder by the second to find some graceful way out of staying. He didn't belong at such a fancy event. "Elizabeth? I could really use your help."

What was he doing, expecting someone he'd only known for a few hours to read his mind and come up with a convenient excuse for his departure?

"He can't be your personal guest," Elizabeth blurted out. Color flooded her cheeks.

Lucky let out the breath he didn't realize he'd been holding. This wedding was an important family occasion. Thankfully, someone had seen sense. He was already counting the minutes until he was on the road.

"Because he's already my plus-one."

Dear Reader,

Welcome to Violet Ridge! Wedding bells are ringing. For Lizzie, her father's nuptials are everyone's focus until she, thanks to an innocent mistake, winds up engaged to Lucky, a cowboy who's determined to keep to his bachelor ways. Fortunately for the unlikely pair, thinking of ways to break their fake engagement and sadly disappoint their families leads to finding out how much they have in common. And the love of a lifetime.

This story brought back memories of my wedding. My car didn't start, and my family helped me transfer the dress and other regalia to another vehicle. I made it to the venue at the same time as my groom. With my family holding on to superstitions, everyone was guiding me away from him and covering my eyes so I wouldn't see him before the ceremony. I hope this book stirs fun memories of your own.

I love to connect with my readers through my website and social media.

Happy reading!

Tanya

HEARTWARMING

Her Temporary Cowboy

———

Tanya Agler

⬦H HARLEQUIN
HEARTWARMING

HARLEQUIN®
HEARTWARMING™

ISBN-13: 978-1-335-47573-2

Recycling programs
for this product may
not exist in your area.

Her Temporary Cowboy

Harlequin Enterprises ULC
22 Adelaide St. West, 41st Floor
Toronto, Ontario M5H 4E3, Canada
www.Harlequin.com

Printed in U.S.A.

Tanya Agler remembers the first set of Harlequin books her grandmother gifted her, and she's been in love with romance novels ever since. An award-winning author, Tanya makes her home in Georgia with her wonderful husband, their four children and a lovable basset, who really rules the roost. When she's not writing, Tanya loves classic movies and a good cup of tea. Visit her at tanyaagler.com or email her at tanyaagler@gmail.com.

Books by Tanya Agler

Harlequin Heartwarming

The Single Dad's Holiday Match
The Soldier's Unexpected Family
The Sheriff's Second Chance
A Ranger for the Twins

Smoky Mountain First Responders

The Firefighter's Christmas Promise
The Paramedic's Forever Family

Rodeo Stars of Violet Ridge

Caught by the Cowgirl
Snowbound with the Rodeo Star

Visit the Author Profile page
at Harlequin.com for more titles.

There are family members whom we know from birth, and then there are people who become part of our families through time, shared experiences and loyalty.

This book is dedicated to my "brother" Matt. He and his family have become a part of my life, and I'm honored to be his little "sister."

CHAPTER ONE

"YOU'RE LIVING UP to your name, Lucky. You must not have a care in the world driving around in this." Lucky Harper's best friend, Sabrina Mac-Grath Darling, let out a long whistle as he ran his hand over the aluminum exterior of his combination horse trailer and RV.

Lucky almost pinched himself so he could make sure this was his home before following Sabrina into the living quarters. All the fourth-place finishes might never have landed him in the year-end rodeo finals, but they added up to a pretty penny, enough to pay off the trailer. Pretty good for a foster kid from upstate New York.

"Butterscotch likes it." His horse's comfort counted for something. Last winter, he'd helped a friend in Texas, not expecting anything in return, let alone the magnificent American quarter horse that knew a thing or two about tie-down roping. This year, he found himself collecting champion belt buckles, rather than landing smack-dab in the middle of the standings, like usual.

Sabrina explored the cabin's interior, where the small kitchen backed up to the tiny dining nook. Good thing he'd cleaned up, not that he skewed toward leaving messes around. That wasn't his nature. Neither was having too many possessions that might weigh him down. Except for Cherry's ring in his small safe. Even though they'd broken up the day before he'd been set to propose over a year ago, he still thought of it as her ring. Guess he shouldn't, as she was now married with a little one on the way.

"Then your horse has excellent taste." She settled herself on the black leather dinette seat and rubbed the granite tabletop that matched the counter near the sink. "Elizabeth Irwin said you can board Butterscotch here at the Double I Ranch. Even with my mother's upcoming wedding to her father, you don't have to worry about whether she'll take good care of him. When I quit my job, Elizabeth rolled my barn-manager position into the rest of her duties. She runs that stable with her usual efficiency."

Lucky shifted on his feet, the hardest part of today's visit upon him. "I'll make some coffee."

He gathered the filter and beans, his nerves getting the best of him. He'd put off telling her he wasn't attending the wedding as long as he could. The next rodeo beckoned, with its earthy smells and camaraderie among the crowd and contestants. He belonged there, in that exhilarating moment in the chute when adrenaline met nerves and anything could happen, spurring him to new arenas.

For a long time, he'd believed his best friends, people he considered his family, felt the same. During his first year on the circuit, he'd met Will Sullivan and they'd bonded over Will's border collie, who traveled with him, and the two became inseparable. A couple of seasons later, rodeo clown Sabrina completed their trio. Together, they'd celebrated their victories and nursed each other through sore muscles and broken bones. They prided themselves on one-upping each other on their birthdays with who could find the most unusual souvenir as a gift from their travels. Sabrina claimed the permanent title when she'd gifted them both tacky ceramic armadillos.

He thought the three of them would continue on their journeys indefinitely. But then Will's parents died, leaving him the Silver Horseshoe and a mound of debt. Will didn't look back—he'd left the rodeo to save his ranch and fallen in love with an energetic whirlwind in the process.

Months later, Sabrina had mysteriously accepted a job at the Double I before she revealed she was pregnant. Last winter, she and rodeo champion Ty Darling rekindled their romance before welcoming their daughter, Genie, and forming plans for a rodeo academy here in Violet Ridge.

Now he counted himself as the lone remaining rider, surprising since he hadn't grown up around horses like Will and Sabrina. But here he was, having his best season to date. Still, he wasn't fooling himself. The rodeo was merely a convenient excuse for turning down Sabrina's kind offer. Witnessing another wedding celebrating love and forever, after things had gone south with Cherry? No, thank you.

Hitting the road with Butterscotch was his chance to continue doing something he loved, somewhere he belonged. Maybe his next cobbled-together family would stick.

He fixed two cups of coffee and handed one to Sabrina. Then he sat across from her, breathing in the rich aroma. He never stinted on good beans. "About that."

Sabrina nodded her thanks. "Would you feel more comfortable boarding Butterscotch at the Silver Horseshoe? Will's been asking about you."

Lucky had spent many a relaxing day at his other best friend's neighboring ranch, but he didn't intend on visiting Will this time around. He shifted in his seat, already counting the minutes until this conversation would be over, and he'd be traveling to the next rodeo in Pueblo, a good three-hour drive from Violet Ridge. This time of year, the marigolds and other late-summer wildflowers would be blooming, although the aspens wouldn't change color for another month. While he wanted to lend his support to Sabrina, seeing as it was her mother getting married and all, this ranch was overwhelming with its rarefied air and all of its affluence. His childhood had been spent moving from foster home to foster home, never knowing where he'd be living the next day. As it was, all his worldly possessions fit into this trailer/RV, a throwback to the days when he had to be ready to shove his belongings into a black trash bag and head to the new family at a second's notice.

"Not really." Especially considering Butterscotch already had a home for tonight, an assigned stall in the rodeo stock pen. The organizers knew they could always count on Lucky to lend a helping hand wherever needed. A jack-of-all-trades, he was as adept at repairing fences as he was at wiring temporary structures.

Sabrina finished her cup of coffee and placed it in the stainless-steel sink. "Good. Then it's settled. Find Elizabeth Irwin. You know her, right? Auburn hair, green eyes and very pretty. Let her know you're ready to unload Butterscotch."

"We've never been formally introduced." That admission came easily. Admitting he wasn't staying for the wedding? That was hard. Disappointing someone he loved like a sister was rougher than eating dirt in the rodeo arena.

"What?" Sabrina laughed before she realized he was serious. "Then today's your lucky day."

Hardly, as he'd be hurting Sabrina. And, for the record, the luckiest days of his life were the days he'd bought a bus ticket for Steamboat Springs, Colorado, and landed at the Cattle Crown Ranch. Little did he know the owner was a hall-of-fame rodeo competitor who'd ended up taking Lucky under his wing and preparing him for the circuit.

Sabrina opened the door and exited, and light flooded into the small space. The August heat was rather stifling, and Lucky tugged at the edge of his T-shirt. He picked up his weathered brown cowboy hat and placed it on his head. She was at the horse trailer part of the RV by the time he caught up with her. "You're going too fast."

She shrugged and introduced herself to his gelding. "That's because there's so much to do." She cooed soft words to Butterscotch, who nudged her as if they'd known each other for years. "As soon as we find out whether Elizabeth wants you in the paddock or a stall, we'll be back for you."

"I'm mighty thankful for the invitation." Lucky fought for control of the situation. The longer he took, the hotter the water he'd find himself treading in.

"I'm the thankful one since you supported me through this. I can't believe my mother's back in my life, let alone marrying the owner of the ranch where I used to work." Sabrina had interrupted him before he could make his excuses. "Evie and Gordon mesh well together. Best of all, Elizabeth will be my stepsister and Genie's aunt. A new family, so to speak. Follow me."

The water went from warm to scalding. *A new family.* He'd give anything for an old family. "It's mighty kind of you to invite me to the rehearsal dinner." Especially since he'd never met the bride before. He'd been taken aback when he'd discovered his friend, who couldn't sing a note, was the daughter of one of the most recognizable singers in the world, Evalynne, known to her friends as Evie. He'd hummed along to Evalynne's hit "Misty Mountain" on the bus ride from New York to Steamboat Springs at least twelve times, if not more.

"Evie's excited to meet you, and Genie loves her uncle Lucky. You have the magic touch with her. I can't believe my daughter is already eight months old."

Sabrina was making his announcement more difficult by the second, but she was happy with her new husband, Ty. He'd kept waiting for an offer to teach at their rodeo academy, but she never broached the subject. Instead, she congratulated Lucky on his season, telling him he still had his best rides ahead of him. She didn't need her old friend anymore, and neither did Will, who'd connected with the love of his life, Kelsea, last May. It wasn't their fault they'd found love. He just wished there was a place for him here in Violet Ridge, one of the prettiest places he'd ever had the fortune of visiting. Staying longer would only make him feel like a third wheel and remind him of what he lost when Cherry chose someone else.

He followed Sabrina past a field where a bull snorted and pawed the ground. "Speaking of the rodeo…"

"What about it?" Sabrina stopped and faced Lucky.

He'd known Sabrina too long to keep up the pretense any longer. "I'm not staying for the wedding."

She searched his face, and her jaw dropped. "You're serious."

He nodded and tipped his hat. "It's a family affair."

As hard as it was to admit it, Will and Sabrina were no longer his family. They'd moved on without him. His heart ached once again at losing the people who'd come to mean everything to him, but he was used to it. He survived before, and he'd carry on.

"You're like the brother I never had and always wanted, Lucky." Sabrina came over and laid her hand on his arm, her engagement-and-wedding-ring set digging into his skin. "You're my family."

Those brown eyes gazed at him with care and concern. Somehow, he had to let her down gently. Ty would more than make up for Lucky's absence. Hadn't she made it clear last Christmas when she and Ty separated themselves at the Mile of Lights holiday display that she was ready to move on without Lucky? At the time, Lucky thought he'd be helping Sabrina, lending his support during the last stages of her pregnancy by surprising her at the apple orchard where the Mile of Lights was being held. Instead of a happy reunion, though, Sabrina had gone off with Ty, leaving Lucky with Will and Kelsea until Lucky found an excuse to head out of town. It was a good thing Ty was the perfect fit for the woman he cared for like a sister. That helped soften the blow.

"You know I'd do anything for you." And he would, except he couldn't stay for the wedding. Anything but that after he thought he and Cherry were destined for each other, only to be dumped without a backward glance. No wedding bells for him, then or ever. "But this might be my only chance to make the finals. Every rodeo counts."

"Of course, you'd bring up the one reason I can't stay mad at you. As it is, I'm taking a three-week leave of absence from my rodeo-clown position to support Evie and Gordon." She released his arm and pushed on the sliding doors of the stable. "At least you'll stay for the prewedding festivities, right?"

"I just came to give Genie the rocking horse." The one he'd carved and then painted in his off-hours. "Hold on a second."

He went back to the trailer's storage compartment and returned with his gift for Genie.

"Lucky, it's beautiful. You made this?" Sabrina

gasped and ran her hand across the sturdy oak that formed the horse's body with connecting wooden legs. He'd painted Genie's name on the strong base. "The craftsmanship is breathtaking. Look at that saddle and the tiny pink heart on each side."

Tears welled in the corners of her eyes, and she hugged him. He'd carved it for Sabrina as much as Genie.

Separating from his friend was almost impossible, but he'd manage. "I'm better with smaller pieces of wood. Whittling's more soothing, but this came out well. Since I delivered it, I'm heading out."

"Already? Lucky Harper, you can stay in one place for longer than ten minutes. Mold won't grow on you." Sabrina popped her hands on her hips and stared at him while something outside the stable caught his eye.

More like a someone. A little someone, probably five or six, by the way she held her teddy bear with tears running down her face. Was she looking for Sabrina? His heart went out to the little girl, those pink cheeks tugging at his heartstrings even though he'd never set eyes on her before. A few feet away from the stable, she stopped on the gravel path and sniffled. Her eyeglasses fell to the ground. She bent over for them and released her grip on her teddy.

Out of nowhere, a UTV barreled toward her. Horror gripped his chest when he noticed the driver was talking to the passenger and probably couldn't see the child. There was only one thing to do and no time to waste.

He sprinted away from the stable and scooped the girl up under his arm. Rolling, he landed on the other side of the path, the UTV missing them by mere inches. Shouts from the vehicle reached him while it parked on the nearby grass. Pain jolted through his shoulder, but the little girl was fine. That was what counted.

At least he thought she was until she burst out crying and wailing at the top of her lungs.

It seemed as though this wasn't his lucky day after all.

IN THE SMALL office next to the tack room, Elizabeth Irwin studied the blueprints for the row of four modern, updated bunkhouses she wanted to build behind the stable. Anything to keep busy and away from the bustle of her father's wedding.

The current bunkhouse needed too much work with the upgrades costing more than new construction. Ten minutes ago, the architect had finally sent her the plans, and she opened each rendering on her tablet. The elevation view gave her a better sense of what they'd look like from the side and back. Constructing these would allow the Double I Ranch to retain long-term employees who wanted to live on site and hire more temporary workers for seasonal work. Female cowhands could have their own facility, and there'd also be ways to accommodate families. The best place for these bunkhouses was her father's favorite riding trail, and he always shut down any discussion of more utilitarian uses for the land. Sometime before the wedding, Elizabeth needed to find a minute alone with her father so she could convince him to approve the architect plans for the bunkhouses.

The Double I was the best ranch around, and these improvements would only make it that much better. While she loved every day riding herd with Andromeda and overseeing the stable, her favorite time of year was upon them, only days away from one of the three annual roundups when she and the cowhands moved the cattle to the autumn field. Preparations for that gave her a reason to hide out here in her stable office, far from the rest of her family.

A commotion arose outside the stable, and the horses whinnied their discontent at the sudden uproar. Elizabeth was unsure of whether to calm them or check on the cause, and it wasn't often she was unsure of anything.

After jamming on her red cowboy hat, she passed the stalls, taking care to keep a calm presence for the horses' benefit. There hadn't been this kind of noisy disruption since that camera crew finished filming the commercial ad last Christmas. She found her beloved Appaloosa, Andromeda, and murmured some sweet words until her mare's agitation settled. Then she quickened her pace and found bedlam outside. Her good friend and future stepsister, Sabrina, was on her knees next to Elizabeth's niece, Audrey, who was practically inconsolable. Two of the newest ranch workers were arguing with each other next to a parked UTV, and a man she didn't know sat on the ground, rubbing his left shoulder.

She hurried over and kneeled beside Audrey, brushing her niece's long auburn hair, which matched her own, away from her face. "Sweetheart, are you okay?"

Audrey sniffled and bit her lip. "Aunt Elizabeth, I want to go home." She threw her arms around Elizabeth, her tears wet and warm against the thin fabric of her tank top under her unbuttoned plaid flannel shirt. "My glasses are dirty, my knee is scraped and Zack says I'm gonna mess up the wedding."

Her chest tightened at her nephew Zack's comment to his younger sister. That sounded like something her brothers would have said to her twenty-five years ago when she was six, the same as Audrey now, although thankfully they'd grown up since then. If anything, she didn't see them enough with Audrey's father, Jeff, working as an attorney in Boston, and Ben stationed in Germany with his United States Air Force unit. Jeff was already here for the wedding, and Ben would arrive late tomorrow night. Elizabeth squeezed her niece tight before reaching for the bandanna she always kept in her rear pocket.

She located Audrey's purple frames on the lush green grass and wiped the dirt from them. With care, she placed them back on the bridge of Audrey's nose. "One problem solved."

Then she removed her hat and plopped it on her niece's head. *Way too big.* Those sniffles turned to giggles, followed by a lone hiccup, since it covered her forehead and most of the frames.

"I like you." Audrey grinned.

Something stirred within Elizabeth, and she wanted to protect her niece, but first she intended to get to the bottom of what had just transpired. "What happened?"

Before Audrey could answer, her father marched over with Evie MacGrath keeping pace beside him. America's favorite bluegrass singer was a perfect match for her father. In sync with their steps, the two also meshed in other ways. They both strived to be the best in their chosen professions while emphasizing their relationships with their adult children. More than anything, though, Evie made Dad happy with her vibrant personality and positivity. He beamed whenever she was around, and they interacted like they'd known each other for decades rather than mere months.

Evie reached Audrey first, and her niece left Elizabeth's side for the older woman who was set to become her grandmother and the new Mrs. Irwin on Saturday, a mere two days away.

"Audrey, sweetheart. Are you okay?" Evie asked.

A second hiccup was Audrey's answer, and Dad pulled the workers aside, the intensity in his dark eyes reflecting his feelings about the matter. The fact that their conversation was too muted for Elizabeth to hear only confirmed how upset her father was. He was using his quiet voice of steel that cut to a person's core. She was watching the workers departing, heads down and shame-faced, when she spotted someone hiding behind an aspen in the distance. She stood and crooked her finger. "Zack, please come here."

Now Elizabeth would get some answers. Her eight-year-old nephew merely gulped and hung his head, but did as ordered. Sweat dripped off his forehead, probably due to the sweltering August day as much as his nerves. He lifted his head in time to catch the tail end of one of his grandfather's patented Irwin glares. "Sorry, Audrey." Zack kicked at the dirt with his new boots. "You're not gonna ruin the wedding."

"Zachary Gordon Irwin, we're going to find your father and have a talk about being a gentleman," Gordon said. "I had several such discussions with your father and your uncle. Somewhere along the line, they received the message."

With a nod in Evie's direction, he reached for

his grandson's hand and headed toward the main house.

So much for finding some time to talk to her father this afternoon. The down payment for those new bunkhouses was coming due soon if they were going to get a head start before winter. She'd have to get his approval some time before he left on his and Evie's honeymoon.

Evie oohed when she saw Audrey's knee. "Shall we get that cleaned up?" She scooped up the little girl with the same care and loving tenderness as she did whenever she reached for her beloved guitar. "A couple of my crew members like colorful bandages, so I have extra."

"I need Teddy." Elizabeth handed her niece her special bear.

Evie smiled as Audrey cleaned the dirt off her bear. "And if your teddy has a boo-boo, too, we'll kiss his knee and make it better," Evie said.

In no time, the crowd thinned to only her, Sabrina and the man sitting on the grass observing everyone, and everything, like a hawk. Unlike those birds of prey, however, the man seemed as though he didn't have a care in the world, but was just watching the world go by.

Sabrina walked over to the man and offered him her arm, making Elizabeth feel rather guilty for not thinking of that sooner. "And that, Lucky, is my mother and future stepfather." She helped him rise and glanced at the main house before tugging on her long brown braid. "Would you mind if I check on Genie and Ty while you talk to Elizabeth about Butterscotch? Something must have happened for Ty to lose track of Audrey and Zack like that."

Without waiting for a response, Sabrina trailed in Evie's footsteps, calling for them to wait for her. That left Elizabeth alone with someone named Lucky. He dusted the grass and dirt off his T-shirt, the color of which matched the electric blue of his eyes. Wincing, he stretched his shoulder, bringing attention to the muscles under the shirt. Then he noticed her and grinned. "You must be Sabrina's friend Elizabeth. It's supposed to be my lucky day meeting you."

"Lucky day? Hardly." Even if he had a grin that would melt ice cream. Elizabeth bristled at Sabrina matchmaking before Evie and Dad's wedding. She'd have a little talk with her friend, and ask her to cease and desist any further efforts to pair Elizabeth with anyone. Just because Sabrina found her true love with Ty Darling didn't mean everyone wanted a relationship. The ranch was enough for her. That, and getting her father to accept her contributions to the family's legacy. All she wanted was a chance to prove to him she could run the ranch.

Then she saw a flicker of pain cross Lucky's face. He wasn't good at hiding secrets, if that look was any indication. "Now that everyone has scattered, can you fill me in on what I missed?"

"Uh, um, the important thing is that little girl is okay…" Lucky averted his gaze and searched the ground until he picked up a battered brown cowboy hat, grimacing as he raised his shoulder. "Congratulations on the upcoming wedding. Couldn't happen to a nicer family."

Taken aback at his sentiment, she concentrated on how he was flexing his biceps. Something had happened to this man on her land, and she'd find out what and fix whatever was wrong. "What happened to your shoulder?"

"Must have landed on it funny." So he knew more about the incident than he was letting on. She bristled at the fact some outsider had inside knowledge about her ranch that she didn't. He covered his longish, dirty blond hair with his hat. "I'll be on my way so your family can enjoy the festivities."

"I'll enjoy them better once you get that shoulder examined. I won't take no for an answer." With a glance toward the stable, she saw one of the grooms bringing out Margarita, her father's favorite mare, for exercise. She needed to deliver some instructions before she accompanied Lucky to urgent care. "Wait here."

In no time, she was back, but Lucky wasn't where she'd left him. She searched the area and came up empty. Where'd he go? He'd injured himself on her ranch and, although she still wasn't clear on the sequence of events, that made him her responsibility.

She passed the field where the wedding would occur in two days. The wildflowers were in full bloom, providing the perfect backdrop for the ceremony, along with the most spectacular view of the Rocky Mountains anywhere. Tomorrow, the arch would be constructed and the chairs assembled for the guests, one hundred of the bride and groom's closest friends and family. As of now, the weather promised a Saturday of sunshine, so the event should be the special day her father deserved.

Glancing this way and that, she found no sign of Lucky and headed to the guesthouse, where Sabrina and her husband were staying. In the driveway sat a behemoth of a horse trailer, and Elizabeth found Lucky at the rear of the vehicle. She stopped at the sight of a gorgeous American quarter horse, and her estimation of the man before her rose considerably. "Beautiful horse. Does she follow instructions better than her owner?"

"His owner. His name's Butterscotch," Lucky corrected her and patted the horse before pulling the door closed. "Thank you for the offer about my shoulder, but I'm due in Pueblo later today."

He retrieved the keys and winced, rubbing that same left shoulder. "You should reconsider.

It won't take long to have someone examine you, and it would set my mind at ease."

"This here's nothing. I've hurt myself worse at the rodeo," Lucky insisted and headed toward the driver's door.

By his own admission, he was well enough to leave. That ought to be enough to satisfy her, but she was convinced he was underplaying the injury for some unknown reason. This close to the wedding, however, she wouldn't press him. "Then have a good day."

Unsure of why he caused such a powerful reaction in her, Elizabeth headed to the stable with a firm intent on checking on Andromeda and the other nine horses, all of whom didn't care for sudden, loud noises. She didn't have time to dwell on cowboys who refused a little attention, not with her ranch chores calling her name, followed by a final fitting for her bridesmaid dress before dinner.

She halted in her boots when she heard her name. Turning, she faced Lucky heading her way. "I changed my mind. Could you keep an eye on Butterscotch while I find the closest urgent-care clinic?"

His earnest face held her gaze. He placed the needs of his horse above his welfare, and that was an admirable trait. Good thing he had plans to compete in this weekend's rodeo. Someone with those eyes and a love of horses could disrupt her schedule in a hurry if she wanted that kind of disturbance. Which she didn't. The best way of ensuring Lucky's quick departure from her life was to get him cleared for the rodeo so he could move on before nightfall.

"Better yet, I'll unload him and get him settled in the stable. Then I'll take you myself."

CHAPTER TWO

THE PUEBLO RODEO would commence tomorrow night, but Lucky wouldn't be a part of it. The physician's assistant had cleared him with a warning. The shoulder was only bruised, yet one wrong fall could leave Lucky sidelined for the rest of the season, if not longer. Rest was recommended, and he'd done the math in his head. Sitting out this weekend shouldn't impact his current position in the standings, and he wasn't scheduled to participate in another rodeo for two weeks after that. Missing the rest of the season, however, would end any chance of heading to Vegas in December for the finals and instead have him searching for a cowhand position to see him through the fall and winter.

Emerging from Elizabeth's new truck at her ranch, and impressed at all the bells and whistles, Lucky considered the road ahead. Will and Sabrina had moved on, and he'd best do the same. He'd drive to Pueblo tonight and offer his help to the rodeo director. Even without competing, there had to be some way Lucky could make himself useful. Wherever he landed, he always met a friend who needed a hand. He slammed the door and gave her a nod. "Thanks for the ride. Appreciate it."

She came around the front of the vehicle and halted some distance from him. "What about dinner? Can I get our cook, Tammy, to prepare you a meal while I see to Butterscotch?"

How had he forgotten his gelding was in Elizabeth's paddock rather than in his trailer? It would take some time to transfer him and get him settled before they hit the road. With dusk approaching, he should really turn down Elizabeth's offer for a bite of supper. "Thanks, but I'd best be loading him so I can be on my way."

It was a shame he had to leave so soon, what with his earlier glimpse at Elizabeth's family. Three generations together at one ranch, looking out for one another. He'd have given anything for a chance to get to know them better. Then again, leaving now was for the best before something happened and he became too attached. Families had a way of closing their ranks inward, leaving him to look in from the outside.

"Did I hear you correctly? You're going to Pueblo tonight? I thought you weren't attending this week's rodeo to let your shoulder heal. My brother Ben isn't arriving until tomorrow. You can sleep in his room, unless you'd be more comfortable in your RV." Elizabeth gave him a once-over and shook her head as if exasperated. "You already decided, didn't you? At least wait until morning and have a good dinner first. Then you can set out bright and early. The deliveries for the wedding will commence shortly after dawn. We're on a tight schedule with the florist, the caterers and the bakers. I usually arrive at the stable around five a.m., and I can help you load Butterscotch then."

More proof of what a special family occasion this was. "Thanks, but it'd be a sight better waking up in Pueblo. I'll gather Butterscotch and be out of your hair within the hour."

"It's your decision, but surely you can stay long enough for dinner. Tonight's the last night Tammy is cooking until after the wedding. She's the best cook west of the Mississippi, and she and her husband, JR, he's our foreman, have worked at the Double I for nearly thirty years. They will be guests, like most of the ranch staff. Dad said, 'Tammy knows me better than most of Violet Ridge. She's family.' The newest hires and a few temporary workers are in charge of the cattle on Saturday. I'll check on them early that morning. I have it down to the minute how long it will take me to get ready."

If he were fortunate enough to be part of her family, one that incorporated its staff into its ranks, he'd lap up every minute with them rather than spending it in the stable. "Why are you spending so much time away from the festivities and your niece and nephew? Aren't you happy about the wedding?"

Elizabeth had already started toward the horses. She stopped and turned toward him, a scowl on her very attractive face. "Of course I am. Evie makes Dad happy. It's just that I'm more comfortable wearing these clothes." She plucked at her jeans and plaid shirt layered over a tank top. "And I'd rather not twist my ankle in the strappy high heels I have to wear in the meadow. I've been told to leave my favorite red cowboy hat in the tack room, too."

She tipped her red hat over her long auburn hair, which was tied back in a ponytail. The dark red highlights were more like the sky at sunrise than the deep orange and pink hues of the setting sun off in the distance. Her fresh heart-shaped face, with its wide apple cheeks and green eyes, had a timeless appeal.

So she was pretty. She was also practically in charge of this ranch and way out of his league.

With no warning, his stomach rumbled, reminding him that Pueblo was three hours away. He'd counted on restocking his RV refrigerator this afternoon after making sure Butterscotch was settled nicely in the stock quarters. With this delay, he hadn't had the chance, and taking up Elizabeth on her offer of a meal would only set him back thirty minutes or so. There weren't that many fast-food places to stop on the highway.

Maybe he could convince Elizabeth to eat dinner with him. He'd love any advice or recommendations she could give for soft-shoe boots for Butterscotch during their long hauls to rodeos. In the waiting room, they'd talked about farriers, and she seemed knowledgeable about the subject, as well as easy to talk to.

Unless she had plans with her family. He blinked. She might even have a boyfriend or husband, for all he knew. Many cowgirls wore their wedding rings on a necklace or took them off for the day, donning them again after ranch chores were completed.

"Elizabeth." His stomach growled again, and she turned and faced him. His sheepish grin summed up everything right now. "I'd be mighty obliged to accept your dinner offer on one condition."

She placed her arms over her chest and arched an eyebrow in that same imperious manner her father had done earlier. If only he'd had an adult give him that type of glare growing up. While there was a hint of rebuke in such a look, someone had to care to stop everything and deliver their two cents.

"Really? We don't know each other well enough to make any conditions on each other." She tapped her dusty red boot and then grimaced. "Then again, you hurt your shoulder on my ranch. Name it."

"I'd like you to eat with me."

She checked her watch and considered his offer. Then she nodded. "Dinner makes sense. I have a long night ahead of me. This wedding is playing havoc with everyone's routine, and the animals don't know the difference between Saturday and any other day." Then her stomach delivered a long growl, and she looked embarrassed. "You're right. Dinner sounds pretty good right about now."

"See, that wasn't too hard to admit, was it?" he asked.

"You already got one concession out of me. Don't press your luck." She laughed, and he knew she was teasing him. She hooked her arm through his right one, almost eye level with him since she was taller than average, and he was a couple inches shy of six feet. "I know a shortcut."

"It's mighty kind of you to accept my invitation." He dipped his head in her direction. Then again, he shouldn't be too surprised. Any future stepsister of Sabrina was bound to be nice.

"I have an ulterior motive. I'm going to observe your shoulder and make sure you can drive." Elizabeth kept her arm entangled in his. "You must have landed on it pretty hard, considering they ordered X-rays."

"I've had worse falls, and there was no calf

struggling to get free." Like in his event of tie-down roping.

Besides, Lucky would throw himself in front of that UTV all over again for this moment with the pretty cowgirl, not to mention that little girl, Audrey.

Elizabeth guided him toward the path leading to the main ranch house, and Lucky's mouth dropped. Never had he seen such an impressive mansion in the mountains. A circular pathway, full of SUVs and newer model trucks, led to an expansive front porch. Huge flagstones lined the facade, and the length of the house went as far as the eye could see. To the right, he spotted a pair of Adirondack rocking chairs on the long wraparound porch. Wisps of smoke curled out of the stone chimneys, rising higher than the golden aspens surrounding the area. This was a far cry from the houses he was shuttled between as a foster child.

She opened the front door, her arm still hooked through his. "What's your preference? Chili? Stuffed jalapeños? Steak? I'm sure Tammy will have something to suit your fancy."

"Steak would sure hit the spot."

Out of nowhere, something latched on to his legs with the force of a stampeding bull. "You're back." Lucky glanced down and found Audrey attached to him.

Someone flicked on the lights in a nearby room. "Surprise!"

Elizabeth released his arm, and his jaw dropped. She led him toward a massive living room filled with people. Over a stone fireplace that extended to the ceiling was a sprawled banner with the words *Thank you, Lucky* drawn with every imaginable shade of crayon. Gordon strode toward him, his hand outstretched.

"Lucky, how's that shoulder?" He whapped him on the back, and Lucky feared his right one now might be worse off than the one he'd injured earlier. "Audrey told us the entire story. You saved her life."

Evie approached and hugged Gordon's arm. "Audrey and her teddy bear told us. It was the cutest thing. We both owe you a world of thanks for saving her and threw this together while Elizabeth and you were spending time together."

Two more adults came over. The man gave Lucky a hard whack on his bad shoulder, and it was all he could do not to cry out in pain. "I'm Jeff Irwin, Audrey's father. My wife, Nicole, and I—" he tilted his head in the woman's direction "—were on a conference call with our law firm back home in Boston. The call went on longer than we expected, and we didn't realize Zack and Audrey went outside to explore the ranch. Thank you for looking out for our little girl."

Elizabeth turned to him, her green eyes clouded with surprise. "We've been together all this time and whenever I asked, you changed the subject. Now I know why."

He caught Audrey staring at him with stars in her young eyes and waved away the praise. "The UTV was slowing down. I'm sure of it."

Jeff and Nicole talked with him for some time, asking all sorts of questions about what he did and where he was from. At the first break in the conversation, Elizabeth passed a plate of food to Lucky. He salivated at the steak and roasted potatoes.

"Sorry, it might be cold," she said. "It's been thirty minutes."

That long? It seemed like five minutes, but it sure was nice feeling like he was part of the family all this time. He accepted it with pleasure. "Thank you."

"Steak and potatoes, along with some appetizers. Your favorite, right?"

"You know it." Always grateful for his favorite fixings, he delivered a wide smile for her thoughtfulness. It might be stereotypical for a rodeo rider to favor steak, but there'd been nights he went to bed with an empty stomach so he never took anything like this for granted.

"That's Elizabeth. Efficient to the core. Most of our friends wanted skis or a new saddle growing up. She asked for a computer," Jeff said, smiling.

Lucky looked Elizabeth's way and saw her smile tighten.

"We already owned the top saddles, and I prefer riding to skiing. To me, it was an easy decision. Lots you could do or find out with a computer," Elizabeth said. "Come on, Jeff. You've called me worse things than efficient, but we're older now and should be past that."

"True, and I'm sorry for sounding like an obnoxious brother." Jeff reached out and brought his wife close. "It's hard not to fall into the same habits now that I'm back. You turned out okay for a little sister."

"Now I see who Zack and Audrey take after with their quibbles. You two make me happy Evie's an only child." An older woman with short silver hair and a metal cane headed their way, her chin held high. Wrinkles lined her sun-beaten face. She stopped and stared at Lucky before giving a swift nod. "I've heard many stories about you from my granddaughter, Sabrina, all good. I'm the mother of the bride, and you can call me Grandma Eloise."

Her eyes twinkled, and Lucky liked her on the spot. What he would have given to have met an honorary grandmother years ago. As it was, he'd take this one in a heartbeat. "Nice to meet you, Grandma Eloise. I thought you and your husband couldn't attend." Sabrina had mentioned their health ailments.

"Bob's waiting for me in Texas." She crooked a finger, and he moved a few steps closer. "Just between us, he's having the time of his life without me looking over his shoulder all the time."

Lucky doubted that and held out his plate. "Care for a stuffed mushroom?"

"I never turn down sharing food with an attractive man." She accepted the one closest to the edge. Eloise's tone was light, and he found her delightful. Her face grew more pensive. "Speaking of attractive men, Bob is beside himself for missing his daughter's wedding."

"I can't attend, either," he said between mouthfuls of food. "I'm leaving tonight."

Audrey let out a gasp. "You can't go yet. My teddy hasn't thanked you."

Evie gave Gordon a firm look. Gordon approached him, his eyes piercing Lucky with the same glare he'd given Zack earlier. "What's this about missing the wedding?"

Lucky placed the plate on the hearth. "I'm heading out for the Pueblo rodeo."

"I should have known you were competing there." Gordon nodded with appreciation in his gaze. He was a longtime supporter of the sport and the primary drive behind the Violet Ridge Rodeo Roundup, the first event of the year. "You're having quite the season. Congratulations."

"We've kept Lucky long enough. Now that

you've finished your dinner, I'll help you load Butterscotch into the trailer," Elizabeth said.

"Slow down, Elizabeth," Gordon admonished his daughter. "We need to show Lucky some hospitality, considering he saved Audrey's life."

This close to Elizabeth, he heard her breath hitch. "I thought I was being hospitable, offering to help with his horse. Gorgeous American quarter horse. Calm temperament and a large eye. One of the finest I've ever seen."

Gordon faced him, his lips drawn in a straight line. "My daughter gets caught up with horses naturally. Now, since Sabrina's one of your best friends, and Evie's happy when Sabrina's happy, I insist you attend the wedding as my personal guest, especially considering you saved Audrey. It won't be any trouble adding an extra seat since Elizabeth's not bringing anyone to the wedding."

By his side, Elizabeth blanched at her father's observation, while Jeff burst out laughing. Lucky tugged at his T-shirt. It was getting harder by the second to find some graceful way out of staying. While he'd do anything for Sabrina and already thought the world of her grandmother, he didn't belong at such a fancy event. He appealed to Elizabeth by reaching out and squeezing her hand. "Elizabeth? I could really use your help."

What was he doing, expecting someone he'd only known for a few hours to read his mind and come up with a convenient excuse for his departure?

"He can't be your personal guest…"

Lucky let out the breath he didn't realize he'd been holding. Color flooded back into Elizabeth's cheeks, and relief flowed through him. This wedding was a family event, and he didn't belong here. As it was, being thanked this much for being in the right place at the right time was downright uncomfortable, and he counted the minutes until he was on the road.

"Because he's already my plus-one."

ELIZABETH GROANED AND rubbed her head before donning her work gloves in the stable. A good hour of mucking out stalls would clear her mind. The horses depended on her and, whether or not her father recognized her contributions, the ranch needed her.

What had she been thinking earlier this evening, announcing to her entire family that Lucky was her date for Dad's wedding? No sooner had she made the biggest mistake she'd made since dating Jared, than her brother scoffed at her declaration. Only after Nicole pointed out that Elizabeth and Lucky had walked into the living room arm in arm, and she knew what his favorite meal was, did Jeff let the matter drop.

Pride, pure and simple, had sucked her into a tight vise. It would serve her right if Lucky loaded

Butterscotch into the trailer in the middle of the night and went on his merry way.

"I don't even know his last name." She exerted extra force in shoveling the hay from Andromeda's stall.

"Harper."

Her heart nearly exploded out of her chest at the sudden sound of his voice. She glanced backward, only to find him picking hay off his jeans. "Oh, I'm sorry." For everything, starting with asking him to stay for dinner and then putting him on the spot like she had. Now she only compounded her error by accidentally pelting him with discarded hay. "Let me get you a towel."

He brushed off his jeans and his T-shirt. "I'm good."

Why did he go along with her? What was in it for him? She was about to ask when her father entered the stable. Normally, Dad left the horses to her care, his entrepreneurial enterprises extending beyond the ranch to the arena named after her family in town. He managed all that while she coordinated management of the extensive stable, the hiring and firing of cowhands and everyone's schedule. While the upcoming wedding and cattle drive had knocked everyone's schedule out of whack, horses didn't care about orange blossoms or cake flavors. Instead, they went about their business, which was comforting in and of itself.

"Lucky, I'm glad you're here. Since the two of you are dating, it figures you'd follow Elizabeth when she left abruptly like that. That's real nice."

Elizabeth bristled at the implication she'd run from the impromptu celebration. She never ran from anything. She had merely waited for what she thought was a reasonable amount of time before making her excuses, namely the horses.

Lucky looked away. "Well, yes, I suppose so… but I also came out here to check on Butterscotch."

Dad murmured some words to his favorite mustang, Margarita. Then he reached into his pocket and brought out apple slices. The mare nuzzled his hand and neighed her thanks. "You're modest. I like that about you, and it's good to meet a man who values a horse. You can tell a lot about a person by how they treat animals. Elizabeth, this one's a keeper. You should have brought your boyfriend to the ranch sooner."

She considered correcting her father's misperception about Lucky, but she'd start with the easier subject first. "Dad, speaking of people and animals, those two temporary cowhands won't work out." She leaned the shovel against the closest stall door. "They didn't show up for their shift. I tried calling their cell phones, but no answer."

If they were this unreliable now, how would

they measure up next week at the annual cattle roundup?

"Didn't you get my message?" Dad folded his arms across his chest. "Those were the men who almost ran over Audrey. Jeff and I discussed the matter with them, and they agreed a future here was out of the question. We cut their final paychecks and sent them on their way."

"Why Jeff? Is there something I should know?" Elizabeth reached for the shovel and gripped the handle so much it hurt. She was always in charge of personnel matters, rather than her brother, who didn't even live in Colorado.

Dad's chest puffed out. "I told Jeff that he and Nicole would be more than welcome to come home to the ranch and offered them a position as my personal attorneys. Or the guesthouse if they practice law in Violet Ridge. I'd regret it someday if I didn't ask them to move back, especially seeing how fast my grandchildren are growing up. It would be great for Audrey and Zack to know how to ride. When I was their age, I collected the eggs and helped with the hay harvest." The same chores she, Jeff and Ben could do before they entered elementary school.

Her jaw slack, Elizabeth couldn't believe what she was hearing. She'd been the child who'd stayed behind and sweated over vaccinations, roundups and every facet of ranch life. Now her father wanted Jeff to return just like that and, most likely, take over what was mostly her role. Once again, her father underestimated her.

"What did Jeff say?" Elizabeth sounded as numb as she felt inside.

"You and Lucky walked into the room before he answered me. There was no time to follow up on the matter." Dad faced Lucky with a smile. "We're being rude to your boyfriend. I don't know why you didn't tell me about your relationship before now."

Elizabeth's stomach tightened. This was the moment. She should come clean and admit the truth. She opened her mouth, but no words tumbled forth.

"You know, it's funny how these things start." Lucky shrugged as if sensing her distress. "Turns out we care about the same people, and you've heard so much about them you feel like you know them. That's the case with us. I'm getting to know the real Lizzie, and she's giving me a test run, so to speak, but the minute I met her it was as if I'd been run over by something stronger than both of us."

How did Lucky do it? Everything he said was true, while glossing over the fact they'd just met. Dad nodded, and Elizabeth squinted. It was as if there were stars in Dad's eyes. "I like that. That's a lot like Evie and me. Evalynne is part of her, but Evie's the whole package." He blinked and cleared his throat. "I trust you'll be at the wedding rehearsal, then?"

"Um…" Lucky tugged at the collar of his blue T-shirt. "That's a family affair."

"Nonsense. You're Elizabeth's plus-one, so you're coming tomorrow night. I insist." Dad patted Lucky on the back. "The dinner will be at Mama Rosa's in Violet Ridge since everything for the wedding is being set up at the ranch tomorrow."

Elizabeth wouldn't let her father drop the other matter so fast. "So you and Jeff fired the two workers who were driving the UTV without consulting me?"

"They were negligent, Elizabeth. A little girl, my granddaughter, could have been injured or worse." Dad stroked Margarita's muzzle. "It was the right thing to do in the moment."

His cool tone made it clear he was acting as the ranch owner in this moment, not her father.

"Probably so, but who will take over their responsibilities during the wedding and for the roundup?" Elizabeth bristled on the inside, but tried not to show it.

"I'm sure you'll find someone. You always do."

So the employee decisions were his to make when it suited, yet she was the one who was expected to produce cowhands out of thin air with the wedding now less than thirty-six hours away and the roundup starting on Tuesday? It would be a sight easier to employ quality staff with extra benefits, including onsite housing.

"Speaking of our cowhands, I'd like to show you something regarding our future prospective employees. It'll only take a few minutes." With more amenities and benefits, the newly hired ranch hands might stick around longer.

"Maybe tomorrow. I don't have time right now. Evie's expecting me, and we're going downtown to pick up the wedding rings. The jeweler is staying late, just for us." Dad tipped his hat in Lucky's direction. "See you at the rehearsal."

Disappointed, she watched her father leave the stable. How would she get everything done before the wedding and hire extra hands for the roundup? It wasn't like Jeff or Ben had handled ranch chores in the past fifteen years, so they'd be more of a hindrance than a help.

She blew out a deep breath and started cleaning the nearest stall.

"Want to talk about it?" She'd almost forgotten Lucky was still here.

"Not really." She was determined the stable would never look better than when she left tonight. At least she had control over that. Efficient Elizabeth to the rescue, like always.

"You know you already cleaned that stall, right?" Lucky pointed out what should have been obvious, but in her state, she had managed to overlook that.

"My horses deserve the best." And that included employees who knew what they were doing.

Lucky laughed. "Can't fault that line of thought."

There was something genuinely nice about this man, and here she'd used him to make herself look good to her family, her father in particular. "I *can* fault myself for using you the way I did tonight. Now you're on the hook for the wedding rehearsal, too, when you wanted to get to Pueblo."

He shrugged and glanced around the stable. "Got another one of those shovels?"

"I'm giving you a chance to leave when no one's looking. Or is there something about you I should know? Are you a glutton for punishment?" She leveled a look at him. "After all, you're supposed to be my date to my father's rehearsal dinner and wedding."

"Maybe I'm a sucker for wedding cake and dancing." He grinned and held out his right hand. "Besides, now that I'm staying longer, Butterscotch will need an extended stay in your stable. He can't be in the trailer that long. Helping with the chores is the least I can do to earn his keep."

"How's your shoulder?" The last thing she wanted was to have him injure himself further on her watch.

"Ibuprofen wore off a couple of hours ago, and I'm fine." That was the first trace of exasperation she'd heard out of him. Guess he was like her and would rather be useful than sitting around doing nothing.

She returned in no time with extra supplies, including a pair of work gloves and another shovel. "Don't suppose you know any cowhands who are looking for temporary work? I have two openings for Saturday and for our annual cattle roundup, which begins on Tuesday. We pay well."

"I'd offer, but apparently I already have plans for Saturday." He winked. "I'll make some calls and get back to you."

Elizabeth had no doubt he would, either. They fell into a companionable silence, getting the horses fresh hay and water. After they finished, he murmured sweet words to his quarter horse, their bond clear.

"How long have the two of you been a team?" she asked.

Butterscotch nickered, and Lucky produced a peppermint from the pocket of his jeans, which looked the worse for wear, the rip near the knee a product from the earlier accident. "A little over six months."

She was impressed. It had taken Andromeda a while to accept her, yet Butterscotch delivered a look of pure devotion to his owner. Probably on account of Lucky being laid-back, yet sweet and kind. It was no secret that some in town called her imperious and thought she was snobbish. That wasn't the case, as her friends knew. She was just more comfortable around animals.

"Thanks for your help." And for bailing her out earlier and not embarrassing her in front of her family. He'd done more than his fair share to help her, and now it was time to return the favor. "Look, I was out of line. Jeff had me on edge, and then I panicked. You don't have to go to the wedding as my plus-one."

"Breaking up with me before our first date?" He crossed his palms over his heart and pretended to stagger backward. "I'm devastated."

Despite everything, she laughed. "There could be worse dates, except I roped you into it because of my pride."

"Then let's make it right." He hung his hat on a nearby hook and then removed his gloves. He reached for her hands and clasped them firmly. She liked his callused palms, a sign he wasn't afraid of hard work. "Ms. Irwin, er, Elizabeth, you don't know me, but my best friends Will and Sabrina will vouch for my character. I've heard there's a little shindig taking place this weekend in Violet Ridge. Would you do me the honors of being my date?"

She giggled and nudged the straw on the ground with the tip of her boot. "I do have the perfect dress."

"I happen to clean up pretty well myself." He released her hands and scrubbed his jaw, his stubble more attractive than it should be. "Then it's a date that's not a date."

Who could argue with logic like that? And why was she suddenly looking forward to the wedding more now than when she'd entered the stable?

CHAPTER THREE

THE NEXT AFTERNOON, Lucky stepped out of Harold's Barbershop in downtown Violet Ridge, feeling a pound lighter with a couple of inches of his shaggy, dark blond hair left behind on the faded linoleum floor. Last night, he told Elizabeth he cleaned up well, and he went for the whole she-bang, treating himself to a close shave and haircut. A promise was a promise, and keeping his word led to a good night's sleep. He was proud to say he hadn't lost out on too many nights.

He rubbed his jaw, the smoothness unusual and a little disconcerting. Was it too obvious, though, that he was trying hard to impress Elizabeth and her family? He still wasn't sure how he felt about last night. He was fine with Elizabeth claiming him as her plus-one. If anything, he was still blown away by her snap decision, trusting him with that kind of privilege.

What was troubling, though, was her family proclaiming him a hero. He was no hero. Far from it. Still, it was nice to have Zack and Audrey claiming his attention for one night. Almost as nice as helping Elizabeth in the stable, working side by side, tending to the horses. Butterscotch seemed most content with his surroundings, and who could blame him? Posh didn't even begin to describe the Double I Ranch. He'd even taken up Elizabeth on the offer of staying in Ben's room. While he'd never thought a ranch could be elegant, what with the cattle, interesting smells and noise, this one was definitely more sophisticated than Cale's down-home Cattle Crown Ranch, where he'd landed on his feet years ago.

He stepped out of the barbershop, a block away from the primary group of shops and parking deck. Sabrina had lent him her SUV so he wouldn't have to drive his large horse trailer/RV.

With only a couple of hours until he was due to escort Elizabeth to the wedding rehearsal and dinner, he'd best pick up his pace. Still, he spared the time and stared at the window display in front of the Reichert Supply Company, an assortment of candles and homeware on one side and toys on the other. Was he supposed to purchase a wedding gift for the happy couple? What did a rodeo com-petitor buy for a successful ranch owner who was marrying a famous singer? Silver candlesticks? A crystal decanter? A kite?

Sighing, he turned and found Sabrina exiting the Think Pink Salon, along with her mother and grandmother. Hurrying toward them, he called out Sabrina's name, and she let out a squeal.

"Lucky!" Sabrina ran over and hugged him. "I almost didn't recognize you with a haircut and a shave."

She elbowed him while Evie and Grandma Eloise caught up to them. He reached for his cowboy hat, forgetting he'd left it back at the ranch, and then moved his hand to hide his mistake. "Ma'am."

He nodded at both and then searched behind them for Elizabeth, but she was nowhere to be found. Evie smiled. "Your girlfriend is back at the ranch. Gordon told me what you said to him last night. That was so romantic." Lucky blinked until he realized Evie was talking about Elizabeth. "We invited her, but she insisted she was too busy. Now we know why. She's working hard while you're in town so the two of you can spend time with each other later. You'll have to pry yourselves away from each other tomorrow when my personal makeup artist and hairstylist arrive early. They'll be staying as guests for the wedding after they finish getting the bridal party ready, too."

Was Elizabeth hiding behind the horses? With a family like this? Either way, he was glad she'd be part of this loving group tomorrow. Families should stick together, and she was gaining a loving stepsister in Sabrina.

"Elizabeth will look beautiful, no matter what."

And that was the truth. Elizabeth's inner radiance stood out last night, impressing him more than he should have let it.

"Good answer." Grandma Eloise tapped her cane on the sidewalk. "Elizabeth is smart to keep you around. I hope the two of you can separate yourselves from each other long enough for you to save this old lady a dance tomorrow."

"I'll be the lucky one if we light up the dance floor together." Lucky grinned.

"You have a silver tongue." Grandma Eloise chuckled and placed both hands on her cane. "The price for that is two dances."

"You're a real taskmaster, Grandma Eloise." He winked his approval.

"We still have to pick up Ben's tuxedo at the alteration shop." Evie patted her watch. "He's missing the rehearsal, but Jeff can fill him in on his usher duties when he arrives late tonight. See you later, Lucky."

Sabrina delivered an extra hug. "I'm keeping my fingers crossed about you and Elizabeth. Evie told me everything. I should have known you were playing with words when you said you'd never been formally introduced. It's obvious you two didn't need a formal introduction and found each other just fine. You're her lucky match."

Hardly, and guilt over not correcting everyone's impression of him and Elizabeth as a couple glued him to the sidewalk, the summer sun beating down on him. What would Will and Sabrina say when they found out the two weren't dating? If he hadn't lost them already, he'd have lost their respect when everything came to light. Families didn't come along every day, and he already missed them. Maybe he should try to confide in them now?

Passing more of the local shops, he considered other options for a wedding present. Maybe Elizabeth would know if Gordon and Evie had announced a charitable foundation for donations instead of gifts. Then a beautiful arrangement in the window of Forever Violets Floral Shop caught his eye. Four huge tissue paper peonies roughly Audrey's size were surrounded at the edge of the display by real bouquets of daisies and violets, arranged in a way that combined whimsy with beauty. Maybe flowers would be a nice thank-you gift.

Lucky entered the shop, and the light wind chimes greeted him along with a cool blast of air-conditioning. He didn't see anyone behind the counter. A minute later, a harried worker in her late fifties hurried over and wiped her forehead with the back of her hand. "Sorry about that. I'm getting ready for a weekend wedding. How can I help you?"

Good question, as he wasn't quite sure himself, but he didn't want to appear at Elizabeth's door empty-handed before the rehearsal dinner.

He glanced at the double refrigerator unit with glass doors beside the counter. Corsages dotted the upper level. He'd never given anyone a corsage, since he'd worked on prom night, busing the tables of his classmates at an upscale restaurant.

"I'd like to buy a corsage." He could write a book about training colts or how to lasso a steer, but what he knew about flowers wouldn't fill a paragraph. "Do you have any suggestions?"

"What color is her dress?" The woman was all business as she pulled out an order pad.

"Um, I don't know. Does that matter?"

"It's a general starting point." She reached under the desk and produced a card. "When you ask her for the details, see if she's willing to give you a picture of the dress. Then I can also match the ribbon to the hue and style of the cut."

Even something as simple as flowers was anything but, the same as everything else on this trip to Violet Ridge. "I need one for tonight." Grandma Eloise seemed as though she'd appreciate one as well. "Actually, two of them. What about those?" He pointed to the top shelf of the refrigerator. "Are any of them for sale?"

She winced and shook her head. "I'm sorry, but those are for the Irwin wedding tomorrow. The co-owner of the shop is at the location, setting up and finishing the prep work."

"Thanks for your help. Mighty obliged." He dipped his head and went to leave.

Sabrina sailed in and stopped next to Lucky without looking at him. "I'm here to make sure the last of the flowers for the Irwin wedding are ready." Then she whipped her head back and laughed. "Lucky Harper. You're everywhere."

"Guilty as charged." Lucky stepped back and reached up, missing his cowboy hat once more. "See you tonight at the rehearsal dinner."

"Wait!" The store owner rolled her eyes. "You know the Irwin family?"

"He's Elizabeth's plus-one." Sabrina hugged Lucky's arm. "Of course, I should have guessed you'd also be at the rehearsal dinner."

"You're Ms. Irwin's date?" The owner's gaze wandered over him, and he couldn't help but feel as though he was lacking the panache of someone worthy of Elizabeth.

"They're perfect for each other." Sabrina let go of his arm. "I knew the two of you would get along."

Uh-oh. He also wasn't sure how Elizabeth would like the news about their date becoming fodder for gossip in Violet Ridge. One date that wasn't a date was one thing; people talking in her hometown about the two of them was another.

"I'll whip up an extra two corsages in no time for you tonight, sir." The owner glanced at Lucky and smiled. "You didn't tell me one of the corsages was for Ms. Irwin. I'll be right back with the best I've got left."

The owner disappeared behind the curtain, and Lucky wasn't sure he liked receiving this type of preferential treatment. If this was the impact of having money and influence, where people treated you differently, he'd rest better at the next rodeo having nothing but a modest sum in his bank account after paying cash for the trailer this year and for the engagement ring last year.

Sabrina leaned on the counter and nodded at him. "I know you too well so I know what you're thinking. Between you and me, I prefer being Sabrina and wearing my rodeo-clown outfit." She squeezed his hand. "Folks living in this area respect the Irwins and how they've always supported not just their home and business, but Violet Ridge, too. This kind of thoughtfulness, at times, is part and parcel of dating an Irwin."

He kept from frowning. His experience centered on the opposite treatment when it came to people judging him based on his family, or lack thereof. Some of his friends' parents had treated him with disdain once they found out he was a foster kid. One even locked her purse in a cabinet right in front of him. Ever since, he'd tried to treat everyone with the same level of respect, whether they were rich or poor, were a foster kid or had a loving family.

Problem was, he wasn't dating an Irwin.

"I'm not..."

Before he could elaborate, the owner reappeared

with a large box with a smaller one nestled on top. She handed them to Lucky. "The colors for the wedding are dusty rose and moss green. So I prepared one large and one small corsage with that as my guide. The rest of the flowers are well in hand."

Sabrina shook her head. "You didn't have to get me anything."

His cheeks grew hot. "Actually, the other corsage is for your grandmother. I thought your grandpa Bob would have bought her one."

She rose on her tiptoes and kissed his cheek. "Elizabeth better not break your heart, or she'll answer to me. Grandma will be tickled pink—" she flashed her hands "—which will match our nails. Gotta run and check on my daughter before the wedding rehearsal. See you there."

Sabrina departed the shop, and Lucky paid for the corsages. An hour later, he rang the doorbell near the ranch house's massive mahogany front door, and Elizabeth answered.

His breath whooshed out of him. She'd been attractive yesterday in her jeans and boots, but tonight she was stunning in a sage-green sundress dotted with dusty pink flowers. The color brought out her emerald eyes, and her auburn hair was swept up, showcasing her long neck. He wobbled in his crisp gray trousers, paired with a white dress shirt and tie. Speechless, he thrust the boxes toward her.

She opened the larger one and gasped. "The corsage is beautiful, but there are two boxes."

The sound of a cane hitting the hardwood reached him before he spotted Evie and Grandma Eloise heading their way. "The second one is for Grandma Eloise." He reached into the box and presented the orchid to the older woman. "I thought Bob wouldn't want me to forget you."

Evie smiled and patted his arm. "I should have thought of that. Thank you, Lucky." She grinned and faced Elizabeth. "This one's a keeper, just like your father."

He thought he saw a tear in Grandma Eloise's eye. She tapped her cane twice on the hardwood floor and nodded. "Bob would approve, and so do I." She then placed her hand over her heart. "Nothing like a corsage to make a woman's heart pitter-patter, right, Elizabeth?"

"When it's the right person, absolutely." Elizabeth snapped the corsage on her wrist. "We're running late to the rehearsal. We better hurry to the meadow since we have to drive into Violet Ridge for the dinner at Mama Rosa's immediately afterward."

She led the group to the outdoor area, where a field had been transformed into a wedding wonderland. Overhead, twinkling lights lit the rows of white chairs that faced an arch decorated with dusty pink roses and sage greenery. The Rocky Mountains rose majestically behind the arch, as if overseeing the wedding itself. Even tomorrow's weather was custom-made for a once-in-a-lifetime day, with the forecast predicting sun and perfect August temperatures.

Gordon separated himself from the group and handed Evie one of the crystal goblets he had been holding. He kissed his future bride on the cheek, his ruddy cheeks deepening to red, his love for her evident in his eyes. "You look lovely, Evie. The best thing I ever did in my life was ask you out."

Beside him, Lucky heard Elizabeth gasp softly and saw her face flame into a deep red before her breathing grew regular again. He leaned in and, soft enough for her ears only, whispered, "One of the best things. I'm sure that's what he meant to say."

Her smile didn't reach her eyes. "My father always says what he means."

"The officiant is here." Gordon's gaze shifted to a man in a solemn gray suit. "Before we start, has anyone received a text from Ben? His plane should have landed by now."

Members of the Irwin family reached into purses or pockets for their phones. Jeff shook his head, but Elizabeth paled. "Excuse me for a minute."

Walking away from Lucky, she pulled her father aside, and Gordon's face turned beet-red. Evie came over to Lucky. "What did the text say?" she asked.

"I don't know."

Gordon proceeded to the archway where the officiant would perform the ceremony while Elizabeth moved to the rear, joining Lucky and Evie. "Attention, everyone."

The small crowd gathered around Gordon. Lucky kept his distance, away from the family, while Evie joined Gordon by his side.

"What's wrong?" Evie asked, placing her arm around her fiancé.

"Ben texted Elizabeth. He missed his flight because of a last-minute emergency. Military business. He isn't coming." Regret and sadness came through in his voice. Gordon dipped his cowboy hat before taking it off and fiddling with it. "We're an usher short."

"Jeff can walk Elizabeth up the aisle, and then go back for Nicole," Evie suggested.

"Or I could escort one on each arm." Jeff held out his elbows as if proving his point.

"I can walk down the aisle by myself," Elizabeth said, with conviction.

With no place for him in this circle, Lucky backed away. In his experience, this type of family dilemma was always settled better with less of a presence from outsiders. He glanced around for something to do, someone to help.

"Lucky!" Evie called out, and he stopped in his tracks. "You look like you're the same size as Ben."

His hands grew clammy. "Nah. I'm shorter than Gordon and Jeff."

"So's Ben." Gordon sized him up and nodded. "You'll fit into his tuxedo with no problem. Congratulations, Lucky. You're promoted to usher, and you'll walk Elizabeth down the aisle."

THE PRIVATE ROOM at Mama Rosa's always promised a special evening, and this night was no exception. Candlelight bathed the walls in a soft glow, highlighting the one covered with pictures of Gordon and Evie. In the background, Evalynne's greatest hits serenaded the small group, but not too loud as to get in the way of good conversation.

With the remnants of her eggplant parmigiana on her plate, Elizabeth motioned for Lucky to lean into her. A whiff of his lime aftershave mixed with a faint scent of horses and sunshine was more calming than she'd have liked. A few days ago, she didn't know him, only what she'd heard about him from Will Sullivan or Sabrina, yet now she found that scent combination was just like him: earthy with a twist of something invigorating.

"I had no idea what your father was planning." Lucky kept his voice low so only Elizabeth could hear him, just as he had several other times throughout the evening. "I couldn't think of a way to bow out gracefully."

Welcome to her world. At least he didn't fault

her for this conundrum, although she wouldn't have blamed him if he had. "Believe me, I've been there, but we need a plan for after the wedding. A reason for us to break up." Especially since everyone now believed they'd been carrying on in secret all this time.

"Hmm. I can fill you in on all of my bad traits, and you can pick the worst. Sometimes I'm in a hurry and don't clean out the sink after I shave."

Elizabeth laughed. "I don't think anyone would believe I broke up with you over that."

The server brought dessert—tiramisu for Lucky and cheesecake with strawberries drizzled with chocolate for her. This time Lucky motioned for her to come close to him. "Anyone who doesn't choose raspberries over strawberries? That's a deal breaker for me."

She burst out laughing. "Good thing they didn't offer me a choice."

"Then we'll just have to stick to the truth. That's always for the best, anyway." Lucky was so close she felt his breath tickling her ear, a quite pleasant way to end the perfect meal.

"Look at the lovebirds." Evie's pronouncement sent her back to her seat as her future stepmother approached with Sabrina at her side. "Whispering to each other as if they're the only two in the room. They've been doing this all night."

"I love seeing you happy, Lucky." Sabrina

beamed at the pair of them. "You deserve all this, and more."

And she had tied this nice guy into her crazy scheme. Elizabeth transferred the mossy green napkin from her lap to her plate. She needed time to think and plan. The nighttime stable duties with the familiarity of the horses and her routine would provide just that. "Can you drive Lucky back to the ranch, Sabrina? Then I can finish the instructions for the crew for the weekend."

"No problem. It'll give me time to get the full scoop." Sabrina winked at Lucky.

Elizabeth rose and ignored the slight flutters when Lucky stood at the same time, his gaze earnest and insightful. "I'll be on my way, then."

Back at the ranch in her bathroom, Elizabeth sent a lingering look at the corsage on her wrist before taking it off and placing it on the counter. Lucky shouldn't have gone to such trouble, but she had the feeling remembering little details like this were part of his personality. Why hadn't she told him how much this unexpected and thoughtful gesture meant to her?

Any other time, under any other circumstances, she'd love to get to know Lucky better. And yet this was the worst time for emotions to get in her way. She'd been preparing to take over management of the ranch her entire life, and now her father wanted to pull her oldest brother back into the fold?

Hardly a ringing endorsement of her abilities as manager. What would Dad say if he found out her pride had goaded her into claiming Lucky as her plus-one? That might make him push for Jeff, and possibly even Ben, to return and run the ranch. Worse still, Lucky had been roped into being part of the wedding party.

What the laid-back rodeo star must think of her now, she didn't want to know.

She hastily scrubbed off her makeup and changed out of the beautiful dress into her favorite jeans and thread-worn flannel shirt. Then she donned her boots and headed for the stable. After a quick check of the notes left by the lead groom, she sent a longing glance toward Andromeda's stall. What she'd give for a nighttime ride under the stars with the cattle lowing nearby. Next week would deliver moments like that with the roundup. Once that was over, her father and Evie would leave on their honeymoon while Elizabeth tended the ranch and monitored the corn being cut up for silage. The resulting product, with its high-energy content, would feed the cattle long into the cold Colorado winter.

Somehow, during the cattle drive, she'd have to get her father on board with her plan for the new bunkhouses. When he returned from his honeymoon, she planned on implementing yet another change that would shore them up for the long term. While the Double I was residence to one thousand head of Angus cattle, she'd been reading up on another popular breed in Colorado: Simmentals. Introducing that breed to the other side of the ten-thousand-acre ranch could reap benefits down the line. She counted on her father being in a good mood for that discussion.

On her way to the tack room for the fly spray she needed to apply to each horse, the stable cat's purrs reached Elizabeth. She rolled up the sleeves of her flannel shirt and climbed the ladder. Once at loft level, she checked on the cat. Content and relaxed, the cat raised its head. She must have been satisfied Elizabeth didn't constitute any kind of threat because she curled up and went to sleep. That type of personality must be nice. In a way, the cat reminded her of Lucky, who seemed to take life in stride.

With reluctance, she gathered her supplies and applied fly spray to each horse, except Butterscotch, texting Lucky that she'd apply it if the gelding had no problems with the brand she favored. As always, she saved Andromeda for last. That way, she could spend extra time with her mare. She placed the spray bottle on the ledge.

"Oh, Drommie." She rested her head against her horse's flank. "What a night!"

"A good one, I hope." Lucky's voice came from behind, and her heart raced.

A glance at him with his white dress shirt stretched across his broad shoulders, the top button unbuttoned, only made her heart beat that much faster. She took a deep breath and pushed aside her reaction to him. It was surprise, that was all. "You scared me. You could have just texted me back."

"I was already on my way." He jerked his thumb toward Butterscotch. "I wanted to check on him before bed. Appeared we had the same idea."

The best idea, in her opinion. She liked how his mind operated almost as much as she liked his droll sense of humor. Still, guilt flooded her about how her pride was causing him all this extra trouble. She grabbed the fly spray and went over to him. After exhaling a deep breath, she said in a rush, "I didn't mean for you to get caught up in my family's issues."

He laughed and then shoved his hands in his pockets. "I don't mind at all, and that's a bit of an exaggeration, isn't it? You're making everything sound so serious. This wedding is a joyous occasion."

"One you weren't going to attend, and now you're in the wedding party."

"A promotion. Who can argue with that?" His gaze held bemusement, and she wondered if anything ever bothered him. "And that dinner tonight more than made up for any inconvenience. Good food, great company, a beautiful woman at my side."

She thrust the bottle of fly spray into his chest. "You seem too good to be true."

Lucky applied it to Butterscotch's legs. "On the contrary. I've just seen too much in my life to get upset over something that's not worth it."

For some reason, she wanted to know more about him. "Like what? Tell me about yourself."

He squirted some of the spray on Butterscotch's flank. "It's too late at night for that, and we have a wedding to attend tomorrow."

Avoidance, pure and simple. Or perhaps he didn't feel comfortable around her. The conversation at the rehearsal dinner had been light and simple, the casual chat of acquaintances who'd never see each other again.

"Another time," she said. Not that there would be one. After the reception, he'd head to the next rodeo, and she had the roundup on the horizon. If anyone asked why they weren't dating anymore, she'd tell the truth. They'd agreed to the one date, and nothing more.

Somehow, though, not getting to know him better or even seeing him again caused a ripple of sadness to run through her.

After he finished, he returned the bottle, and she returned to Andromeda. He followed her and murmured sweet words to her mare. Was he a horse whisperer, or did he make everyone feel special, allowing them to open up to him?

"What do you get for a rancher and a singer as a wedding gift, anyway?"

"They specifically asked for no gifts. Guests can make a charitable donation to a local horse shelter or causes Evalynne supports in her professional capacity, but it's not like anyone's going to check for a receipt at the door." She rubbed the spray into Andromeda's coat, taking care there was a fine sheen afterward.

"I like that idea. I don't think Cherry would have gone for anything like that, but I would."

"Cherry?" All this time she thought he was single and unattached, but she must have figured wrong. "Is she your girlfriend?"

Her voice sounded too high-pitched and garbled for her liking.

"My ex-girlfriend." That revelation shouldn't have made her as happy as it did. "She's married to someone else now."

She had no idea if Jared had ever married, nor did she care enough to find out if he did. "That must have been rough." Elizabeth set down the spray bottle and reached into her pocket for some apple slices for Andromeda.

"I've handled worse." He reached for a slice and fed one to her mare, who nuzzled his hand searching for more.

"Breakups are never easy." She should know, although losing Jared ended up being a blessing in disguise. He'd been interested in signing a lucrative contract with her father rather than pursuing her out of sheer love. Even though that was a while ago, it still left an unpleasant taste in her mouth. She reached for the fly spray and held up her right index finger. "If you have a minute, I'll walk with you back to the house. I need to put this away first."

"Thanks. I'm meeting Evie and Grandma Eloise to try on that tuxedo, and I appreciate the company." Lucky followed her into the tack room.

In no time, everything was in its proper place for the night. She found a supply of peppermints and raised one. "I remember Butterscotch likes these. Can he have the special treat tonight?"

"He *loves* them, so, yes." They walked together to the gelding's temporary stall. "Thanks for boarding him. Maybe Sabrina was right after all. I guess it was lucky for me you didn't have a date for the wedding."

"Guess you're living up to your nickname." She smiled and reached into her pocket for the peppermint.

He stared at her, squinting those electric blue eyes that observed far more than he let on. "The men of Violet Ridge's loss is my gain."

She met his gaze, and something stirred within her. His calmness seemed to balance out her constant need for activity. Too bad they had to meet like this. Too bad that he'd be heading to the next rodeo and out of her life by nightfall tomorrow. "I'll take your word for it."

"It's the truth." He reached out and stroked Butterscotch's muzzle.

"Cherry seems to be the one who missed out on something." The air crackled around them, but there was a wedding taking place on the ranch tomorrow. That, along with the balmy summer night, explained everything.

"At the time I wasn't happy about it, but now I'm relieved I never asked her to marry me." He shrugged and shook his head. "It must be that glass of wine at dinner. I don't like to talk about myself."

Was this his first flaw? Or was it refreshing to find someone who didn't spend every minute talking about himself the way Jared had? "Well, for the record, no one's ever asked me."

She reached into her pocket, and the peppermint fell to the hay. About to bend down, he beat her to a kneeling position. "Allow me." He picked up the peppermint and held it up to her, a smile lighting up that friendly face. "I can't believe you've never heard the words *will you marry me* before."

She laughed and reached for the peppermint so he could rise more gracefully without crushing the candy. "Yes—"

Shrieks came from behind her. Her blood chilled, and her eyes grew wide. Lucky rose to a standing position, and they both turned to find Zack and Audrey standing there.

"A proposal. Yuck." Zack scrunched up his nose and made a face. "Mom and Dad were wrong, and you were right, Audrey."

"I get to tell them." Audrey ran out of the stable toward the house. "They're engaged!"

Elizabeth stood rooted to the spot, her legs too heavy to move. Her mouth dropped as she glanced at the peppermint in her hand. How could anyone mistake a peppermint for a ring?

Worse yet, the date that wasn't a date might just have turned into the engagement that wasn't an engagement.

CHAPTER FOUR

LUCKY DUSTED BITS of straw off his good gray dress pants. A glance at Elizabeth confirmed she was as shell-shocked as he felt inside. Seemed as if he wasn't living up to his nickname after all.

Then again, there was a simple explanation for this misunderstanding, and everyone would laugh afterward. "If anyone else comes, we'll show them the peppermint." Lucky held out the candy, and Butterscotch whinnied for the treat. Before Lucky could move his hand out of the way, he felt the gelding's tongue and mouth tickling his palm as Butterscotch lapped up the peppermint.

"The peppermint you just fed to your horse?" Elizabeth's wry voice was a stark reminder about the real reason they were in the stable.

"Yeah, that one." He wiped his hands on his pants and kept from sighing. Who was he kidding? Once Gordon and Evie heard the entire story and he became a laughingstock the night before their wedding, they'd probably rescind

Lucky's invitation as acting usher. That would be the end of his time here, period.

Elizabeth leaned her ear toward the stable entrance, and her face softened. Then a peal of nervous laughter swept over her. "Nothing. No one's coming, so they're either busy, or Zack and Audrey got sidetracked. Thank goodness no one believes we're really engaged."

A brief pang of regret over how relieved she sounded flitted through him. He couldn't blame her, though. Who'd believe someone as beautiful and accomplished as her would end up with this kid from upstate New York who only had two nickels to rub together?

"Well, then, I have a tuxedo to try on." If it didn't fit, that would be another sign he shouldn't be in the wedding party and might be able to leave town with some grace. "Unless you want me to go, Elizabeth. Just say the word and I'm out of here."

Even though he hadn't known her long, he enjoyed her company and liked what he'd seen, but if his absence would help her, he'd follow through on his offer in a heartbeat. His gaze met hers in the dim lighting of the stable. Her emerald eyes glistened with uncertainty. Somehow, he knew that scared her more than anything. He understood that kind of fear.

Before she could answer, shouts and exclamations came from the direction of the house. Elizabeth reached for his hand and pulled him outside. "Uh-oh. This kind of excitement's not good for the horses."

And, by association, for her, either, but he stayed silent, as a throng of Elizabeth's family members headed for them with Audrey and Zack leading the pack. Lucky squeezed Elizabeth's hand for courage.

"See, Mommy. They are happy. They're holding hands just like you and Daddy," Audrey insisted as everyone stopped a decent distance from him and Elizabeth. "I told you she said yes."

From the opposite direction, Sabrina and Ty arrived with baby Genie quiet and content in her mother's arms. "What's going on?" Sabrina was out of breath. "We were changing Genie when we got a text to come to the stable at once."

Jeff huffed. "Really, Elizabeth and Lucky? You couldn't let Evie and Dad have the spotlight to themselves?" He shook his head and let go of Zack's hand. "This weekend is about them, not the both of you."

All the wind left Lucky's sails. He had been so happy to be included in the Irwin family wedding, but Jeff was right. This disruption was taking the focus away from Gordon and Evie. He glanced at Gordon, who wiped a tear from the corner of his eye. It appeared as if he'd overstayed his welcome at yet another home.

"I'm sorry, sir," Lucky said, releasing Elizabeth's hand.

"Wait a minute, Jeff," Sabrina said. She handed Genie to Ty, who didn't miss a beat and tickled Genie's nose, the baby's giggle a sweet sound in a sea of disapproving faces. Then she marched over to her future stepbrother and popped her hands on her hips. "Lucky Harper is one of the most selfless people I've ever met."

He appreciated Sabrina coming to his defense. "Thanks, but..." Lucky began, but bedlam was breaking out with everyone talking at once. Jeff and Nicole were arguing with Sabrina, and Elizabeth was saying something to Gordon and Evie.

What had he done, bringing dissension into this wonderful family who'd opened their home to him?

Something, or someone, tugged at his pants. He glanced down at Audrey, whose smile was almost as wide as the frames of her purple glasses. "I'm glad you'll be my uncle."

Lucky's chest expanded with something warm and fuzzy filling his heart. Thank goodness, he'd been in the right place at the right time, so she wasn't hurt. At that moment, a whistle pierced the air. Everyone stilled.

Evie held her head high and smiled once she had everyone's full attention. "Good." She fanned her face. "This was getting too heated for my comfort. Gordon has something to say."

"Thank you, darlin'. That was perfect." Mr. Irwin hugged his fiancée. "I never knew you could whistle like that."

"There's a lot you don't know about me yet." She winked, her eyes holding a hint of mystery and humor. "Still want to marry me?"

"Wouldn't miss it for all the acres in Colorado." Gordon grinned, a look of admiration spreading across his face. Then he cleared his throat, and that serious glare returned. "Now, there seems to be some misapprehension that Lucky and Elizabeth are stealing our thunder. Evie and I are more than capable of speaking for ourselves, and she just showed how she's capable of getting anyone's attention when she wants it."

"And don't you forget it." She nudged him and brought forth a burst of laughter.

Gordon grew serious once more. "Having Evie by my side, supporting me, loving me, is something beyond my wildest dreams." He wound his arm around her slighter frame. "If you're lucky enough to have a whirlwind of love in your path, sometimes you have to ride into the storm rather than get out of its path."

"You're adding to our celebration." Evie leaned into Gordon's solid frame. "And you have our blessing."

Gordon nodded. "You'll make an excellent addition to our family, Lucky. I can already tell you and Elizabeth are a perfect match."

TANYA AGLER 79

Sabrina extended her hand toward Jeff. "You'll come to love Lucky as much as Ty and I do. I promise."

Jeff accepted her offer of a truce while his wife Nicole stepped forward. "Let me see the ring."

Nicole's gaze shifted to Elizabeth's bare left hand. The light from the full moon shone brightly enough for him to see Elizabeth blanch. "Well, you see, this is all a big…"

She glanced at Lucky as if appealing to him to bail her out of the situation.

Gordon looked at him with anticipation, and Lucky gulped. "The ring's still in my trailer."

"Really?" Jeff asked. "How did you propose to her? With a horse bit? Elizabeth, this is Dad's special occasion."

Elizabeth stood there like a statue, hurt on her face. Lucky had to say something. "It might have been on the spur of the moment, but Zack and Audrey witnessed it. She said yes, and the ring is waiting for her."

"This cold air and all this excitement is too much for me tonight." Grandma Eloise double tapped her cane into the soft grass. "I need my beauty sleep, so I look gorgeous in the wedding pictures. Besides, the lovebirds need some time alone. And I mean all the sets of lovebirds."

Zack scrunched up his face. "Ew, gross. Come on, Audrey. I'll race you inside."

Gordon and Evie escorted the older woman

along the path with everyone else dispersing in different directions. In no time, he was alone with Elizabeth.

"Thank you for defending me to Jeff, but a ring in your trailer? That's a little far-fetched. I'll explain everything to my father." She groaned and placed her face in her palms, her chest falling and rising with a deep breath. With a shiver, she rubbed at her arms. "Dad looked so happy. Bursting his bubble before the wedding—"

Guilt over the position he'd put Elizabeth in gnawed at his insides. He couldn't leave her in the lurch any more than he could stand by while that UTV barreled toward Audrey.

"Come on, Lizzie. I really have a ring in my RV. We have a fake engagement to plan." He reached for her hand and squeezed it. "And a fake breakup, too."

LIZZIE? HE'D CALLED her Lizzie out in the courtyard. Where did that come from? Why that and not Beth or Bessie? Everyone had stuck with Elizabeth since her mother, who always called her Lizzie, had died. Elizabeth set her red cowboy hat on Lucky's dinette table and bit back a laugh. Of all the problems from tonight, she was dwelling on a nickname? She had to get her head out of the clouds and her boots planted on brown Colorado soil again.

Collapsing into the plush black leather seat, she

rested her head next to her hat. She needed time to think. What she'd give for a long ride on Andromeda right about now.

Plunk! Something plopped next to her, and she raised her head and found a small black velvet jeweler's box. "What's this?" she asked.

"It's an engagement ring." Lucky settled across from her and clicked on the lamp on the wall, illuminating her surroundings.

She liked what she saw, an efficient setup that would allow him to go anywhere at any time. Perfect for him, and while she craved that type of freedom this second, this ranch was her home, her livelihood, her first love. She'd do anything for the Double I and her father, including letting her family believe she was engaged to a rodeo star on the eve of Dad's wedding. She wouldn't place a damper on the proceedings, especially now that her father had finally approved of something she'd done. Or didn't do, as the case may be.

Her gaze locked on the box and she picked it up.

"You happen to drive around with an engagement ring?" She pushed the case back toward him. "Just one or more than one? I'm not sure this isn't a little creepy."

"Just the one." He nudged it back in her direction. "I intended on proposing to Cherry and never did."

She snapped the case open. Unlike the clean,

classic lines of her surroundings, the ring, an oval diamond of at least two carats surrounded by little diamond chips, was rather ostentatious and over-the-top. Not her style at all, but it didn't look like a genuine diamond, and for that she was thankful. "This is quite a ring."

He shrugged. "I know it's flashy, but it's available." He reached for the box and pulled out the ring. "Try it on."

While she summoned the nerve to see if it fit, skepticism bubbled inside her. Why had Lucky gone along with this? Jared's duplicity popped into mind. That experience had ended badly. Her ex-boyfriend claimed to love her, but he'd only been after her father's signature on a lucrative contract that would have lined Jared's pockets for life. He wanted the Irwin name, not her. Her first impression of Lucky had been different, especially with Sabrina vouching for him, but only time would tell if he was different from Jared. She brushed aside the unpleasant memory, but she had to dig further and find out what Lucky was after.

"I don't get it. What's in this for you?"

He flinched. "Why does there have to be anything in it for me?"

"Everyone always wants something." That was why she liked horses.

"Maybe I'm not most people." He leaned back on his side of the dinette, raising his arms until they rested on the top of the cushions. "You go first. What do you want out of our fake engagement?"

Guilt churned in her stomach. She'd stood rooted in the spot, unable to defend herself. It was just that Jeff's attitude had rankled almost as much as Dad's immediate acceptance of Lucky. Her father was known for his quick judgments, which usually proved correct. With all his business acuity, why couldn't Dad recognize she was a genuine asset to the Irwin family? "I insist you start." Then she might read him better.

"I like to think I'm a gentleman. Ladies first." He dipped his head in her direction.

"Do you make everything difficult?" She fidgeted with the box, unable to keep her hands from fluttering around, the same as she couldn't control the flutters in her stomach every time she looked at him.

"Just fake engagements." He chuckled, a low sound that also played havoc with her insides.

"How do we end this without anyone getting hurt?" She hadn't known him long, but she valued his feelings. Hurting him was the last thing she wanted to do.

"Same way as I tie the calves in the rodeo, fast and careful."

"Not tomorrow, though. This wedding should be a joyous occasion. Dad deserves it." She wouldn't do anything to ruin tomorrow for Dad and Evie.

"Agreed." He moved his arms and leaned forward. "So why didn't you speak up?"

While she'd have thought her *why* was as obvious as that diamond, she owed him an explanation. She continued fiddling with the case, turning it this way and that, until he rested his hands on hers, the callused fingers calm and steadfast, good qualities in anyone. Maybe she could trust him. There was only one way to find out. "Growing up an Irwin is not as easy as it looks. Growing up the remaining Irwin on the ranch is even harder."

"I'll take your word for that." Lucky's stiff posture was different from his usual laid-back stance. She didn't know much about the man she was supposedly engaged to. This could be a good time to get to know him better.

But there was a wedding tomorrow, and they still had to figure out how to foil an engagement: namely, their own. "We need a good cover story for our breakup."

"I'd think that would be the easiest part." He leaned back again as if attempting to put distance between them. So much for believing there was an attraction brewing, as it was obviously one-sided with her imagination working overtime. Who could blame him for not wanting to get involved with someone who should have spoken up and admitted this was a big misunderstanding?

She nodded and reached for the simplest explanation. "After you leave for the rodeo, I'll explain we had too many differences to make it work. You wanted your freedom, and I agreed." After all, she'd lived in one place her whole life, but he must love to travel. Even his home was on wheels.

"Except I'll come back to see Will and Sabrina. We have to think of an excuse that won't paint me in a poor light." A shadow fell over him, and he shook his head. "Never mind. That'll work. We just have to get through the wedding and afterward I'll leave as planned."

"Wait. You're right." She hadn't considered how her refusal to speak up in the courtyard would impact his relationship with Will and Sabrina. She might not know much about her fake fiancé, but she knew Sabrina counted him and Will Sullivan as her best friends.

"How about we concern ourselves with the breakup down the road? No sense inviting trouble yet where there's none." He tapped his watch. "And I really need to go try on that tuxedo."

A rather cavalier approach, but it was late, and she had a lot to do before tomorrow's wedding as well. There was her nightly discussion with the head groom, followed by a quick check on Andromeda to make sure she hadn't been spooked by the commotion.

"Lizzie?" Lucky broke into her thoughts.

That was at least the third time he'd called her that. "I prefer Elizabeth."

"Okay." He scrutinized her face. "Elizabeth, are you thinking about the stable?"

"Always. The ranch comes first. It's everything to me."

"And you have a competent staff who will perform their jobs so you can enjoy the wedding." He pointed at the ring. "Does it fit?"

She removed the gaudy gold ring, heavier than she'd anticipated, from its slot. Whenever she'd envisioned this minute in her life, she always thought her fiancé would always be the one sliding the ring onto her finger, yet this wasn't a real engagement, so she did the honors.

To her surprise, it fit as if it was made for her. For some reason, relief flooded her at one problem solved. The fact that it presented a host of others wasn't lost on her.

"Yes, it fits." She twisted it and found her first impression was wrong. It was a little loose, but nothing a bit of clear tape couldn't handle.

Then again, maybe that was a sign she should let Lucky keep the fake ring, and she should march to the house and explain that this was a big misunderstanding before anyone's feelings could be hurt.

"Thank you for sharing your family with me." *What did he mean by that?*

Before she could ask, he rose from the table and headed to the door. "I'll walk you back. I have that tuxedo fitting."

She'd almost forgotten that, even though he'd just told her. He was distracting her. She usually prided herself on being the observant Irwin who remembered details and kept the family organized. That was her role, and she usually filled those boots well.

"On Sunday, once the wedding is over, we'll nail down the ending to this charade."

With that note of certainty, she brushed past him. Electricity traveled down her spine more than that time she'd been jolted by some live barbed wire. Somehow, she wondered if her feelings were already involved. Looking at her left hand, she'd just have to play the part for a few days before she'd return this rhinestone ring, and that would be that. No one would be the wiser, and everyone would get on with their lives.

One look at him, and she wasn't sure if it would be that simple.

CHAPTER FIVE

LUCKY STRAIGHTENED HIS bow tie, but no matter how many times he positioned it, he just didn't look like himself in this custom-tailored tuxedo made for someone else. He fingered the fine silk of the lapel. While he possessed the same measurements as Ben Irwin, he'd never fill his boots in the family. He resisted the urge to untie the bow tie and head for Casper.

Someone knocked, and Will Sullivan entered the guest room where Lucky was staying so as not to exhaust his RV's electric reserves. Actually, it was Ben's room, but Lucky had to remember staying here and wearing the middle brother's clothes didn't make him part of the Irwin family.

"I miss one rehearsal dinner and have to find out from Sabrina that you're engaged?" Will folded his arms from his stance at the doorjamb.

With the late-night fitting followed by a long talk with Butterscotch in the stable, Lucky knew he'd forgotten something. Namely, to let his best friend in on what was happening at the Double I Ranch.

"Surprise?" Lucky tried to laugh it off, but one look at Will confirmed that wouldn't work. He had assumed he'd be able to keep his story simple, including the breakup, but maybe that was a little naïve. Someone had to take the fall and Elizabeth lived here. The Sullivan ranch bordered the Double I. Long-term neighbors supported each other. It made far more sense for him to position himself as the heartbreaker.

"That's putting it mildly. Don't keep anything this important from me again." Will frowned before he embraced Lucky, patting him on the back for a second before separating.

"Don't worry. I won't." A swift pang of guilt brought a shudder through him, and he tamped it down the best he could.

Here he was keeping a huge secret from his best friends, especially Will, who'd taken him into his fold when Lucky was a greenhorn. The three of them had celebrated countless holidays together on the circuit. Definitely more than he'd ever celebrated with any one foster family. They'd taken side trips, too. The three of them had visited Yellowstone and the Grand Canyon and every barbecue joint in between seeking out the best brisket in the West. Sabrina always sampled whatever cobbler Lucky ordered and usually ate more of his dessert than he did.

Will and Sabrina were like family, but there was a hidden layer of vulnerability to Elizabeth underneath that efficient exterior. How she talked to the horses appealed to something deep inside him, something that recognized a common kinship with animals.

Will shook his head and pointed at Lucky's attempt at tying the bow tie. "Before he passed, my father taught me how to do that. Do you mind?"

"It would be my honor." Lucky appreciated Will's discretion of delicately handling the matter of Lucky's past, including stints in countless foster homes, each one progressively worse. There were many great foster families out there, and someday he would love nothing more than to be a foster father to a child in need, but his experience wasn't one of the positive ones. It didn't stop him from hoping that one day, though, he'd be part of a loving family.

Too bad it couldn't be the Irwins.

Will unknotted the tuxedo tie and held the long black strip in his hands. "It's an honor for Kelsea and me to be invited."

"Your ranch borders the Double I." Lucky breathed more easily once his bow tie wasn't constricting his throat. "And you and Kelsea are Sabrina and Ty's best friends."

Kelsea and Will had met a little over a year ago, but Lucky credited her with bringing out the best in his friend's personality. Marriage suited Will.

"The Sullivans and Irwins have been friends for years. Evie and Gordon's wedding will only cement the bond between all of us. One thing bothers me, though."

"Only one thing?" Not much slipped past Will's notice.

Will quirked one eyebrow, and he gestured to Lucky to raise the lapels of his shirt collar. "It's actually a pretty big thing. Sabrina said you just met Elizabeth the other day."

"She said that, huh?" With Sabrina and Ty building their rodeo academy near Will's ranch, she and Will would have many more conversations in the future and remain close. This was extra proof they'd be just fine without him. He could return to the circuit any time. "Her mother's getting married today. I'm sure she has a lot on her mind."

"The first step when you tie a bow tie is to make sure the right side is shorter than the left." Will looped the tie around Lucky's neck, and Lucky felt the tight fit.

"Got it." Lucky made mental notes but gave up. He understood the calves who were darting out of the chute looking for a safe place to hide a sight better at this moment. Besides, it wasn't like he'd have another occasion anytime soon to wear a tuxedo and bow tie. In the rodeo, a bolo tie suited formal events just fine.

"Then you put the longer side over the shorter end and loop it under," said Will, demonstrating the procedure. "Getting back to Sabrina. You know she's sharp and doesn't miss much."

Countering Sabrina's strengths with Elizabeth's seemed the best way out at this point. "Elizabeth also has a mind of her own, and she's pretty strong-willed."

Will pinched the fold of the looped end and pushed it through the small opening. He pulled on the folded parts and tightened the bow. "You know her better than I thought." Will adjusted the bow tie until it was balanced and straight. "You know Gordon tried to matchmake the two of us a long time ago? Something about the Silver Horseshoe and the Double I being stronger if they were merged."

Something tore at Lucky's chest at Elizabeth getting together with Will. "You seem a little too intense for each other." Besides, he couldn't see Will with anyone other than his wife, Kelsea.

"That's true, but Elizabeth says it's because I knew her when she wore braces."

"I'd like to have seen that." Lucky laughed at the image of a serious yet gangly teenage Elizabeth with braces and her red cowboy hat.

Will stepped back and examined his handiwork. "Sabrina and Elizabeth are important to me."

Lucky met his gaze, and the laughter faded from his lips. "Not denying that."

"So why are you and Elizabeth pretending to be

engaged?" Will flicked a piece of lint off Lucky's coat and then crossed his arms.

"Who said we're pretending?" Lucky would tread carefully, toeing the line as closely as he could. He wouldn't do anything to hurt Elizabeth, or ruin Gordon and Evie's wedding day. He and Elizabeth had agreed to stage a breakup after the wedding so her father could marry Evie with his happiness intact.

Protecting Elizabeth through this experience was the best and only wedding present he could give the Irwin family.

Someone knocked at the door. Jeff stuck his head through the crack. "Wedding pictures are taking place at the meadow in ten minutes. Dad and Evie want to get them done before the guests trample the grass."

"Lucky will be there," Will confirmed. As soon as Jeff left, he held up his hands. "Whenever you're ready to tell me everything, I'll listen. No judgments."

Will left Lucky behind without a backward glance. Lucky picked up a high school half-marathon trophy from Ben's bookcase and wished he'd left Violet Ridge when he'd had the chance. But that didn't seem true, either. He'd enjoyed being with Elizabeth every moment they'd had together, so far. The best he could do was enjoy the wedding and hold on to what he had a little longer.

Grabbing his new cowboy hat, a present from

Gordon to all the ushers and the best man, he was determined to do just that. Then he'd walk away, exactly as planned.

WHILE THE PHOTOGRAPHER snapped pictures of the bridal party in the meadow, Elizabeth's cheeks hurt from all the smiling. After a new set of instructions from the photographer, she held the bouquet of roses close to her chest and tried not to glance in the direction of the stable. The ranch animals would be fine without her for one day, just like Lucky said. Concentrating at the task on hand, she drank in the beauty of the day that couldn't have been any more perfect if it had been made to order.

"Everyone except Evie, hold up your bouquet and pretend you're about to throw them." The photographer snapped more pictures. "Have fun. The joy will reflect on your face."

As Elizabeth raised her arm, the morning sunlight glinted off the engagement ring on her left finger. Rather than joy, guilt over what she'd done to Lucky and her family made her stomach clench. She should just come clean so they could get on with the important day.

Except one look at her father stopped her in her dusty pink calf-high cowboy boots. Dad radiated happiness, something he'd done every day since meeting Evie, but he'd never looked as happy as he did today. As it was, Elizabeth would disappoint him all too soon when her and Lucky's fake engagement came to an end, but today she couldn't—and wouldn't—do anything to spoil this happy occasion.

Dad's gaze didn't leave Evie, who was flanked by three on each side. Elizabeth stood to her immediate right, with Nicole and Audrey beside her. To her future stepmother's left were Grandma Eloise, Sabrina and Evie's best friend, Robyn, her longtime drummer.

"Time for something different!" The photographer set her camera in a safe spot and handed out the new dusty rose cowboy hats Evie and Gordon had given the bridesmaids and flower girl.

"This is one gorgeous Stetson." Robyn placed her hat on her head and whistled. "Evie, you and Gordon sure know how to throw a party."

"This will ruin my hair." Nicole cringed with disdain and smoothed her moss-green tea-length dress, which was a twin of Sabrina's.

"Stuff and nonsense. There's nothing like a cowboy hat at a ranch wedding." Grandma Eloise grinned and placed hers on her head at an angle, the pink nicely accenting her silver lace dress, which matched her hair. The older woman glowed with the attention of being the mother of the bride. "Besides, that's what a brush is for."

Along with the can of hair spray Evie's hairdresser had insisted on using this morning, Elizabeth mused. Her hair would stay in place like this for the rest of the year. Elizabeth accepted the hat and helped Audrey with hers. Both she and her niece, along with Robyn, wore dusty rose dresses, which matched their hats.

Something was wrong, though, as her cowboy hat didn't fit right. Elizabeth looked inside at the inner lining near the sweatband, where their names were embroidered. "I have your hat, Nicole."

They traded, and the photographer encouraged them to hold them high over their heads, adjusting the group until the Rockies provided the perfect backdrop. More clicks and more smiles.

Evie faced Elizabeth, who admired the bride's champagne-colored wedding dress embroidered with tiny dusty pink roses, her trademark color, along with moss-green leaves. "Your wedding will be here before you know it. Are you holding the ceremony here or in town?"

Considering she and Lucky had no intention of getting married, she hadn't thought of an answer. While she and Jared were dating, she'd dreamed of having the ceremony at the ranch. This site would still be her preferred venue, but she'd need a groom for that. "I don't know."

"Do you have a date yet?" Nicole left the line and picked up her moss-green clutch from the front row of chairs. She returned with her phone and swiped on the screen. "Jeff and I have a packed schedule over the next few months between Zack and Audrey and work, but I know he won't want to miss his sister's wedding."

Audrey tugged at Elizabeth's skirt. "Can I be your flower girl?"

"When I get married, you can be my flower girl." Elizabeth was purposefully vague, disliking this hole she was digging for herself.

Audrey touched her glasses and straightened them on her face. "I like bright purple. It's my favorite color." She twirled around in her flower girl dress, the skirt made for dancing. "I love this dress, Grandma Evie. It's so pretty."

"Thank you, sweetheart. Just hearing you say 'Grandma Evie' made my day." She bent down and hugged Audrey before standing and facing Elizabeth again. "There's a good chance Lucky will make the year-end finals. If so, he'll be busy until December. What about a Christmas wedding?"

Elizabeth's heart thundered, and she was surprised everyone didn't hear it almost pounding out of her chest. To make matters worse, Dad appeared out of nowhere. "This conversation seems serious. You're not getting cold feet, are you, Evie?" His voice held a note of frantic worry with just enough humor inserted so he could sound nonchalant. A fine sheen of sweat broke out on his forehead despite this being one of the prettiest August days in Elizabeth's memory—crisp and clear, with nary a cloud in the cerulean sky.

"Never." Evie hugged Gordon. "You and the Double I are a part of my life now."

As it was a part of Elizabeth's life. Once Dad realized Elizabeth loved it with the same devotion as him, he might finally listen to her about her plans for its future.

"This day, and you, mean everything to me, Evie. The only thing that made it even better is Elizabeth's engagement."

Evie beamed and slipped her arm around Dad. "We were just talking about Elizabeth's wedding. Nicole asked if she and Lucky had set a date. Nicole, will you and Jeff fly here for the holidays if it's a Christmas wedding?" She smiled at Elizabeth. "Having your family around makes the big day even more special."

"My parents are hosting a New Year's party, but I'll talk to Jeff about Christmas." Nicole swiped the screen. "We'd have to arrange the time off with our law firm, and we won't stay as long."

Dad faced the photographer. "How far ahead are you booked? Are you available either the weekend before or after Christmas? Add their wedding deposit to our balance." Then he turned to Evie. "We can also talk to the other vendors when we pay the bills. I'm sure they'll accommodate another wedding at the Double I."

"I'm available the weekend after Christmas." The photographer started texting. "I'm engaged to the caterer, and I'm checking with him about his schedule."

This was getting out of hand fast.

"I haven't checked with Lucky," she protested, trying to figure out how to stop this madness from escaping her control. "He should have a say in this."

Evie winked at her. "He's in love and will go along with any date you choose. That is, unless you two want to get married even sooner than that?"

Elizabeth wasn't planning on getting married at all.

She grasped at anything to draw the attention away from plans for a ceremony that would never happen and back to the one that would. "Your wedding is in two hours. Shouldn't we finish this?"

The photographer took back control and called for Elizabeth, Nicole and Audrey to surround Gordon. She assumed her place before the photographer lowered her camera and stared right at her. "Elizabeth, your expression went wonky. Smile this time, okay?"

In the distance, Lucky and Will walked toward the picture area. Her stomach did a funny flip, and she took a deep breath. It wasn't anticipation about Lucky's presence that caused that inner dance. Embarrassment did funny things to a person, and that's all it was. She'd roped him into this mess on her behalf. If the photographer's down payment was nonrefundable, Elizabeth would repay her father the fee, but that was the least of her quandaries. How was she going to explain to Lucky that they now had a date for the wedding?

Sabrina spotted the group walking toward them. "That's what happens when your fiancé heads this way." Laughing, she lowered her bouquet and faced Elizabeth. "But one thing bothers me."

Grandma Eloise started coughing and everyone crowded around her. Will rushed over while Lucky diverted in the other direction. Evie patted her mother's hand. "Sit down. All this excitement must be affecting you more than I realized..."

"Here's some water, Grandma Eloise." Lucky appeared with a glass, the liquid sloshing over the top.

"That's just what I needed, Lucky. Thank you." Grandma Eloise accepted the drink with a smile.

"Maybe you should lie down until it's time for the wedding." Concern laced Evie's tone, and she appealed to Gordon with her eyes.

"Stuff and nonsense." Grandma Eloise drank a few long sips and reached for her cane. "Sabrina will help me freshen up. Afterward, I'd like the photographer to take a picture of me and Genie together."

"Of course, Grandma." Sabrina reached for her grandmother's arm and led her away.

While Sabrina ushered Grandma Eloise toward the main house, Gordon pulled aside the photographer, and the two had a private discussion. As much as she wanted to interrupt them and confide that her wedding to Lucky was off because it was never on to begin with, she couldn't ruin her father's important day.

A minute later, her father reappeared with a big grin. "Before the guests arrive, the photographer is going to take Lucky and Elizabeth's engagement pictures." He patted Lucky on the back. "Congratulations! Elizabeth and Evie talked, and the Saturday after Christmas works well for everyone. You and Elizabeth can talk about it before the reception and finalize the date. With this much notice, we might even get Ben to come home for the holidays. Welcome to the family."

The photographer came over and led Elizabeth and Lucky away from the crowd.

Lucky mouthed "Christmas" at her, a shocked expression spread over his face. She grimaced and nodded. Somehow, a wedding date, engagement photos and deposits made the disaster of this more real.

Then his gaze swept over her, and his mouth dropped open. Wonder lit his eyes, and she looked around her, expecting a reason for the change in his reaction. Her head stilled, and she sent him a questioning glance. He smiled, pointed at her and mouthed "beautiful." Somehow, amid the impending storm, his presence calmed the roiling emotions inside her.

Suddenly, she didn't know which was worse—his presence growing on her to the point where she felt lighter when he was around, or facing the inevitable music when their ruse was discovered.

Falling in love was too real and too painful. Keeping her wits about her and heart out of this arrangement was the only way she'd be able to get through the fallout when this facade ended.

CHAPTER SIX

LUCKY RETURNED TO the rear, having seated the final guests, friends of the groom. Before today, he'd only attended two other weddings: Will and Kelsea's, followed by Sabrina and Ty's, both times in clothes that belonged to him. He tugged at the tuxedo shirt collar, the stiff fabric unfamiliar and chafing, until he spotted Elizabeth kneeling in front of Audrey. Suddenly his discomfort faded as he concentrated on the pair. Elizabeth straightened her niece's purple frames and tipped the cowboy hat upward so Audrey's face was more visible. Elizabeth winked at her niece and hugged her before rising and handing her the basket of pink rose flower petals.

Lucky swallowed, the intimate moment between the two family members not lost on him. Elizabeth cared more than she let on to others. He understood that too well, but maybe it was time to change all that. Maybe it was time to express his appreciation in words as well as deeds.

Then, Elizabeth donned her hat and approached

him, sunlight bathing her in a golden glow. She held out her elbow for him, and his heart raced at the woman by his side. It didn't matter whether she wore flannel or silk. Her inner radiance set her apart from every other woman he'd known.

"Ready to walk me down the aisle?" Her cheeks grew as pink as her hat. "You've done so much for me and my family today. Thank you for staying." She hesitated and switched her bouquet to her other hand. "There's something else you should know."

"Tomorrow. Today is a day for happiness." He was the one who should be thanking her, and he recalled his new promise to himself. "Elizabeth, thank you. There's nowhere else I'd rather be."

Someone tapped them, and they proceeded down the aisle, where she took her place next to Nicole and he stood beside Jeff before the string quartet ceased the processional music. Then everyone rose to their feet as the musicians launched into the wedding march. Evie appeared and glided down the aisle, smiling at some guests who were dotting at the corners of their eyes with tissue.

Gordon and Evie exchanged vows they'd written themselves, and Lucky snuck another glance at Elizabeth, her gaze locked on his as if they were the only ones here. No matter what else happened after today, this shared moment would stay with him.

The wedding ended without a hitch, and Lucky

walked into the reception tent. Someone he didn't know came up and patted him on the back. "Welcome to Violet Ridge. The Irwins are a fine family."

Others followed, their congratulations sincere yet foreboding. It would be a total disaster when they learned his engagement to Elizabeth was a sham. Instead of finding a place to belong, this was merely another rest stop on his way to his ultimate destination, wherever that may be.

This wasn't the time or place, though, for those kinds of thoughts. Gordon and Evie had spared no expense with the festivities, and he, along with everyone else, settled back and enjoyed the dinner. He'd never tasted a meal this exquisite, and he'd never seen anyone as beautiful as Elizabeth, who was whispering something to Sabrina.

The band was now warming up, and Grandma Eloise tapped her silver boot tip against the wooden floor under the reception tent.

Someone clinked their crystal goblet, and the guests turned their attention to Jeff, who was rising to his feet a few seats away from Lucky at the head table. It must be time for the toasts. Lucky listened while stealing glances at Elizabeth, who didn't realize the vision she was in that dark pink dress with her burnished auburn hair cascading in curls over her shoulders.

More people spoke until Gordon finally rose, with Evie joining him at his side. She spoke first, expressed her thanks and then turned over the microphone to her new husband.

"Tonight, I look out and see so many colleagues and friends who've come here to celebrate with me. Thank you for spending your evening with us and for your friendship, which has enriched my life." Gordon dipped his head and waited for the applause to fade away before he continued. "A special thanks to Evie's family for bringing me and mine into your fold. To my family, a special thank-you for the love you've extended to my new wife, and just when I thought my happiness bucket was so full, it now runneth over with the addition of Lucky Harper, who's engaged to my daughter, Elizabeth. Save the weekend after Christmas for a return trip to the Double I, as that's the Saturday they're getting married. A toast to my daughter and future son-in-law."

Gordon raised his glass, and the crowd chimed in with their congratulations. Elizabeth's cheeks turned a brighter shade of red than her hair, and Lucky barely kept from falling off his seat. How had this engagement gotten so far out of hand so fast?

Grandma Eloise scrambled to her feet, reaching for her cane and standing steady. "Gordon, I speak for Bob and myself when I welcome you to the MacGrath family. Lucky and Elizabeth, I hold both of you in my heart and am always here for you as your honorary grandmother. As the mother of the bride, I think I've earned the privilege of announcing the first dance between Gordon and Evie. Then, it's every person for themselves as I am a mean line dancer. Watch out that my cane doesn't stub your toe."

Laughter filled the room as the band began the familiar chords of "Misty Mountain," Evie's signature song, which Lucky figured was now hers and Gordon's as well. Evie nodded at Gordon, who escorted her to the middle of the dance floor. Lucky darted a look at Elizabeth, still bright red from the announcement, as guests came over and congratulated her. Her tight smile didn't waver, and she twisted her engagement ring. She glanced down and must have realized what she was doing as her blush deepened.

In his rush to become accepted by her family, he'd placed Elizabeth in quite a predicament. Why he'd thought the news would only stay among her family until they ended it, he wasn't sure. Somehow, he had to make this right for her before he left town.

Or should he sneak out and leave her to handle the aftermath? No, that was wrong, and Cale had taught him a sight better at the Cattle Crown Ranch in Steamboat Springs all those years ago.

He fiddled with his fork while guests began congratulating him. After the tenth or so, he lost track of how many, he needed a minute to himself, as the well-wishers' good intentions were biting at his conscience. With a smile he didn't feel on the inside, he left the reception tent for a breath of fresh mountain air.

Walking a short distance away from the tent, he heard sniffles. That halted him in his tracks. Was someone crying? And why? Had he made Elizabeth cry on her father's wedding day? His breath caught, and he peeked behind the closest aspen. His heart skipped a beat at the sad sight. Audrey Irwin sat under the tree, crying. What was the girl doing outside by herself?

"Audrey?" He went over and sat by her side.

She glanced up and blinked. "Uncle Lucky!" She threw her arms around him and hugged him. "Whatcha doing out here?"

"I could ask you the same thing." Lucky reached into his pocket and pulled out the linen square. "Did you tell anyone where you were going?"

She started nodding before she met his gaze and slowly shook her head. "Mommy and Daddy are dancing, and so are Grandma Evie and Grandpa Gordon. Zack is busy with his video-game player. There's nothing for me to do."

He handed her the cloth and motioned for her to wipe her eyes. "I know what it's like to feel left out. It's not fun." Growing up, though, he hadn't had anyone who'd be upset about him disappearing, like she had now. "You know, though, you have to tell an adult before you go anywhere.

When people care about you and love you, they want to make sure you're okay."

She sniffled and removed her glasses. After she blotted her eyes, she handed him back the square, but he folded her hand over it and told her to keep it. She gave him a slight smile before she winced. "Am I in trouble?"

He didn't want to think about the irony of her question, as he'd be in far worse trouble if the residents of Violet Ridge discovered he had no intention of marrying Elizabeth. Not that he didn't want to get married someday, and not that Elizabeth wasn't the most beautiful, intelligent, kind woman he'd ever met. He'd be, well, lucky to have someone like her in his life.

Any other time, he'd have loved to be friends with someone like her, if not more than friends. But he was out of his league here with all the surrounding opulence.

Audrey's face looked expectantly at him, and at least he could solve this problem. "Not if we both get back to the reception tent, where we belong." He used the aspen for leverage as he rose. "And I might be able to help you with your boredom."

He reached for her hand and helped her off the ground. "It's all icky adult stuff in there." She wrinkled her nose and her purple-rimmed glasses fell a few inches.

"Depends on your perspective." He raised his chin and grinned. "You're speaking to someone who's a big kid at heart. I'll bet you your piece of wedding cake we'll have fun."

"Cake? There'll be cake?" Audrey looked skeptical. "I don't believe you."

"I'm wounded to the core." He clasped his hands over his chest. "Of course there's cake. You saw it. The pretty one with the pink flowers."

"We get to eat that? It's not just a decoration?" Her big green eyes lit up behind those frames. "Let's go."

She grabbed his hand and pulled him toward the tent, but not before he caught sight of Elizabeth standing behind an aspen, relief all over her face as she pointed toward Audrey. How much of that exchange had she witnessed? Still, she'd noticed Audrey was missing and had searched for her.

The Irwins did stick together, an enviable trait indeed.

ELIZABETH TAPPED HER toe under the table. She watched Lucky demonstrating to Audrey how to move her feet for the line dance.

Grandma Eloise sat next to Elizabeth and huffed out a breath. "That was fun." She tapped her cane before placing it between them. "Why aren't you out there?"

Elizabeth pointed to her cowboy boots. "Two left feet."

"Maybe you just haven't danced with the right

person." Grandma Eloise pointed toward the dance floor. "Lucky saved two dances for me. Your fiancé has some moves."

Elizabeth reached for her water and downed the last drop. "He's having fun with Audrey."

Grandma Eloise clucked her tongue. "I think he wants to dance with his fiancée."

At that moment, Lucky glanced their way and wiggled his finger at Elizabeth to join them. Not only did that tuxedo show off rather broad shoulders, but Lucky was also a genuinely nice person. She'd gone looking for Audrey earlier, only to duck behind an aspen tree so she wouldn't interrupt their conversation. The way he'd coaxed Audrey back had pulled at her heartstrings. If only they'd met under other circumstances…

Who was she kidding? The time still wouldn't have been right. Not with those architect plans waiting to come to fruition and possibly introducing a new breed of cattle to the ranch. A question about Simmentals came to mind, and she grabbed her phone. Her fingers flew across the screen.

A boot stopping inches from her led her gaze to Lucky, who shook his head. "I know that look. Even your father is taking today off, and deservedly so." Lucky pointed toward Dad, who was laughing as he stumbled and bumped into Evie. His new wife righted Dad, and they resumed their dance. "Ranch business can wait until tomorrow."

Grandma Eloise rose and reached out for Audrey's hand. "Come with me. You can help me with something before we tell Evie it's time to cut the cake."

The pair left, the older leading the younger, and Elizabeth never realized you could be alone with someone in a crowded room before. Lucky tilted his head toward the dance floor. "You need more fun in your life."

"I need two working feet in my life." She laughed away her nervousness, not sure whether the offer to dance or Lucky's presence was the culprit. Either way, her stomach was doing backflips at the sight of him, so handsome in his tuxedo.

"One dance, and if I hurt your feet, I'll rub the soreness out myself." He flexed his hands and cracked his knuckles.

"That isn't a rousing endorsement of your skills."

"It's best to show you, anyway. Telling you isn't half as fun." He waggled his eyebrows until she stood and threw her napkin on the table.

"You're incorrigible."

"Thank you. May I have this line dance?" Lucky bowed at the waist.

"Be careful with my feet. They're tender."

Her breath caught as she met his gaze. Without further ado, she grabbed his hand and led him to the back of the dance floor. "What do I do first?" she asked.

The song ended, and the singer announced

there'd be one slow song before Evie threw the bouquet and cut the cake. Elizabeth headed for the table, but Lucky tapped her arm. "Afraid of a little dance?"

She raised her chin. "You should be afraid for your feet."

"I take my chances inside a rodeo arena. I can manage this." He reached for her, and she dipped her head.

"You can't say you weren't warned."

Without another word, she slipped into his waiting arms, and he placed his arm around her waist. Her breath hitched at the close contact, and he stepped back, obviously thinking she didn't want him so close when his presence was actually throwing her for a loop. "I was surprised, that's all."

At feelings she shouldn't be feeling for her fake fiancé who was getting under her skin more than she wanted to admit.

"I promise. You're in safe hands for the next few minutes."

The band started playing a ballad, and other couples swayed to the sweet music. Enjoying one dance with Lucky wouldn't harm anything, or anyone. She met his gaze and regretted her last thought. This dance could irreparably harm her heart.

He pulled her closer, and they began dancing. She laid her head next to his chin, his skin warm. "I'm sorry about earlier."

"Why? You were looking for Audrey, weren't you?"

Yes, but that was beside the point. "You were so sweet with her, but that's not why I'm apologizing. The whole Christmas wedding date happened so fast."

"Elizabeth, there will be time for that later." He waited until she met his gaze, still sweet but with a note of warning. "I have a beautiful woman in my arms at a wedding I'd never imagined anyone like me would ever be invited to. When was the last time you enjoyed something for the sheer fun of it without worrying about the future?"

Her insides felt light and carefree. He thought she was beautiful. Maybe she should let go of worrying about how they were going to end this with no one getting hurt and go with the flow for tonight at least. The animals and plans could wait a little longer as the ranch hands were taking good care of the former, and the latter weren't going anywhere today, anyway. She snuggled close to him and let the song's rhythm seep into her.

But it ended too fast, and everyone was gathering around the cake table. Audrey approached Lucky and gestured for him to pick her up. He obliged and swept her into his arms. She hid her face in his shoulder. "I don't think I can watch Grandma Evie cut the cake," Audrey said.

Lucky tapped her until she looked at him. "Why not?"

"It's so pretty." She resumed her earlier position as he cracked a smile that showed he was doing his best not to laugh and hurt Audrey's feelings.

While the crowd watched her father and Evie, Elizabeth couldn't keep her eyes off Lucky. He'd make someone a very happy spouse someday. An image of him with another woman sent a shock through her system.

Was that a twinge of jealousy that zapped her? It couldn't be. This wasn't real. What her father and Evie had was real. Her gaze floated to Sabrina, the back of her head resting against Ty's chest, their love also genuine and inspiring. Her and Lucky's relationship was as fake as the ring on her finger.

Applause greeted the couple, and an attendant started handing out slices of cake to the crowd. Elizabeth accepted hers, the raspberry mousse filling complementing the buttery richness of the vanilla cake. She couldn't help but miss her brother Ben. Raspberries were his favorite.

The energy of the crowd, though, was electric with everyone buzzing about the wedding and the delicious cake. No sooner had she finished her slice and set down her plate than someone tapped at the microphone. "It's time for Evie Irwin to throw the bouquet."

More applause and Elizabeth started to walk toward the sidelines. At least her engagement to Lucky would get her out of this part of the reception. She approached the crowd off to the side, only to see Grandma Eloise shake her head and point her cane toward Audrey, Robyn and the others, waiting for Evie to toss the flowers. "You're still eligible to catch the bouquet."

Sabrina and Nicole nodded and pushed a protesting Elizabeth back toward the dance floor. *Fine.* She'd go out there, but she'd stand at the back, where she'd have no chance of drawing any more attention toward her.

After an announcement asking if anyone else wanted to join in the fun, Evie glanced over her shoulder. "Where's my stepdaughter? I hope you catch this, because you're next. I can't wait for Christmas now."

Elizabeth hid behind Violet Ridge's favorite identical twins, one of whom was widowed, while the other was divorced. If Evie aimed for the rear, one of them would surely snag the floral arrangement.

Squeals accompanied the toss, and the flowers were batted from person to person like a hot potato until they finally hit Elizabeth in the head and fell into her hands. Her cheeks burned hot as everyone turned to congratulate her on catching the bouquet and her December wedding.

CHAPTER SEVEN

IT WAS SO early on this Sunday morning that it was actually the middle of the night. Lucky listened to the crickets chirp and the lowing of the cattle before he slid open the stable door as quietly as possible. Growing still, he searched the area in case any ranch hands might raise an alarm about his presence. One of the outside dogs, an alert border collie, ran over and sniffed him.

"It's okay, Moose." Audrey had laughed upon learning the dog's name, and Lucky kept his voice low as a barn owl screeched in the distance. "It's just me."

Fortunately for him, Moose wagged his tail before returning to his guard post. With this first hurdle cleared, Lucky patted his jacket, the letter he'd written to Elizabeth secure in his pocket. He'd leave the note on her office desk, load Butter-scotch in his trailer and be on his merry way to Casper for the next rodeo.

Yesterday's wedding had been a real barn buster, and so much more. The Irwin family had included him in everything, and for that, he'd always be grateful. For one day, he'd had a grandmother and so much more. Others may take that for granted, but he never would.

Once inside, he noticed Butterscotch at the front of his stall, awake and alert, a slight whinny his greeting for Lucky.

"Shh. I'll be right back, and we'll move on to other pastures." Maybe not as green as those here at the Double I, but something good always waited on the horizon.

He made his way to Elizabeth's tiny office and entered, flicking on the light.

"Going somewhere?" Elizabeth's voice startled him, and he turned.

He waited a few seconds until his breathing returned to a normal, steady rhythm. "What are you doing here?"

"It's my office. I was in the tack room about to start my morning routine when I heard someone in here and came to investigate." Passing him, he noticed she was already dressed in a flannel shirt layered over a red tank top paired with blue jeans and red boots. She looked just as beautiful in the fluorescent light and her cowgirl clothes as she had in the bridesmaid dress. A brief flicker of hurt crossed her face. "Were you really going to sneak out without saying goodbye?"

He reached into his pocket and pulled out the

letter he'd spent so much time composing last night. "I was going to leave this behind."

She stepped forward and reached for it. "May I?"

"No need." He crumpled it and replaced it in his pocket. "You can simply tell your family it didn't work out because you were caught up in the whirlwind of Evie and Gordon's wedding."

Her wry chuckle filled the air. "You must have me mixed up with someone else if you think my family would ever believe that excuse."

She stood so close it was hard not to reach out and smooth her hair. Touching her, though, might cross the invisible line.

"You have some hay in your hair," he said, wincing at how ridiculous he sounded. She reached up and the lone straw fell to the ground while he leaned against the door post. "You'll think of something. You're intelligent and perceptive."

Conflict warred in those expressive eyes, and she put a gentle hand on his flannel shirtsleeve. "I'm sorry I put you in a tight spot. I'll take the blame, so Will and Sabrina won't be upset with you."

His jaw clenched. Will and Sabrina had each found love. They didn't need him anymore, and he accepted that. Somewhere out there, someone needed him. "I'm not worried about that."

"Then think of my taking the blame as a way of thanking you for yesterday."

"Thanking me?" Her statement was almost as much of a surprise as her presence in her office this early in the day. "I'm the one who gained everything yesterday. I should be the one expressing my gratitude."

"You encouraged me to live in the moment and enjoy myself, which I did. That'll make the aftermath more than worth it." Elizabeth delivered a winsome smile, one he could find himself wanting to see often. "But why don't you take your own advice and stay one more day? It's recovery day, and we can both use that. Tomorrow's the preparation for the cattle roundup, which starts bright and early Tuesday and goes through Friday. It makes more sense to leave in the morning when you're well rested."

He hesitated. If he left now, he wouldn't get attached to this family and Elizabeth. Who was he kidding? He already cared about her. Look at how often he thought of her when she wasn't around. No matter how he looked at it, he'd need time over the following weeks to bounce back from once again being so close to a family and having it yanked away.

She was right. He needed time to regain his bearings. Could one day really make his departure worse?

She must have sensed his hesitancy. "Tammy

is making dinner with all the fixings tonight. You'll love her huckleberry pie with homemade ice cream."

"I've never had huckleberry pie before." He hadn't texted his friend that he'd arrive in Casper today, leaving his arrival time vague and open-ended.

"And you've never seen a sunrise at the Double I on horseback. How about we take Andromeda and Butterscotch for an early morning ride? We can discuss the best way to end this charade. As I see it, we can break up after dinner, or you can take your leave while I'm away on the cattle roundup. While this is fake, I'm sure you want your ring back." She held up her finger and twisted it so he could see the clear tape on the back. "I'm worth more than a mere letter. Let me be in on the details, okay?"

Saying goodbye to Audrey and Grandma Eloise were added bonuses. And one more day with Elizabeth? That was priceless. "I've seen some mighty pretty sunrises in my life. You think this one can compare?"

She grabbed her red cowboy hat and plopped it on her head. "Once you see one on the Double I, it'll ruin you for all others."

That was exactly what he was afraid of.

ELIZABETH REINED IN Andromeda and gasped at the ribbons of orange on the horizon meeting the lush green landscape. No longer was the mountainside bathed in shadow, but there was a glow that promised a full day ahead. Was it only the scenery that catapulted this sunrise into the magnificent category?

Or did Lucky astride Butterscotch add something to the fullness of this moment?

"You're right. That sunrise is unlike any other." Lucky pulled up beside her, his eyes soaking in the beauty of the day.

That made what she had to say all that much harder. "Well, so is our engagement." The early rays caught the diamond, and a rainbow prism seemed to bounce on the saddle's pommel. "We need a plan to get out of it."

"I like pineapple on my pizza. You could say that was the ultimate dealbreaker."

She laughed. "Except everyone knows I order it the same way."

"Then that won't work." He shrugged and flicked the reins so Butterscotch proceeded at a slow trot. "How do you like your French fries?"

Andromeda kept pace with Butterscotch. "I dunk mine in my puddle of ketchup."

Lucky shook his head. "While barbecue sauce is better, I drizzle ketchup over fries. That way it's even."

"They get soggy like that. My way's much better." How was he making something so serious as staging a fake breakup so much fun?

He brought Butterscotch to a stop and searched the mountainside, his smile fading like the colors on the horizon. "Why now? This sunrise is something special."

And just like that, the day was upon them. "The sooner we end it, the less likely anyone will discover how everything spiraled out of control."

He stared at her a long time, and she held her head high. So he didn't eat his French fries the same way she did. He liked pineapple pizza and horses and made dreaded family occasions into something special. She had to break up with him now, or else…?

She could fall for him.

"Tonight, then. We'll stage a pretend fight, and then I'll leave for the rodeo." There was a slight movement near his jawline, enough for her to want to reach out and reassure him that his presence at the wedding had changed everything for her.

But then she'd never know if he could fall for her, just her, and not the whole Irwin family, who'd been on their best behavior during the wedding. "I think it needs to be convincing."

"Elizabeth, you leave your imprint on everything. They'll believe you." This was sounding too real, too fast. Nothing came this quickly and lasted.

"For good measure, I'll talk about the ranch and how much it means to me." She remembered his earlier advice about sticking as close to the truth as possible.

"And I can't imagine any other life than going from rodeo to rodeo. We simply couldn't make it work."

They practiced their mock argument, and the light faded from his eyes. She couldn't let it end like this.

The sunrise moment, that was. "I'll race you across the meadow. You haven't lived until you feel the morning breeze kissing your cheeks with sunflowers all around you."

A hint of a smile curled up his lips. "You're on, in three. One, two..." He spurred on Butterscotch before he said *three*, his laughter the real cue to resume their fun.

Her laughter met his as she joined him for one last horseback ride.

Hours later, with the down payment for the construction of the bunkhouses due a week from tomorrow, Elizabeth stilled her hand on the doorknob to her father's study. No doubt she'd find him here, as he and Evie were waiting until the end of the cattle roundup to leave for their Hawaiian honeymoon. The day after the wedding should be the perfect time to broach business, just as tonight should be the perfect time to end the sham of an engagement.

If Dad agreed to the construction and everything proceeded as planned with Lucky, Tuesday would be the beginning of the best roundup yet.

Not that her days with Lucky hadn't been special. And this morning was the most special time of all with her and Andromeda keeping pace once he and Butterscotch galloped across the meadow.

Now, though, she had to return to reality and leave the splendor of Lucky's company in the past. Otherwise, one of them might get hurt, and she didn't want him to get so involved that there might be any heartache on his part as well as on hers. Once the line was crossed on either side, it was impossible to keep emotion at bay.

"It's an afternoon made for riding." Her father's booming voice could be heard down the hall.

Dad wasn't in the study. Instead, she found him in the living room with Zack. "Fresh air and horses are more fun than any video game."

"No way. I'm almost leveling up." Zack's gaze didn't leave his handheld game unit. "Then I can get more stuff and be faster."

Dad turned toward Jeff and Nicole, who were involved in a deep conversation that made them oblivious to what was happening around them. Dad tapped Jeff's shoulder. "What about a family horseback excursion? Then I can gauge how long Zack and Audrey can ride on Tuesday. They've been doing really well in our riding lessons. Audrey's a natural."

That was high praise from her father.

Nicole glared at Jeff and nudged his side. "Go on, tell him."

"Tell me what?" Dad crossed his arms as Lucky approached the living room from the opposite direction from Elizabeth. "Ah, here are Elizabeth and Lucky. Perfect. Now I won't have to repeat myself."

Elizabeth let out a long, slow breath, knowing improved housing was a necessity to attract long-term workers. "I have something I need to talk to you about before the roundup."

"I thought we weren't bringing this up until after dinner." Lucky paled under his tan.

"I have some plans I want to run by you," Elizabeth said to her father, before widening her eyes in Lucky's direction, hoping he would realize she wasn't referring to their breakup before he said anything more.

Nicole crossed her arms over her chest, a frown marring her face. "I can't go on the roundup. There's an important deposition this week that I must attend. Fortunately, it's virtual."

Dad shrugged. "We'll miss you, but we'll keep Audrey and Zack so busy they won't even notice you're gone." He waved away Nicole's concern like it was nothing and faced Lucky and Elizabeth. "Now, you two don't have to worry about a thing to do with your wedding. Evie and I paid the caterer last night and placed the deposit for your reception with him. Same with the photographer and florist."

Elizabeth couldn't seem to catch her breath. Her father was a force of nature. While her father and Evie had employed the best in Violet Ridge, the same as she most likely would have hired, that was beside the point. When she married someone, she wanted to plan everything and hire everyone herself. "Thank you, but that's not what I wanted to talk to you about..." Her mouth went dry. She knew exactly what she wanted to say about the bunkhouses. Why was it harder now when there was an audience?

"What Elizabeth is trying to say is—"

Lucky was interrupted when Evie burst into the room, waving her phone in the air, a huge smile gracing her face. "You'll never believe it!" She ran over and hugged Gordon, then Zack, then Audrey. "I have the best news."

"Nicole's not going on the roundup. She has legal matters," Dad began before he blinked, as if Evie's words had penetrated his senses. "Sorry, darlin'. What's your news?"

"Oh, the roundup." Evie gulped and shook her head. "For a minute, I forgot about it. Never mind."

Dad placed his hands on her shoulders. "What's your news, darlin'?"

She held her phone up to his face. "The producers asked me to be a guest host on *Your Next Favorite Song.*"

Dad's face lit up, and he hugged his new wife. "That's wonderful. I know how much you've wanted to appear on that television show."

"I'd have to be in California tomorrow night. The show films this week." Evie's smile wobbled, and then her shoulders slumped. "I grew up on a ranch and remember how important this cattle roundup is. I'll see if they'll have me a month from now."

"This is important to you. I promised you yesterday I'd be there for better or worse, and this qualifies for the better part of my vows. You're going to be the prettiest, most talented guest host ever." Dad faced Lucky. "You'll be riding along with Elizabeth, right? And Jeff's an old hand, too. You rode on these for what, ten years, before leaving for college if my memory is right."

Elizabeth struggled to maintain her composure. What was going on here? He was turning to Lucky and Jeff when she'd been the one accompanying him for the past twenty years. "Dad, I can do this in my sleep. Our cowhands are the best." At last, an opening appeared for her to bring up the bunkhouses. "And speaking of our staff—"

"You're right, Elizabeth. Our staff, along with Jeff and Lucky, can handle this." A wide grin broadened across Dad's face. "Evie, you text your acceptance, and we'll start our honeymoon early.

I'll go with you to California, and then we'll head to Hawaii as planned."

Once again, her father had undermined her, bringing Jeff and Lucky into the equation. This only seemed to confirm those fears. Was this the best time and place, though, to confront him about it?

"I'm sorry, sir." Lucky leaned against the wall. "But my horse isn't outfitted for the roundup. It was one thing to ride with Elizabeth this morning, but his shoes aren't right for the terrain."

"Not a problem." Gordon dismissed his concern, too. "You can use Margarita."

She winced. Dad never let anyone ride Margarita on the trail.

"Thank you, but the rodeo—"

"Doesn't start for another week and a half. This is only a four-day event. Besides, this will give you time together. Plus, you can decide where you want to honeymoon, our treat, now that all the deposits have been paid." Gordon nodded and reached for Evie's hand. "Elizabeth, Lucky and Jeff have everything in hand. That takes a load off my mind, so I can sit back and bask in everyone adoring my talented wife. We can leave whenever you're ready."

Evie smiled, and the two left the room, oblivious to the rising tension. There went a chance to get Dad's approval for the bunkhouses. Worse yet, this only confirmed her fears it was an up-hill battle to get his approval at all.

Lucky joined her and rubbed her shoulders, her tension melting under his fingers. She soaked in his presence. His sense of calm and his down-home common sense were rare qualities indeed. She could use a little of that in her life, even if it was just temporary. To her surprise, she wouldn't mind if he made Violet Ridge his permanent home base.

Stop it, Elizabeth. He wasn't her actual boyfriend any more than the ring on her finger was made of genuine diamonds. This was a fake engagement, but the feelings she was beginning to feel for him weren't fake.

Her father's pronouncement added a new wrinkle to this dilemma. Her father wanted Jeff and Lucky on the trail with her. She was more than capable of handling everything herself, but her father wanted them by her side. For the sake of his happiness and well-being, she'd go along with it for now.

Maybe this was a blessing in disguise. The trail might provide the perfect place for her and Lucky's so-called breakup. Without her father's disruptive presence, she and Lucky could end this charade, once and for all.

Then she'd also find a way to close the door on the jumbled emotions his presence caused whenever he entered the room.

CHAPTER EIGHT

LATE MONDAY AFTERNOON, Elizabeth entered the grocery store and selected a cart. With Tammy's list in hand, as well as requests from several of the cowhands and her brother's family, she headed for the produce stand. Even though she rarely ran ranch errands, she'd jumped at the chance to head into town and get away from the constant scrutiny of the engagement. Even the grooms had been asking questions about her wedding, and she longed for a respite from the constant barrage.

"Elizabeth Irwin, one of my favorite students." Mrs. Sanderson, her fifth-grade teacher, hailed her from a spot near the peaches. "A little birdie told me you're engaged!"

So much for keeping the engagement under wraps. Elizabeth propelled her cart toward the nectarines and stopped near one of her favorite teachers. She twisted the ring on her finger, the tape a temporary fix, but then again, this was a temporary engagement. "You heard about it already?"

"I just had my hair done." She fluffed her blue-gray pageboy and smiled. "It was all the talk at the Think Pink Salon."

Of course it was.

"You know, a lot can happen between now and December." Maybe laying the groundwork now for the broken engagement would help her escape scrutiny down the line, although that seemed unlikely in a town the size of Violet Ridge.

"Does that mean you might move up the date?" Mrs. Sanderson clapped her hands. "I'm so happy for you."

Elizabeth sent her the woman a wobbly smile while Mrs. Sanderson pulled her into an embrace. After she escaped, Elizabeth gathered the items on her list while even more town residents stopped her and congratulated her on the news. Distracted, she threw anything in the cart and blinked at the register. Cookies, processed cupcakes and kettle potato chips weren't part of her regular diet, and she never purchased them. Yet that and every other form of junk food had made its way into her cart.

The cashier greeted her and made a big deal about the ring on Elizabeth's finger, leaving no chance to ask for the food to be returned to the shelves.

Was there any graceful way of getting out of this?

SUMMER IN VIOLET RIDGE was crowded with tourists taking pictures of the metal buffalo in front of a restaurant that served bison burgers. While crossing Main Street from the parking area to the shops, Lucky held on to Zack's and Audrey's hands. This town had always been one of his favorite stops on the rodeo tour, with its picturesque downtown, the pastel facades showcasing some fun stores and delicious food. Today, he had one destination in mind: Reichert Trading Company, where he'd seen children's fishing poles next to those bright and colorful kites. Earlier, Jeff had pulled him aside and asked him if he wanted to spend some time getting to know his future niece and nephew. There was no way Lucky could turn down such an offer, his happiness overflowing at making it onto the list of approved caretakers for these two.

"I have a fun afternoon planned." Lucky released their hands and warned them to stay by his side. "What do you say to a horse ride to the meadow with the duck pond? We'll go fishing and have a great time." Audrey pulled him over to Rocky Mountain Chocolatiers. "Can we have a treat, too?"

It was next to impossible to say no to that elfin face framed with those big purple glasses. A customer opened the door and delicious smells of chocolate and sugar filled the air. "All that fresh air and exercise calls for something special."

Even Zack's face lit up when they entered the shop. They waited in line, and Lucky laughed at hearing the siblings change their mind umpteen times about what they'd choose for their treat. He'd never had a day like this when he'd shuttled from foster home to foster home, and he'd savor every moment as much as he'd enjoy a chocolate turtle the size of his hand, his favorite chocolate confection with pecans and caramel.

When it was their turn to deliver their orders, Zack asked Lucky's permission for an apple covered with caramel and nuts while Audrey's eyes grew wide at the sheer number of varieties of fudge. The attendant laughed and pointed at the second row. "My daughter's a little younger than you are. The strawberry tuxedo fudge is her favorite. It's white chocolate fudge with chocolate chips and swirls of strawberry flavoring."

"Yes, please." Audrey looked at Lucky for approval, and he nodded at both children.

"Aren't you Elizabeth's fiancé?" The attendant boxed up the order. "She's a sweetheart."

Lucky nodded, and Audrey jumped on her toes. "You know my aunt Elizabeth?"

"You must be Jeff's son and daughter." The woman, who appeared to be about the same age as Lucky's thirty-one, smiled at the pair and gave them each a tiny plastic spoon with a sample of the fudge. "I attended school with your aunt, and she's really smart. She helped me with my business plan, and she knows everything about horses."

That was quite a compliment. Then again, Elizabeth was quite a woman.

"I'm Zack, and this is my sister, Audrey." Zack placed his hands on Audrey's shoulders in a protective way.

"Nice to meet you. Tell Elizabeth that Emma said hello." Emma gave them a big smile.

They finished the transaction, and Lucky dipped his cowboy hat at Emma. When they stepped out the door, bright sunshine flooded their eyes, and it took a minute to adjust. Then they made their way to Reichert Supply Company. What should have been a two-minute walk turned into a half hour as nearly everybody they met told him a story about Elizabeth, all of them positive.

The townspeople loved her, and he couldn't blame them.

Lucky headed for the sporting goods section and studied the display for the best equipment.

Zack tugged at Lucky's sleeve. "We don't know how to fish." Then the young boy picked up the longest pole and swung it around.

"I can teach you." Lucky stopped the pole before it hit Audrey. "But these are more your size."

He gestured to some smaller poles, then selected ones that would work. Audrey looked with longing at the bright kites. "Can we fly a kite, too?"

"Why not?" He had them all day, thanks to Jeff and Nicole's afternoon and evening with phone conference meetings. "More fun stuff to tell your parents."

After a great deal of back and forth between a dragon or a unicorn kite, Lucky suggested a compromise. He paid for the sunflower kite, and they found themselves back at the ranch a short time later.

Never one to stand on formality, Lucky entered through the kitchen rather than the more impressive front door. He found Elizabeth helping Tammy unload groceries.

Tammy clicked her tongue. "It must be love," she said as she reached in for the fourth package of chocolate sandwich cookies. "You never buy junk food."

"Aunt Elizabeth." Zack reached her first and began telling her about the trip to Violet Ridge.

"Emma says hello," Lucky added at the end.

Elizabeth reached for her red cowboy hat on a nearby hook. "Sounds like a great day. I'll be at the stable if anyone needs me."

"Why don't you go for a horse ride with us?" Lucky offered. "I'll wager you have everything ready for the cattle roundup."

She scoffed. "Of course, but I can't leave all of my work for the grooms."

"They're looking after the stable, right?" He waited for her acknowledgment. "Then I'll sweeten the deal. I bought two turtles, but you can have one."

She narrowed her eyes, and yet that didn't hide

the twinkle in them. "You drive a hard bargain. Emma makes really good turtles."

"I'll be the judge of that." He'd be getting more out of this day than she realized. "Come with us."

Within minutes, the four of them were riding out to the field of sunflowers, the long green stalks bending in the strong breeze. Nearby the sun glistened along the ripples of water where a mother duck swam with her ducklings following behind. They tethered the ponies, and Audrey ran over to the lake's edge.

"One, two, three, four duckies! Aunt Elizabeth, come see them," Audrey said.

Elizabeth hurried over and talked to Audrey while Lucky extracted his portable fishing pole and gear from Butterscotch's saddle. He demonstrated how to hook the fly and cast off. Elizabeth pulled Lucky aside.

"Audrey wants to pick some flowers for her mom, and then we're going to go in search of more ducks." Elizabeth leaned into Lucky, close enough for her soft hair to brush his cheek. "I think she just wants to observe everything, and she's too sweet to resist."

The females waved goodbye, and Lucky was patient with Zack, giving him pointers on staying quiet and observing everything around them. Still, the fish weren't biting this afternoon. Elizabeth and Audrey returned with a bouquet of wildflowers and the kite, and Lucky stowed the fishing gear.

Sunlight reflected off Elizabeth's auburn hair, revealing spun-gold highlights. The day was perfect for kite flying. He extracted the kite from its packaging and stood with his back to the wind. He held it aloft and let out the string line. The kite sailed upward, and he ran the length of the field until it gained enough altitude for it to stay in the air.

"Can I hold it?" Audrey and Zack said in unison.

"How about Aunt Elizabeth gets a turn first?" Lucky waved away her protests until she stood close enough for him to smell the light scent of her perfume.

Elizabeth held up the line and kept the kite steady in the air. "You're good at this. You must have done a lot of kite flying with your parents."

"Never." This wasn't the time for her to hear his life story, although there was no one he wanted to share it with more, and that included Cherry, the woman he'd almost asked to marry him.

Elizabeth handed the kite to Zack, and he and his sister alternated turns while Lucky spread a blanket on the grass. Then he checked on the horses, making sure they had water and everything they needed. Afterward, he relaxed on a blanket and patted the open spot next to him. She hesitated and remained standing. "Maybe I should get back to work now?"

"All work and no play make Elizabeth a tired person." He opened the box of turtles, using his hand so the aroma of the chocolate would entice her to stay.

She settled next to him and kept her gaze on her niece and nephew. "You're great with kids. You'll make a good father."

Whether that was true had entered his mind hundreds of times over the years. Without a father figure or even a father, period, he'd struggled with the idea of bringing a child into the world. Would he make a good dad? That was one reason it had taken him so long to cozy up to the idea of a serious relationship. Cale and Will gave him hope, though, that he'd rise to the task.

He bit into his turtle, the pecan salty and crisp, the caramel oozing out of the sweet chocolate shell. "This is the life for now."

He watched her enjoy her treat, and he relished the time in the sweet summer sunshine to do the same.

BEFORE DAWN ON this dry Tuesday morning, Elizabeth yawned and approached the stable, yesterday's afternoon of relaxation and fun behind her. Time for hard work and getting the second of the ranch's three annual cattle roundups on the trail underway. The roundup involved quite a bit of labor as she and the crew checked on the cattle before moving them to their fall field, but there was also time for fun. Tammy's chuckwagon cooking, nighttime campfires and a singalong. Not much about it had changed since she started accompanying her father when she was eleven, and she wouldn't have it any other way. She stopped and let her eyes acclimate to the dim surroundings. The shadows of the mountains rising majestically in the background hid the muted colors she loved so much. Far away, the distant howl of a coyote sent a shiver through her. On the horse ride out to the summer pasture, she'd keep a close eye on the fences. The ranch didn't need to lose any cattle to a nocturnal visitor.

Moose, the outside border collie she'd known since he was a pup, ran over as if he also felt the excitement and energy in the air. He ran circles around her, and she laughed. "Yes, you're coming along. I couldn't do this without you."

"That sure is a pretty way to start the day." Lucky's smooth voice could melt butter, but it still startled her.

She caught her breath. "You scared me."

"Didn't mean to. I just wanted to thank you kindly for letting me go on the roundup with your family." Moose increased the radius of his circles until he herded the two of them together. In close proximity to Lucky, she felt those cartwheels in her stomach twist more rapidly than ever. "How can I help you this morning? Fun is fun, but there's also a time for hard work."

Elizabeth slid open the stable doors and greeted a groom coming from the opposite direction. Then she faced Lucky. "You can stay out of the way while we work."

He shook his head. "I have to earn my keep. I've worked on many a ranch over the past thirteen years."

Those blue eyes were pleading his case. His pride was at stake, and she recognized that emotion all too well. "Okay. You can check the saddlebags." She listed everything she expected in each, except for Zack's and Audrey's, since their packs would be lighter.

She was concerned about her niece and nephew coming along, but Tammy had assured her she'd look after them while the others checked on the cattle's welfare. The promise of campfires and no showers had cinched the deal for Zack, and Audrey was looking forward to sleeping in Aunt Elizabeth's tent.

In no time, they readied all the equipment and animals as sunrise greeted them. Elizabeth glanced at her watch and tapped her cowboy boot on the brown dirt outside the stable. Where was everyone?

Lucky must have noticed her agitation. "They're coming. So much has happened over the past few days, and not everyone's used to this schedule, but they're coming."

He was right, but that coyote howl had her on

edge. Okay, so did Lucky, who had no more intention of staying in one place than she did about leaving the Double I Ranch. She was letting her heart cloud her better judgement. Hadn't she learned anything from the debacle that was her relationship with Jared?

For the umpteenth time, she reminded herself this situation was different. Once they ended their "engagement," though, she wasn't sure whether she could call Lucky for a pep talk or ask his advice on the new watering post she'd read about. Sabrina said Lucky dropped everything at a minute's notice for a close friend, and yet when this was over, would they consider themselves friends? She knew one thing for certain. Lucky Harper's friendship was a treasure beyond compare.

As if on cue, a line of people headed toward the stable with Grandma Eloise leading the group. Something was different about the older woman, but Elizabeth couldn't discern what it was. Still, it was sweet that Evie's mother wanted to send them on their way. Most likely, the older lady would say her goodbyes now and return to Texas while they were gone. It was a shame she and Bob lived so far away. Sabrina glowed whenever her grandmother was in the room, and Elizabeth wasn't surprised. Grandma Eloise had a resiliency and strength about her that brought out the best in people.

Jeff held Audrey's hand while Zack followed,

his fingers flying across his handheld video game. Elizabeth considered asking him for the unit and giving it back to him tonight, if for no other reason than his safety around the horses, but decided against calling him out in front of an audience. She'd make sure it was safely ensconced at the bottom of his saddlebag. Who needed a game console when there was this beautiful scenery and excitement all around?

Grandma Eloise came over, and Elizabeth finally put her finger on what was different. Her cane was nowhere in sight. "Do you have room for one more?"

"One more what?" Elizabeth blinked as Grandma Eloise pointed to herself.

Elizabeth blew out a long, deep breath. She disliked having to turn down the sweet woman, who was now as dear as a grandmother to her, but she'd already have to slow the pace with Jeff, Zack and Audrey coming along. At least Tammy was helping with the younger pair so that they'd be out of the way once everyone arrived at the campsite. Elizabeth, a good four decades younger, sometimes returned from the roundups happier for the experience but drained, both physically and mentally, from the activity. How could Grandma Eloise keep up with everyone? Letting her down gently seemed the best approach. "It's going to be rugged out there. We'll be in tents and riding for four days."

She looked toward Lucky, who approached Grandma Eloise, his face calm and kind. "Elizabeth's worried about you."

Grandma Eloise raised her head and pointed toward her cowboy boots. "I've been on more roundups than your ages combined."

"Horseback riding requires a certain amount of agility." Elizabeth was hoping against hope the woman would take the hint. The ranch was her responsibility, as were the health and welfare of those on the roundup.

"Horseback riding is one of the most therapeutic activities." Grandma Eloise delivered a curt nod. "There's increased range of motion, and it helps develop muscle strength. I won't beg, but I'd be a real help with Audrey and Zack."

Elizabeth inhaled a deep breath. Grandma Eloise was right, especially with Nicole staying behind to work on the deposition. Tammy could only do so much with Zack and Audrey while cooking. With the coyote making his presence known this morning, she'd have to keep a close eye on the fences, making Grandma Eloise's presence a necessity. She asked the groom to prepare Maisy, a gentle mare able to make the trip, then turned to the older woman. "We'll try it out this morning. If you feel like you need to return to the ranch, just say the word at lunchtime. Tammy's riding out with the catering chuck wagon and joining us after that. You can go back this afternoon, if necessary. After that, it'll be harder for anyone to reach us because of the rocky terrain. Promise you'll come back if you're exhausted?" She looked at Jeff and the children. "If it's too much on them, I want you to make the same promise."

Jeff nodded, and then Elizabeth turned to Grandma Eloise.

"Of course. Thanks, I won't be a bother. Be back in a jiffy." Grandma Eloise's eyes glinted in the dim lights of the stable.

"We'll wait for you," Elizabeth said while adding fifteen minutes to the departure time.

"No need." Grandma Eloise ducked into the stable and returned a minute later with her sleeping roll. "Had my gear in the tack room."

Elizabeth called everyone together. "This is a long trek, but there's nothing else like it. Is everyone ready for a great time?"

"Can I stay with Mom?" Zack kept his gaze glued to his game player. "I can play my game and be really quiet while she works."

Jeff reached out his hand for the console. "I'll take that for now. You can have it back tonight when we break camp. It will be good for you to spend some of your summer vacation outside."

With reluctance, Zack handed it over and trudged over to the horse he'd been riding during his lessons. Elizabeth approached Jeff. "Nice job with Zack."

"Thanks. He's a good kid, and I don't get to spend

enough time with him or Audrey." Jeff glanced at the cowhands. "Time to load up and head on the trail."

Bristling at Jeff's taking hold of authority, she felt better when JR, the foreman, looked at her for confirmation. She gave a slight nod, and each member of their group checked their saddlebags and cinches. As casually as possible, Elizabeth monitored Grandma Eloise while she adjusted her gear and climbed into the saddle.

Elizabeth sensed Lucky's presence by recognizing the spicy scent of his aftershave. "She's a wonder, isn't she?" he asked.

She faced him and nodded. "I hope I'm like her someday."

"You'll be just as feisty at her age." Admiration lurked in Lucky's gaze. "I'll watch out for her and the kids."

He mounted Margarita with a smooth motion. Everyone set off, and Elizabeth rode next to JR. He and his wife, Tammy, had been employed at the Double I since before she was born. "Tammy's meeting us with the chuck wagon, right?"

"Yep. She's looking forward to riding with us to the summer pasture after that." JR nodded and reined in his American quarter horse, Copper. "We should be there by nightfall."

"I'm looking forward to Tammy's flapjacks tomorrow morning." Elizabeth's mouth watered. "There's nothing like her campfire pancakes."

"Pancakes?" Zack turned around, his smile evident at the mention of food. "Those are my favorite."

Elizabeth returned his smile while checking on the fences. So far, no signs of any disrepair or coyote tracks, either. The morning passed by quickly as the group made their way to the checkpoint, where Tammy greeted them with a veritable feast. Elizabeth cared for the horses and then checked on Grandma Eloise, who insisted she was having the time of her life, before heading for food.

"Turkey or ham with fresh-baked buns." Tammy ushered everyone through the line, scooping out mashed potatoes and green beans on plates, along with biscuits the size of Elizabeth's hand. "Brownies for dessert."

Elizabeth sidled next to Jeff, determined to bond with her brother over these next four days. With Ben stationed a thousand miles away and unable to come home on a regular basis, maybe it was time to gauge Jeff's interest in Dad's offer. "Hi, Jeff."

Jeff nodded at Tammy. "No gravy for me. As it is, Nicole is already discussing how soon we need to resume our diets." Jeff patted his flat stomach and then faced Elizabeth. "I'd have thought you'd have wanted to eat lunch with your fiancé."

"I thought I'd spend some time with my brother. Get to know you again."

Jeff thanked Tammy. "I'd like that. Nicole told me I owe you an apology for accusing you of trying to steal Dad and Evie's thunder. Now that I've seen you and Lucky over the past few days, I'm just surprised you didn't announce your engagement sooner."

Why did people keep saying that?

She glanced at Lucky with a day's stubble gracing his face, a good look on him. Whatever story he was recounting to Grandma Eloise, Zack and Audrey must be captivating, as they seemed to be hanging on his every word.

Despite everything, she couldn't take her eyes off Lucky. She caught some of what he was saying, namely his preparations for the Casper rodeo. Another reminder he would be on the road soon enough. She'd relied on him too much this morning, and there was no use getting attached to someone who intended to leave.

Too late. She already liked having him around. Best to raise her guard and protect her heart.

She led Jeff over to one of the makeshift tables. "I thought we could talk about the ranch." Maybe she'd been approaching the discussion of the architect plans with the wrong person. If the past few days were any indication of Jeff's continued sway over Dad, getting Jeff on her side would maybe help gain Dad's approval. That would make it easier, and then he'd authorize the down payment and the project in general. "Did you know

JR and Tammy live in Violet Ridge instead of on the ranch?"

The foreman and the cook would have their pick of the bunkhouses if this went through, or even work with the architect on a home of their own. That was, if they wanted to live on the ranch. Jeff slathered his biscuit with Tammy's homemade huckleberry preserve. "If I did, I'd forgotten." He took a big bite and moaned. "I'd also forgotten how much I love Tammy's cooking."

"Does that mean you're considering Dad's offer to move here?" How could he choose Boston when he could have the open range and spend every day on the ranch?

"I thought that was settled."

Yes, but which way? She watched her brother closely as he swallowed the last bite of his biscuit. Her father was a hard customer to resist, and it was better to have Jeff as an ally if he moved here. "According to Dad, you're moving here." While she'd started out with mixed feelings about it, Jeff was family. "He's counting on you, and JR told me you've been asking the cowhands about water rights and discussing property issues. I have a couple of ideas to run by you about how to better guarantee employment retention along with some cattle-breed improvements."

"Hold up." Jeff's cell phone rang, and he startled. "I didn't think I'd be able to get reception out here."

"After Sabrina and Ty were caught in a blizzard, Dad invested in top-of-the-line signal boosters." For a few days last winter, everyone in the Irwin household was on edge when Sabrina, who'd been pregnant and the barn manager at the time, had found herself stranded at the family cabin with Ty. That same blizzard had trapped Evie at the Double I and had been the catalyst for her and Dad to find out how much they had in common, and they'd ended up falling in love.

"I have to take this. Excuse me." Jeff walked away while Moose approached.

She threw the border collie some of her green beans. Moose gobbled them and then proceeded to run in circles around the group, narrowing the distance each time as if he was herding them instead of cattle. With a casual glance toward Lucky, she marveled at how he still had Grandma Eloise and Audrey eating out of the palm of his hand.

Jeff muttered something, and she focused on her brother again. He wrung the back of his neck and then transferred his phone from one ear to the other. Something was bothering him as he swiped on the screen. He sent a longing glance toward Zack and Audrey. Then his lips narrowed into a thin line.

"That was Nicole. There's been a development in one of my cases, and the junior associate can't handle it." There was an edge to her brother's voice she'd never heard before. "I should have known this was a bad idea."

"What? Getting away from work or spending time with Zack and Audrey?" She echoed his tone, unclear of his meaning, just as she was unsure whether she knew Jeff anymore. As it was, the ten-year age difference had caused a chasm between them growing up, when she'd trailed him everywhere while he sought solitude.

"This action-oriented business demeanor is a new side of you. I wish we could have spent more time getting reacquainted." He sighed and ate his last bite of mashed potatoes. "Then you might not be thinking the worst about me. For the record, Nicole wanted all of us to fly back this morning, but I wanted Zack and Audrey to spend some time on the ranch. See if they liked it here more than I did growing up. It was a bad idea allowing them to start something I had a feeling we wouldn't be able to finish."

"I never realized you didn't like growing up on the ranch." What wasn't to love? These were ten thousand of the prettiest acres anywhere in the world, and there was always something new in terms of cattle management or in the stable. As far as Elizabeth was concerned, there was no other place she ever wanted to live. Did that mean Jeff wasn't moving back? He still hadn't answered her directly.

"I might look like Dad, but I take after Mom. You're our father to the core. Ben's the only one whose personality combines the both of them."

Jeff stood and motioned for her to follow him to the trash receptacle. "I'll take Zack and Audrey back to the stable with me."

She finally had new insight concerning Jeff's feelings regarding the ranch, but the verdict was still out about Audrey and Zack's perception of life out west. "Why not let them finish what they started? Grandma Eloise is here, and Audrey loves Lucky."

As if on cue, Lucky hefted Audrey onto his back, her giggles echoing in the mountain air. "Faster, Lucky!"

Lucky sped up and darted around the area. Then he made a beeline for Elizabeth and Jeff. With a slight grimace, Lucky lowered Audrey to the ground and dipped his cowboy hat. "Sorry that I've been monopolizing your daughter."

"No more than I was monopolizing Elizabeth, but I'm happy Audrey enjoyed her lunch. I need to talk to her and her brother. Zack!" Jeff's gaze traveled to Zack, who stood next to Grandma Eloise and their horses. He acknowledged his dad, and Jeff motioned for them to join the group. Grandma Eloise walked over with Zack, and they laughed along the way.

Jeff updated Zack and Audrey on the change of plans, and her niece and nephew let out groans. Audrey's eyes filled with tears behind her purple glasses, and Zack stomped the ground. "I want to stay."

Elizabeth blinked. A few hours ago, her nephew had wanted to stay at the ranch house, so Elizabeth took Zack's outburst as a win for the great outdoors. Over the years, she'd grown apart from Jeff, and perhaps this time on the trail was important for her to bond with her niece and nephew. "My offer stands," Elizabeth said. "That is, if Zack and Audrey would feel comfortable riding without you, and vice versa."

"Can we, Dad?" Zack's large blue eyes pleaded with his father.

"I want to stay, too." Audrey wiggled her front tooth. "You might not even recognize me if I lose my tooth."

She grinned as if reassuring Jeff that would clinch the deal instead of the opposite. Her brother looked conflicted, but nodded. "You'll have more fun here. School starts next month, and you'll be cooped up in the classroom then."

"You bet your briefcase, they will," Grandma Eloise said, her eyes twinkling.

They made arrangements, and Jeff kissed them both before heading back to the stable on Rocky. Elizabeth smiled at Audrey and Zack, who'd finish what they'd started here. Best yet, they'd act as a buffer between her and Lucky.

Her niece and nephew crowded around Lucky, who obliged them by showing them some lasso tricks. Despite the myriad tasks on her shoulders, Elizabeth let herself get lost in his mastery and clapped with the cowhands, Zack and Audrey. Realizing everyone had stopped and watched him, Lucky blushed to the roots of his dirty blond hair. That type of modesty was a rarity.

With moves like that, guarding her heart just became that much more imperative, so Lucky wouldn't break it when he left, as he inevitably would.

"TAMMY, I DIDN'T know how you were going to top this afternoon's lunch, but you certainly did with this dinner." Lucky patted his stomach and paid his compliments to the chef.

Tammy's husband, JR, chimed in his appreciation and then delivered a kiss to her cheek, and the older lady blushed. "Get on with you. Neither of you are on cleanup duty tonight."

JR sneaked in one more kiss before Tammy shooed them away. He tipped his hat, then excused himself for the campfire preparations.

Dusk was approaching, and more shadows dotted the Rockies. Lucky went toward the campsite, only to find everyone was still finishing dinner. With some time on his hands, he retrieved his whittling knife and latest project, a set of miniature animals for Sabrina's birthday. His stomach wobbled. After he and Elizabeth broke up and he moved on from Violet Ridge, Sabrina would have ties to Elizabeth and her family through her mother's marriage to Elizabeth's father. Of course, she'd have to support Elizabeth. More than ever, the realization of damaging his close friendship with Sabrina and Will, something he thought he'd accepted, sank into him.

Returning to the rodeo as soon as this roundup ended became that much more necessary. A clean break and distractions had always helped him whenever he moved to a new foster home. Remaining here was only prolonging the agony.

He found a seat some distance away from everyone. Holding the basswood that would become a miniature version of Butterscotch with his left hand, he picked up his whittling knife with his right hand. Humming under his breath, he braced his thumb against the wood and used short strokes to whittle the legs.

"Whatcha doin'?" He'd been so engrossed with the wood he hadn't seen Audrey appear. She wrinkled her nose and her glasses slid slightly. "Why are you cutting that piece of wood?"

"It's called whittling. I'm carving Butterscotch."

Zack joined them and whistled. "Is that a real knife?" Zack asked. "How do you carve the wood so that you don't get splinters? Are you afraid you're going to cut yourself?"

That was the most he'd ever heard out of Zack at one time. "Yes, this is a real carbon-steel whittling knife. I use basswood although pine and cedar work well. Basswood doesn't splinter easily, and my friend and mentor, Cale, went over the safety rules for using a knife before he taught me. I've been doing this for quite a while now." Lucky showed them two other figures he'd carved. "These are my friend Will's goats, Snow and Flake."

Then he handed one to Zack and one to Audrey, who jumped up and down. "Can you make doggies?" She tapped her chin. "Or a unicorn?"

"I'll see what I can do," Lucky promised.

"I like horses now. Blaze is amazing. He likes me a lot." Zack puffed out his chest before his stomach and posture deflated. "Then again, you might not have time for us. Dad was supposed to be here, and he has to work."

Lucky's heart went out to the pair, who went from excited to forlorn in the space of a second. He'd never known his father, but that wasn't the case with them. And he knew Jeff was trying. After all, he'd seen the longing and love in Jeff's face as he rode away earlier. "Your parents love you."

"I guess." Zack kicked at the dirt.

Elizabeth joined them and cringed, a pained expression on her face, as if she was the bearer of bad news. "Hey, Zack," she said. Lucky braced himself. "I guess you're upset about your console. I forgot to ask your father for it before he left."

"I forgot, too. It'll be there when I get back." Zack shrugged and then held up one of the carved goats. "Could you teach me how to make something like this?"

"And me?" Audrey clearly didn't want to be left out.

"Did you make these?" Elizabeth sounded impressed, and Audrey handed her goat to Elizabeth. She studied it and smiled before returning it to Lucky. "It's beautiful."

"I'm not as good as Cale, but it's relaxing, and it keeps my fingers nimble." His mentor had carved a chess set and had taught Lucky how to play. That set had gotten plenty of use, as he'd spent many evenings playing chess with Sabrina while Will read a book in the same room.

"Nonsense. You're very talented with woodworking," Grandma Eloise said as she came over and popped her hands on her hips. "You made Genie's rocking horse."

"I remember now." Elizabeth whistled. "It's gorgeous."

JR called out from the campfire and motioned at Lucky. "Hey, Lucky. Could you give me a hand?"

Thankful for the interruption, Lucky excused himself after collecting the figurines. He helped JR with the preparations by laying hickory logs in the center of a circle of stones well away from a grove of aspens to the east and the meadow with the cattle a good distance off in the north. Dusk fell upon the site. Grandma Eloise excused herself, choosing to turn in early, while JR lit the fire. Smoke plumed in the balmy summer air, and the heat felt good now with the temperature quickly cooling this high in the mountains.

In no time, JR handed out long metal skewers while Tammy trailed behind with a package of marshmallows and gave them to everyone. Zack ate his without toasting it while Audrey held up her skewer. "What's this for?"

"S'mores." Elizabeth followed and opened a box of graham crackers. She handed two to Zack. "I'll show you how to toast your marshmallow so it'll melt the chocolate on your graham cracker."

Elizabeth aided Zack while Lucky helped Audrey.

"Do you like your marshmallows burnt on the outside or lightly toasted?" Lucky asked while twirling the stick over the fire.

Audrey licked her lips. "I don't know. I've never done this before."

He caught his marshmallow on fire and then blew it out, the exterior all brown and charred. "I like them toasty."

She looked skeptical and then her lower lip went all quivery. "It caught on fire."

He ruffled her hair. "I promise it's delicious." He presented the skewer to her. "Try this one and then we'll make a s'more."

She scrunched her nose and accepted it, and then bounced up and down on the log, excited for more. They chatted and laughed while eating the treats. He glanced over at Elizabeth, the fire's glow bathing her in soft light and highlighting her natural beauty. She caught him staring at her, and he grasped for a reason to have been looking her way. "You have a dot of chocolate on your nose."

"I'm not sure I believe you." She raised her chin. "I'm usually meticulous."

He reached out his hand and wiped some of the brown smear, holding it out for her to see. Their gazes met, and something between them changed in that moment. The racing of his heart and these escalating feelings were very much real. No longer did this seem like a fake romance.

"Good grief. Just kiss her. It's not like Audrey and Zack have never seen adults kiss before." Grandma Eloise emerged from her tent and reached for a skewer, making a s'more of her own. "It smelled too enticing out here to sleep."

Elizabeth's wide green eyes connected with his, and he hadn't thought about this part of their fake engagement. Of course people would expect them to kiss. Somehow, they'd fooled everyone at the reception, with no one expressing any doubt, at least not to their faces. Apparently they'd been so convincing they now had a wedding date. She braced herself and nodded.

No matter that it was just for show, he didn't want their first kiss to be in front of everyone like this. When he kissed someone, he wanted it to be special. So he kissed her nose and stepped back. "Mmm, chocolate. That was too good to go to waste."

She opened her eyes, and relief seemed to lurk there, as well as gratitude. "My hero."

JR unlocked a guitar case and pulled out the instrument. "It's time for some music," the foreman said. "I'm not in Evie's league, but I can carry a tune."

With the awkward moment passed, everyone started singing familiar favorites. Above, the stars twinkled bright, extending as far as the eye could see. The fire popped, and an ember escaped, landing on his arm. He brushed away the spark and made sure everyone else was far enough away so no harm would come to any of them.

Elizabeth expressed her concern and checked his arm. He reassured her he was fine. The ember hadn't burned him, but he'd been scorched in the past when families took him into their fold and then rejected him. The last chords of the song lingered for a few seconds before fading away in the night. Nothing lasted forever, and Lucky would do well to remember that before this relationship seared him and branded him for life.

CHAPTER NINE

WITH THE SECOND day of the roundup almost over and quite successful, they'd be moving the cattle to the fall pasture tomorrow morning. So far, the medical checks on the cattle had progressed faster than expected, with no major issues. Still, something wasn't right. Then Elizabeth heard the sound again. She tracked the plaintive mooing until she found the young weaner on the side of the mountain, stuck in a ravine. There was always one stray on these roundups. Soon, this cow would be reunited with the rest of the herd.

She dismounted from Andromeda and tied her Appaloosa to a nearby aspen. Maybe she should contact JR on her two-way radio for assistance, she thought, then scoffed at the idea. Why bother her foreman when this weaner wasn't that big, only around six months old? Rolling up her sleeves, she approached the animal, still mooing, a sign she hadn't been standing here too long. It simply needed incentive to leave its cool shady spot in the creek and return to the pasture.

Wading into the creek, she spotted the problem. The weaner's hoof was trapped between two rocks. The poor thing was stuck and couldn't free itself. Even if this had started as a way to beat the summer heat, it could have ended badly if Elizabeth hadn't arrived in time. She exerted some force, but the cow didn't budge, its hoof wedged in tight. Another angle might work better, and she waded into the stream until she was ankle deep.

Grunting, she attempted to move the rocks so she could dislodge the young cow. Instead, her arms flailed, and she lost her balance.

She fell backward on her bottom. Frustrated, she sat in the creek, droplets dripping off her brow, the water flowing past her with the sun beating down overhead. Then she laughed. Truth be told, the cool creek felt good. It was just her ego that was bruised. At least no one was around to witness her fall.

She tilted her head and tried to figure out how to free the weaner.

An exclamation came from the western ridge, and hooves thundered toward her. She struggled to her feet, but the slippery rocks had other plans for her. She landed in the creek once more. So much for a graceful move. Lucky dismounted and tied Margarita near Andromeda. "Elizabeth!"

He hurried over and reached out his hand. With a murmured word of thanks, she accepted his help and made it to the water's edge. "Her hoof is caught in the rocks."

"You should have called me. I know a thing or two about calves' hooves." He crouched into position and gauged the water's depth. Then he searched the area. "Do you see anything we can use as a lever?"

She spotted a long, sturdy oak branch on the opposite side of the bank. "Over there."

"I'll get it." Lucky forded the stream and returned with the branch. "I'll wedge this under the rock while you help the weaner."

"The rocks are more slippery than they look. Be careful," Elizabeth said.

"Thanks for the concern. There's nothing like a cool, refreshing swim in summer, but I prefer my swim trunks." He winked, and her stomach did a funny flip.

The weaner's moos were getting weaker, and they turned their attention to the animal. On the count of three, Lucky pushed against the rock while she helped the weaner. In no time, the young cow was free, and she scrambled out of the creek, bleating her happiness at being on firm ground again. The cow shook the excess water off her coat and proceeded in the herd's direction, not needing any encouragement from Elizabeth or Lucky.

She glanced in his direction, his smile and expression a sign of his relief. Then his grin faded.

"Why didn't you call me on your two-way radio?" Lucky cautiously moved to the creek bed, still holding the branch.

Elizabeth kept a careful eye on the cow, making sure it headed in the right direction. Moose appeared and took the lead. Only when the weaner and dog were out of sight did she address Lucky. "At first, I thought she was enjoying the water on a hot day. She obviously wanted to escape the heat, but she didn't count on the rocks trapping her. It wasn't until I fell into the water that I realized the severity of the situation."

Her words hit her hard. She'd also wanted to escape—from being the unattached member of the wedding party—but hadn't counted on circumstances tying her to Lucky. Now, the weaner might have gotten away without any injuries—but would she be as fortunate?

"You could have been hurt." He leaned the branch against a nearby aspen and then wiped the water off her face. His callused fingers brushed against her soft cheek, and she leaned into his touch. Suddenly, she knew without a doubt that getting out of this without injury was impossible. She had fallen too hard, too quickly, and Lucky meant too much to her now.

"I'm tough." Her whispered and warbled words hung in the air, and their gazes met.

His electric blue eyes had anything but a calming effect on her as she sniffed, his spicy after-shave lingering in the air.

"I know, but relying on others isn't a sign you're weak." He reached into his pocket and pulled out a dry cloth, blotting the moisture from the other side of her face. "Having people in your life who will stand by you is everything."

Electricity sparked the charged air around them. Everything surrounding her stilled. The nearby lowing of the cattle blurred into a silence that captivated her. She nodded, and he leaned toward her, his lips nearing hers for their first kiss.

"Aunt Elizabeth! Lucky!" Zack's shouts of glee reached them, and Elizabeth scooted away from Lucky.

She glanced around until she found Zack at the top of the ridge. "Grandma Eloise is giving me and Audrey more pointers about how to fish." He held up a good-size trout. "She says I caught dinner!"

Elizabeth and Lucky mounted their horses and met Zack, then rode back to the campsite, where she heard sniffles. Elizabeth dismounted and handed her reins to Lucky. She ran over to Audrey. "What's wrong, sweetheart?"

Her niece's bottom lip quivered. "We don't get to keep the fishies to take home." She pointed at Grandma Eloise. "*She* said we're eating them for dinner."

Elizabeth embraced her niece. Grandma Eloise came over. "I'm sorry, Elizabeth. Living on a ranch for so long…"

Elizabeth raised her head and nodded at Grandma Eloise over Audrey's shoulder. "I think she misses her parents." She leaned back but slipped her hand into Audrey's and gave it a light squeeze. "Hey, Audrey, darling. This is a ranch—"

That lip kept quivering, and Audrey sniffled. "Daddy wouldn't have hurt the fishie."

"Why don't we take a walk and watch Moose herd the cattle until dinner is ready," Elizabeth offered.

More sniffles came before Audrey gave a little nod. After a brief word with JR and Sweeney, the longtime cowhand who was also on the trip, Elizabeth spent time with her niece, whose tears dried in no time, until Tammy called them all together for dinner. Audrey bounced into the chow line, her resilience remarkable. Irwin females took everything in stride. Elizabeth filed that away for reference for when Lucky left the ranch for good.

Tammy offered Audrey a turkey drumstick instead of grilled fish, and Elizabeth mouthed "thank you" to the wise cook. Everyone settled at the campsite, and Audrey situated herself between Elizabeth and Lucky. At least that move prevented any awkwardness that might have resulted from that near kiss.

What would it be like to kiss Lucky? Would

his kisses be soft and gentle like his everyday personality? Or would his rodeo persona, full of energy and charisma, make for a kiss of flashing fireworks?

Elizabeth pushed aside that thought, same as she pushed around the pieces of fish on her plate. She had just raised her fork to her mouth when Audrey jumped in the air.

"My tooth! It's out." She held up a small pearly tooth and went around showing it off to everyone in the circle, finishing at Elizabeth. "See, Aunt Elith, Elith…"

Lucky had called her Lizzie a couple of times, the same nickname her mother had used before she died when Elizabeth was Audrey's age. Elizabeth sounded formal and stiff, and she wanted Zack and Audrey to feel comfortable around her. "How about you call me Aunt Lizzie? That might be easier to say."

Audrey grinned, that gap-toothed smile as endearing as Andromeda's nuzzles. "Aunt Lizzie, look at my tooth." Then the grin disappeared. "Will the tooth fairy visit me? How does she know where I am?"

Zack scoffed. "Aw, Audrey, everyone knows." He stopped and looked around. Grandma Eloise and Lucky both sent him unspoken warnings. He rolled his eyes. "Everyone knows the tooth fairy keeps track of where the teeth are."

Lucky rose and placed his hands on Audrey's

shoulders. "Don't worry. The tooth fairy will love it. Looks like a perfect addition to her collection."

Lucky must have a wonderful family to understand kids so well. Suddenly, Elizabeth had an overwhelming urge to know everything about his childhood and family. His parents must be pretty special people to produce such a loving son.

Audrey came over and hugged Elizabeth, her purple glasses digging into her shoulder. "Thank you, Aunt Lizzie."

Then Lizzie it was. She choked back the emotion and held the embrace for a bit longer, soaking in her niece's joy. If Jeff did move to Violet Ridge, she'd be a bigger part of Zack's and Audrey's lives. For the first time, the thought of Jeff rejoining the ranch family didn't seem so bad.

LUCKY TAPPED ON the side of Elizabeth's tent. "Hey, are we still taking the first shift together?"

Elizabeth murmured something that sounded like "come in," and he opened the flap only to find Elizabeth with one index finger on her lips while the other pointed to a sleeping Audrey, who was sprawled over Elizabeth's sleeping bag. "She misses her mom."

"Is the tooth fairy here?" Audrey flew into a sitting position and reached for her glasses. "Oh, hi, Lucky."

"Audrey wants to stay awake all night for the tooth fairy." Elizabeth hugged her niece, conflict written all over her expressive face. "Sweetheart, I have to help make sure the cattle are safe and protected."

"I can do that," Lucky volunteered. There was no way he wanted Audrey disappointed this young in life, as he'd been even younger than she was now when he'd entered the foster system and was confronted with reality.

"But you don't have to," Elizabeth protested.

"I want to." Lucky sent a smile in their direction, both Irwin females appealing in different ways.

"Audrey, sweetie, I need to give Lucky some instructions, and I'll be right back." Elizabeth finagled her way out of the tent and joined him.

"JR and I can work together," Lucky said. "If you have any directions, tell me now."

"Hold on a second."

She sent a thumbs-up toward Audrey and closed the flap behind her when she caught sight of Grandma Eloise coming toward them. The older woman tightened the shawl around her shoulders. "Good. You two lovebirds get to spend some time under the stars."

"Actually, Elizabeth and Audrey are setting a tooth-fairy trap," said Lucky. "She's giving me some orders for my night shift watching over the cattle."

Elizabeth ran a hand over her hair. "Grandma Eloise, can you keep an eye on Audrey for a minute? Lucky and I have something important to discuss."

"Of course I'll stay with Audrey, dear." The older woman smiled and neared Elizabeth. "You know the best things all have a little magic in them and take on a life of their own."

Elizabeth tugged on her boots while Grandma Eloise entered the tent and situated herself next to Audrey. The young girl snuggled against the older woman, showing her the tooth. Together, they radiated contentment.

Elizabeth neared him, and her cheek brushed his. Her soft skin was still warm from the tent. "I need your help."

There was a nip in the air, the higher mountain altitude bringing a nighttime chill. He led her over to the campfire, and he couldn't help but notice how she was wringing her hands. "What's wrong?"

She pulled her flannel shirt closer until it hugged her chest. "I don't have a dollar."

"Excuse me." He blinked and tapped his ear. "The fire crackled as you spoke."

"I never carry money with me on the round-ups." She sent a nervous glance toward the tent. "The tooth fairy."

He excused himself for a few moments, then returned with a dollar. She stood on her tiptoes and kissed his cheek, her lips burning an imprint on his cool skin. "Thanks! You saved me." She stepped back and pocketed the bill. "We make a good team."

With that, she outlined some instructions for him and JR and then returned to the tent. They did make a good team. Was there any way to explore a possibility of that teamwork turning into a real friendship and then possibly more?

Or had this fake engagement already doomed any chance of a future for them?

CHAPTER TEN

THE NEXT AFTERNOON, Lizzie admired Moose's tenacity while the border collie pursued a stray head of cattle and brought it back to the herd. Moose's innate ability was a sight to behold.

At last, they reached the autumn pasture, the green fields stretching as far as the eye could see with only clumps of silver aspens dotting the hillside. The end of the summer months had brought little in terms of precipitation, but that would change with the fall rains. Moose watched over the herd as the cattle filed into the new spacious grazing fields.

JR reined in his horse near Lizzie. "Right on schedule." He sounded shocked, and she couldn't blame him. With the extra riders, she hadn't been sure they'd arrive here on time, but life surprised her sometimes. One look at Lucky cemented that.

Her gaze returned to the cattle. "And they're all accounted for. They're safe and ready for autumn. That's what's important."

"Your father will be proud of how well you

handled the drive. Of course, he wouldn't have gone to California if he didn't think you'd manage everything."

Lizzie started at the foreman's praise. She wished her father would take a page from JR's playbook. "He thought Jeff would be along for the ride."

JR shook his head. "He knows you're more than capable."

Why was it easier for JR to see that? But was he on to something? Did her father appreciate her efforts more than she acknowledged? "Thanks for the vote of confidence, JR."

"Your father will come around, especially now that he's found love with Evie. He's pleased as punch that you've found that same type of happiness with Lucky," JR said.

This line of talk cut too deep. This engagement was a sham she'd gone along with so as not to further disrupt her father's wedding day. Now that he was on his honeymoon, this thing with Lucky had to end so it wouldn't be hanging over them any longer.

But there was one topic she could broach with the foreman right now. Since JR was proving more amenable to her leadership, she decided to confide in him and start making her own imprint. "What do you think of adding some Simmentals to our ranch? They're more docile and resistant to stress."

JR's gaze narrowed, and his head waffled to the point she could see the gears turning in his mind. "Their large frames sometimes make the calving process more difficult. Mastitis is a real problem with that breed."

"I've heard that's better with some of the black Simmentals, and they're also known for their milk production and a high yield of flavorful beef." After pleading her case, the foreman seemed swayed by her arguments.

He rubbed his chin. "Hmm. We could start with a small sample group for a few seasons. Slow and steady, and see if we get good results," he said.

Getting JR on her side would help her when she presented the same idea to her father. She spotted a problem with the fence at the far western end of the pasture and eased up on the reins. "We need to check out that hole. Ride that way with me."

As they neared the problem area, JR pulled up on the reins and squinted. "Uh-oh. I see the problem." They both dismounted, and JR followed her to the damaged portion of the fence, a big hole near the bottom. He studied some nearby tracks. "Looks like a pronghorn crawled under it."

"And ripped the bottom out," she said, finishing for him. "I don't want any of the cattle escaping. It shouldn't take me too long to fix this. Tell Tammy to save me a plate."

She rolled up the sleeves of her flannel shirt and

rummaged through her saddlebag for the tools she'd need for taking out the damaged section.

"Will do, boss." JR tipped his cowboy hat and rode toward the rest of the group.

A little hard work was just what she needed so she wouldn't dwell on Lucky, especially seeing how she'd been thinking of him far too much on this roundup.

LUCKY RODE MARGARITA over to the section where Elizabeth was fixing the fence. He unloaded the new wire and brought it over to her, along with some water.

"Thought you might need this." He handed her the drink, and she removed her cream-colored leather-and-canvas work gloves before accepting the reusable bottle.

"Thanks." She stood and swigged a big sip, the sunlight reflecting off the diamonds in the engagement ring, and then wiped her mouth with the back of her arm. "You didn't have to do this."

"Maybe I wanted to." He was getting the feeling he'd like to do more for her with each passing day. "Teamwork, remember?"

Her smile brightened his day, already memorable from the moment Audrey had awakened the entire camp with the news the tooth fairy had come, then waved the dollar bill around as if it was a golden belt buckle.

"As if I could forget." She set the bottle on the ground next to the post.

"How can I help?"

"You brought the supplies I need. That's more than plenty for now." She kneeled and donned her gloves before picking up the electric fencing pliers.

He tapped her on her shoulder. "I'm more than a pretty face."

He scrunched up his nose and crossed his eyes, bringing forth a laugh, the prettiest sound in Colorado as far as he was concerned.

"Have a pair of work gloves?" she asked.

"Sure do." He extracted them from the back pocket of his jeans.

"Good. Can you use the fence stretcher to pull the broken sides back together?"

In his sleep, but he merely nodded. Over the next few hours, they worked together, laughing at times, a pleasant silence at others. Then she slid the pieces of wire together through a crimping sleeve while he bound the sleeve in place. They stood and checked out their handiwork. "Clear of debris and safe for the cattle. Good work, partner," he said.

He extended his hand until they shook in a firm handshake, shivers running through him at the contact. He kept that to himself.

"Thanks, Lucky." It was her turn to scrunch up

her nose. "Some fiancée I am. I don't even know your real name."

He removed his cowboy hat and dipped his head. "Lucas Harper at your disposal."

She laughed. "Nice to meet you, Lucas Harper."

He joined in the laughter. There was something about Elizabeth that put him at ease. While she had a slightly formal manner about her, fitting for the future owner of the Double I, she wasn't pretentious or fussy. He'd never felt this comfortable around anyone, not even Cale, Will or Sabrina. "And I'd say Audrey's on to something. You seem more like a Lizzie than an Elizabeth to me."

Her slight sigh was almost lost in the breeze, but he noticed everything about her. "I have a feeling my nickname might be one thing that endures after this trip."

Too bad their relationship couldn't have had that same lasting power. He'd like it if her last name was Harper someday, but he roped calves and she owned them. "Would that be a bad thing?"

She shrugged. "My mother called me Lizzie."

Her use of the past tense also didn't go unnoticed. "What happened to her?"

"My mother died of cancer when I was Audrey's age. I always think of her when the gardenias bloom. It reminds me of her perfume." She removed her gloves and averted her eyes, as if she didn't want him to see her weakness, although her sharing this with him was anything but weak. It was a sign she was starting to trust him.

"And after she passed away, you insisted on going by Elizabeth again." He waited for her confirmation.

"I always preferred Lizzie, though. What about you? Did your parents nickname you Lucky when you were a baby or was it from a cute incident in your childhood?" She added a light note to her question, enough for him to go with the flow and focus the attention on him, something he didn't like around others. Around her, talking about himself didn't seem so bad.

He packed the tools in her saddlebag. "I barely knew my parents. I was raised in the New York foster-care system. When I landed on Cale Padilla's doorstep a week after I graduated high school, I stuttered over my name. He put me at ease by telling me to slow down. Arriving at his ranch was the best thing that happened to me up to that point, so I told him to call me Lucky."

Her mouth dropped open. "I didn't know you were raised in foster care."

"Why would you?" He snapped the bag closed. "It's not a first-date kind of discussion. More like a third."

He grinned so she wouldn't see the hurt inside him. She must have picked up on his discomfort, and that mask of pity was replaced by a far more impish look. "This might be stretching it, but the rehearsal dinner could be called our first date. Then the wedding was our second, and dinner last night was our third."

"If that's your idea of dating," he laughed.

"No, but this isn't my idea of an engagement, either." She giggled, and the absurdity of the situation seemed to overtake both of them. Her giggles turned into full-blown gales of laughter until she doubled over. "I haven't laughed like that in forever."

"Well, if we can't laugh at ourselves…" He stopped and let one last chuckle escape. Then he wiped a tear from the side of her eye, the softness of her skin a balm to his calluses.

"You're a good man, Lucas Harper."

She neared him, and he removed his cowboy hat, resting it next to his leg. The scent of wildflowers drifted toward him, and he knew he'd always associate the smell of them with his Lizzie. He stepped toward her, but the sound of hooves in the background caused her to jump away from him.

JR approached, and he directed his gaze at the fence, repaired and good as new. "Tammy sent me to tell you your dinner's getting cold, but I should've known better than to volunteer to check on the engaged couple." A twinkle sparked in his eye, and he busted out laughing. "When you're done here, it's spooky story night." He made ghost noises and then clucked his tongue, leading his horse away from them. "Don't worry. I'll keep it tame for the kiddos."

The moment for kissing her had already passed. Without a word, Lucky mounted his horse and headed back to the campsite.

SPOOKY STORY NIGHT was always Lizzie's favorite part of the roundups. With the cattle grazing in their fall pasture, JR popped popcorn over the campfire before tomorrow's ride led them home. The rhythmic sound of the kernels exploding should have lightened her mood, but one glance at Lucky sent her spirits plummeting again.

He hadn't said a word after JR had interrupted them earlier that evening. Who could blame him? Here he'd told her something deeply personal about growing up in the foster-care system, and she'd ended up in tears from laughing. What he must think of her and her manners. She was mortified at her treating anybody with anything less than the utmost respect. In just a week, Lucky's perception of her mattered a great deal.

Instead of getting comfortable, she found she couldn't enjoy herself while knowing he thought less of her for her reaction to his childhood. Resolved, she rose and tapped his shoulder. "Have you seen the different flavors Tammy brought along with her for sprinkling on the popcorn? There's butter, cheddar cheese, cinnamon sugar and more."

"Plain works for me." Lucky kept his gaze on the fire.

From across the way, JR laughed. "Son, she's trying to get you alone."

Even in the dim light, she noted that Lucky's cheeks blushed to a deep red under that tan of his. "Right."

Everyone's gazes seemed to be on them as she led him toward the supply wagon. Satisfied no one could hear them, she reached for his hand. "I'm sorry…"

"For what, Lizzie?" He shoved his hands in his pockets. "I'm the one who went along with this."

That was another thing. For the life of her, she didn't understand why he didn't call her out at the beginning, when everyone congratulated them at the stable. "Why haven't you said anything?" She drew in a deep breath and exhaled. "That's not why I dragged you over here. I have to say this, or I won't be able to enjoy tonight. Please let me finish and don't distract me."

"I'm distracting?" His wicked grin kicked her in the gut. He leaned against the supply wagon. "That's nice to know."

Did the man not understand his appeal with that cowboy hat hung low, shading his eyes? And that didn't even take into account the flannel shirt stretched tight across his shoulders…

She pulled herself together. "I'm sorry for laughing earlier."

He frowned. "Why? You weren't laughing at me. Sometimes a good laugh is exactly what the body needs."

"Then why did you leave so suddenly after JR told us dinner was ready?"

He raised his eyebrows. "Guess we both find each other a tad distracting." His low but steady tone sent a thrill through her. Despite everything, she stood there, grinning like she'd already eaten the bucket of popcorn. He continued, "And considering I have a full rodeo slate ahead of me, one of us had to dial it back. Tomorrow, I leave for Casper."

Cold creek water couldn't have put more of a damper on her.

He just confirmed that he had no intention of settling here, no intentions with her.

"Aunt Lizzie! Lucky?" Audrey's voice reached them.

"Over here." Lucky responded faster than she could, and Audrey headed their way.

"Zack said he's gonna eat all your popcorn." Audrey pushed up her purple glasses. "I won't let him."

Lizzie hid her smile at her niece's concern. She walked over and scooped her into her arms, thankful for the interruption that came before she did something foolish, like ask Lucky to reconsider his plans and stay at the ranch. He was a rodeo cowboy with his own life to lead, just as she had hers. "JR makes enough for everyone in Violet Ridge. That's probably just Zack's way of saying he's tired of waiting for us."

Audrey indicated she wanted down. Once her feet were back on the ground, a good place for them rather than hovering in the air, as hers had been just a few minutes earlier, she ran over to Lucky.

"Zack said the stories are gonna be scary." She bit her lip and squished her nose. "I don't like scary stories."

Lizzie kept a straight face. "I'll tell JR to tell some funny ones, too."

Audrey grinned and then yawned. "Good, because I'm tired from waiting for the tooth fairy. I still can't believe she got away."

"You have the dollar, though," Lucky said, as he hefted Audrey into his arms and carried her back to the campsite.

Even with the smoke and the light, the firmament of stars winked at her as if letting her know that even for one night, all was right with the world. Lucky's nearby presence added to that, but she couldn't commit to anything knowing he wasn't staying in Violet Ridge. Her chest constricted at the very thought of leaving the ranch to follow him.

After whispering to JR to take it easy with the stories, she settled next to Lucky. He smiled and held up his bucket of popcorn, offering to share with her. "The cattle are lowing and are just fine. Go with the flow and lose yourself in the story."

Audrey tucked into Lucky's side, and Zack sidled up next to Lizzie. "I'll share my popcorn with you, Aunt Lizzie."

He held out his bowl, and Lizzie smiled. "I'd be honored to share your popcorn, Zack."

Lucky leaned his head in her direction. "Aunt Lizzie suits you. So does the glow from the fire."

Her insides warmed, and she settled in her spot, intent on staying in the moment. JR began weaving words together in spellbinding fashion, keeping them all on the edge of their seats. Zack snuggled up to her, and his soft, downy hair brushed against her flannel shirtsleeve. He shoveled popcorn into his mouth without taking his eyes off JR, hanging on the foreman's description of the stinky sneakers that could walk on their own.

She glanced over at Audrey, concerned about whether the story was too intense, but she needn't have worried. Audrey wore a content look and her eyes were half-closed. Every few seconds, her head would jerk up, and she gazed at JR like she was trying to piece together what she'd missed.

Lizzie transferred her gaze to Lucky, the tenderness in his eyes striking. He'd be wonderful with his own children someday. That was, if he ever settled in one place long enough. The man lived in a combination RV and horse trailer while she lived and breathed the happenings of the Double I Ranch. There was no future for them, even if everyone else was convinced their future was as bright as the glow of the fire.

For now, though, she let herself be lulled by the snap and crackle of the flickering flames.

"Do I KNOW how to put everyone to sleep, or do I?" JR looked pleased with his pronouncement and then excused himself.

Lucky remained behind. It was hard to move considering Audrey was splayed across him, her deep breaths proof she was sound asleep. These types of memories were precious, and he should know. Growing up in foster care, he never knew where he'd be sleeping the following week.

There was that one month he'd stayed in three different foster homes. He'd never forget the couple who'd barged into his current foster home and accused him of planting a six-pack of beer in their son's room. The man, who was the best friend of Lucky's foster father, had railed at him, his face mere inches away from Lucky's own, each sentence louder than the last, while the man's son stood behind him, out of sight, sneering at Lucky. That night, the state worker had arrived at the foster home and accused him of underage possession while removing him from the house, unwilling to give Lucky the benefit of the doubt. Fortunately, he'd turned eighteen and graduated high school soon thereafter. For one of his last projects, he'd written a report about cowboys and had been enthralled by the photos of majestic sunsets and mountains hinting at natural wonders unlike any he'd ever seen.

That had spurred him to buying a one-way ticket out west, where he stumbled onto Cale's ranch. Cale and Vivi had brought him into their fold and taught him the ways of cowboy and rodeo life. After Cale and Vivi had welcomed their fourth grandchild into their family, Lucky had moved on to the rodeo circuit and responded to anyone who sent out a plea for help. During his second season, he'd met Will and then they'd added Sabrina to their little family a couple of years later.

Moving on had always served him well. A sharp stabbing pain went through him at having to do the same once more.

How he'd extricate himself from Audrey without waking her up was as baffling as how he'd leave Violet Ridge without his heart breaking. Lizzie Irwin had no idea of how appealing she was. With her head bent in slumber against Zack's, she was even more beautiful.

A coyote's howl cut through the night, and everyone bolted to an upright position. Lizzie's gaze was immediately focused, and Grandma Eloise and Tammy both popped out of their respective tents. They hustled Zack and Audrey away, and Lizzie joined JR, their heads huddled in deep conversation. Lucky hurried to join them as Moose rushed over from his area of slumber by the fire.

"How can I help?" Lucky offered, unwilling to wait around for any interlopers to harm anyone at the campsite or any of the cattle.

Lizzie glanced his way. "Guard the camp."

While he loved those kids like they were his own niece and nephew, he wanted to ride the range. "Tammy and Grandma Eloise can do that." Lucky decided to plead his case. "I've been on plenty of night watches."

JR nodded. "We always pair up if we're riding horses around the perimeter at night. He would round out the search party."

She seemed to absorb the advice of her foreman and nodded. "Okay, then. JR, you and Sweeney ride south with Moose while Lucky and I head north. We'll meet you on the other side of the pasture."

In no time, he and Lizzie were riding the open range, side by side. The smoky smell of the campfire dissipated the farther they traveled. Only the soft lowing of the cattle and the light sound of the horses' hooves trotting along the grassy plain broke the silence of the night. He glanced at her, alert and on guard, her spine straight as she and Andromeda created an impressive sight. Another memory to file and cherish after he moved on to the next rodeo.

"Thanks for recruiting me on your team," Lucky said.

She pulled up on the reins and searched the

area, vigilant for any signs of wildlife or other disturbances. "That's not even a dent in all I owe you for what you're doing for me."

She still didn't get it. She thought he was doing this for her when the pull of her family was everything. His chest tightened, the sharp pain forcing him to confront the truth. That was why he'd gone along with the setup, but that wasn't why he continued the farce any longer. Lizzie was a strong, independent woman, a force to be reckoned with, and he'd also seen glimpses of her caring nature. Her layers reflected a yearning for someone to see past the polish and let her be Lizzie, efficient to the core with the added bonuses of laughter and affection.

"You let me into your family for a week. That's enough for me." He couldn't be greedy and expect someone like her to want him as a permanent fixture in her life.

"You deserve more than a week, Lucky Harper. Don't cut yourself short." Her voice grew deep. Another howl cut through the mountainside, and she dug her heels into Andromeda's side, sending the Appaloosa into a gallop.

Lucky did likewise to Margarita until he caught up to her. They kept pace with each other, riding to protect the cattle and the loved ones as much as for the pure enjoyment of a midnight gallop under the stars. Finally, she transitioned from galloping to a brisk trot, and he kept up with her, Margarita more than capable of doing whatever he asked of her. The trot turned into a canter, and she led Andromeda over to the fence they'd repaired earlier. There was no sign of any predator. She dismounted, then reached into her saddlebag and pulled out a handful of oats, taking care of her horse before turning her attention to the cattle and then, at last, him. He'd already followed her lead and was looking after Margarita, a pure joy to ride.

"Not many could have kept up with me."

"I had to learn how to adapt." Especially helpful when he always had to be ready to leave at a second's notice.

"I couldn't." Her voice cracked like her admission wrenched something deep inside of her, a perceived weakness that was anything but. "Adapt, that is. When I was six."

"When your mother died?" He moved closer to her and away from Margarita. She gave a brief nod, and his heart ached for that little girl. "You were so young."

She turned her back to him under the guise of watching over the cattle, but he understood why. Sometimes it was easier to talk with no one's eyes on you—people could make rush judgments on something they didn't understand or want to fathom. "And I had the ranch to sustain me, along with Jeff, Ben and Dad. I had everything I could ever want at my fingertips."

Wants and needs were different. He knew that better than anyone. He held her, her back pressed against his front, willing to be a part of her world and listen for a little while. "Kids need a parent or a caring adult looking out for them. What happened to your mother?"

"The doctors discovered her stage-four cancer right after she and Dad separated. They reconciled after that, but the end came quickly." Lizzie didn't glance his way, but he listened with a stillness that equaled the surrounding night. "Then Dad threw himself into his work. For so long, all he did was work, and his distance put up a wall between him and my brothers. I think he was devastated when Jeff came home from college and announced he was going to law school, following Ben's decision to join the military a year before."

"And you stepped into the void." He could see Lizzie with a stiff upper lip, so efficient in her tasks that even those close to her forgot about her caring heart and need for approval.

"It wasn't hard. I love this ranch." At last she turned to him, her face showing how conflicted she was. "I feel like I'm letting everyone down by keeping up with this sham of an engagement."

Now he understood her better. A father, caught up in his grief, projected responsibility onto a young girl's shoulders, a girl too young for such a large load, and he should know. That kind of responsibility before you were ready for it was overwhelming. Even the strongest shoulders needed rest and recovery, or, at the very least, another person to lighten the load.

"People love you, Lizzie." She arched an eyebrow as if she expected him to still call her Elizabeth. He brushed his finger against her smooth cheek. "You're always going to be Lizzie to me. Elizabeth is the more formal side you present to the world, but I saw you a bit ago with Zack snuggled up against you. You love being Aunt Lizzie. It's just another side of you, one you shouldn't be afraid to let everyone see."

"Does that mean I get to call you Lucas?"

He chuckled at the challenge in her voice. "I chose Lucky, and it's your choice from here of whether you prefer Lizzie or Elizabeth. You have wonderful memories of being Lizzie to your mom." It was his turn to watch the cattle and search the area for any signs of anything in their midst that could sneak up and attack at a second's notice. "You're reconnecting with that side of you, and the good that comes with it. But I'll respect your decision about your name."

"So Lucas brings back bad memories." She fixed him with a curious stare until he had no choice but to look at her.

He shrugged. "Let's just say it doesn't evoke any good ones." She was bright and light, and he didn't want to ruin this moment with bringing up his past. He stepped back, before those dark moments threatened to take away everything again.

"And yet you didn't lose your innate optimism." She reached for the sides of his flannel shirt and pulled him back toward her. "I think it's time for you to have one good memory of someone saying your real name, Lucas."

He didn't object when she brought him so close he could feel her breath on his neck. She kept her long fingers curled around his shirt, the knuckles brushing against the cotton of his T-shirt. Her green gaze met his own, and he nodded. "Are you always right, Elizabeth?"

"Just about the important things, and that's Lizzie to you." An impish gleam he'd never seen before twinkled in those bright emeralds.

He lowered his lips to hers, and shivers cascaded to his toes. She kept her hands between them as he curled his arms around her waist. The kiss deepened, and it was like the stars sparkled even brighter in this moment. The sweet scent of wildflowers tickled his nose along with the salty goodness of the popcorn, and he lost track of time and everything around them until a single solitary howl brought him to his senses.

They backed away, and the sound of hooves barreling toward them sent them to their respective horses. She mounted Andromeda with an ease he envied and pulled up on the reins. While JR and Sweeney were still specks in the distance with Moose trotting alongside, she clucked her tongue for Andromeda to hold up.

"You know, maybe we've been approaching this all wrong," she said, hesitating before licking her lips. "We're both intelligent people. It's time for us to find a way to move forward and begin something instead of ending it outright."

Hope flickered in him and then exploded out of the chute while he steadied Margarita with a firm grip on the reins. She found him, Lucky Harper, intelligent, and this could be the start of a real family. He nodded. "Beginnings herald promise. I've always looked forward to whatever life holds on the horizon."

Then JR and Sweeney crystallized into view, no longer silhouettes, with their features defined, their gazes on full alert about whatever might threaten the well-being of this ranch.

Lizzie's home and place of employment, where people looked up to her and counted on her sound judgment.

"Then it's settled." She smiled, the moonlight creating a soft glow around her that he'd never forget. Same as he'd never forget her, but he couldn't accept what she was offering.

"Lizzie, the rodeo is my new beginning this year."

And just like that, her posture stiffened in the saddle. "I see."

JR and Sweeney approached, and they all conferred together. Lizzie and JR headed toward the sound, while Sweeney and Lucky agreed to take the first shift guarding the pasture perimeter.

Thankful for one memory where someone called him by his given name, he regretted it would be the last kiss he and Lizzie would ever share together. He saw the level of respect Sweeney and JR afforded her as the owner's daughter, who'd eventually take over the care of the ranch. That type of respect had been hard-earned over a number of years. If anyone found out that this engagement wasn't real, she could lose that respect, no matter that she'd started this as a way of protecting her father on his special day. He wouldn't let that happen.

The same bittersweet feeling clenched his chest now. He and Butterscotch would leave after the roundup with the memory of that kiss sustaining him while his heart once again shattered into a thousand pieces.

CHAPTER ELEVEN

WITH LAST WEEK'S cattle roundup in the rearview mirror, Lizzie had business in town at the architect's office that couldn't wait any longer. Running behind this afternoon, she arrived with only a minute to spare. She listened as Mr. Krakowski elaborated on why they'd have to delay the construction until next spring. In order to proceed, he needed the down payment now for the cost of the materials. With Dad and Evie in Hawaii, she had no choice but to cut the check from her personal account. Once they'd returned, she'd have to come clean to her father about everything and get reimbursed then.

What would she do if Dad wasn't on board with the new construction? This was a sizable amount of money. She didn't hesitate to sign her name. Her father always looked out for the employees. She just needed to be open with him and confide in him the reasons behind her decision.

Thanking the head architect, she left the building and stopped short on the sidewalk. Was that Jeff leaving Wayne Coltrane Realty?

Maybe her brother and Nicole had changed their minds during the roundup and decided to move to Violet Ridge after all. Instead of managing the Double I by herself, it would become a family enterprise. For the past ten years, she believed she'd be her father's successor, having toiled in the stable and out in the pastures, birthing and vaccinating calves and taking over the barn management after Sabrina and Ty married and rejoined the rodeo circuit on a part-time basis.

The topsy-turvy nature of it all brought back the mixed emotions, but Dad would be even happier when he returned, if that was even possible, at this latest development. While it wasn't her ideal choice, she couldn't blame her father for wanting his family around and working together. Besides, it would be fun watching Audrey and Zack grow up, something she wouldn't have been able to do if they had continued living in Boston.

Jeff was busy talking on his cell and must not have seen her. She yelled out his name, and he glanced around and acknowledged her. "I didn't expect to see you in Violet Ridge this afternoon."

"I could say the same." She pointed toward the window, with its display of posted available properties in the area.

His breath hitched, and he pocketed his phone. "It's not what it looks like."

She laughed. If anyone could appreciate appearances not being what they seemed, it was her, but the evidence here was as striking as the fake diamond in the engagement ring still ensconced on her left hand. "If you're worried about my reaction to your moving back to Violet Ridge, don't be. I loved spending time with Audrey and Zack last week on the roundup. They're delightful, but I don't understand why you and Nicole don't just move into the guesthouse instead of approaching a real-estate agent for your own place." Even though she had set her sights on the guesthouse for her own use. She was getting too old to live in her father's house any longer.

Jeff shook his head. "Have time for a cup of coffee before you head back to the Double I?"

Whatever he had to talk about must be something he wanted to tell her away from the prying ears of everyone at the ranch. "Blue Skies is only a block from here. They're open for another hour."

Lizzie led her brother along Canyon Drive until it intersected with Main Street, and there was the Blue Skies Coffee House. Jeff held the door open for her, and she entered, removing her sunglasses. The cooler interior air was a pleasant change from the summer heat. Before she could make her way to the counter, a friend from high school waylaid her and exclaimed over the ring. By the time she finished their conversation, Jeff had grabbed a table, and she joined him.

He pushed a beverage toward her. "Plain black with two sugars." That was exactly how she preferred it.

"Thanks. Good powers of observation about how I drink my coffee. I'm impressed." She opened the plastic lid and let the steam and aroma waft out.

"In my profession, you have to be observant."

She kept from stating the obvious about his biggest miss, namely her and Lucky's engagement. "Well, I observed you coming out of the realtor's office. Even though I wouldn't have felt happy about it a month ago, I'm glad you and Nicole will be moving here."

Jeff held up his hand. "Slow down. We have no intention of moving to Violet Ridge."

She blew on her beverage, confused for a second before realizing she had jumped to conclusions the same way as everyone else had about her and Lucky. "Then why were you at the realtors'?" She pieced together his other actions of the past few weeks. "Does it have anything to do with why you've been asking my cowhands questions about property rights?"

"They told you. The staff is loyal to you." He used a wooden stirrer and then placed it out of reach. "My questions relate to a big case Nicole and I are working on. That was why we agreed to come to Dad's wedding."

She leaned back against the cold black metal of the iron chair. Apparently, she'd given him too much credit for choosing family over work commitments. Then she stopped herself, as she'd done the same when she hid out in the stable. "You weren't going to come otherwise?"

Jeff huffed out a breath before his shoulders fell, a sheepish look breaking out on his face. "Well, our nanny is also on vacation."

She leveled her brother a look to let him know he was treading on even thinner ice. Not coming home for his own father's wedding? She'd talked to Ben last night, his genuine regret about not coming home for the wedding evident. Ben would have been there if his military service hadn't prevented it.

In the end, though, did it matter why Jeff came to Colorado? She felt as though this was her last chance to bond. If she let it slip away...

He was family. "Maybe Zack and Audrey could visit every summer. Then you and Nicole could spend a weekend here when they're ready to fly home."

"I could talk to Nicole about that," he said, building on her effort, "but I need your help with something."

Her older brother needed her help? That was a change from the teenager who'd always shooed away his younger sister. "There's a first time for everything. Is this about your legal case or something else?"

"Actually, you're the person who can convince

Dad I'm not moving back. No matter how many times I try to correct him about Nicole and myself staying in Boston, he's still holding out hope I'm going to cave." Jeff's green gaze, so like her own, met hers.

Maybe Jeff was her ace in the hole. This very situation might help him understand how everything had snowballed. If so, he might be able to assist her and Lucky in finding a graceful avenue of escape. "Dad has a forceful personality."

"Tell me about it. Zack reminds me of him while I see some of Mom in Audrey." Jeff looked wistful for a minute before he gripped his coffee again. "You were in kindergarten when Mom and Dad's differences caused some intense arguments. Then Mom was diagnosed with cancer and they agreed to reconcile to make her last month easier for her and us. It took Dad a long time to recover from all of that. Evie and Dad are so suited for each other. I'm glad he's happy, but my life is in Boston. I talked to Nicole, and we're flying here for Christmas with Audrey and Zack. Audrey is ecstatic about your wedding. Nicole will get in touch with you about bridal studios in Boston and coordinating dresses and tuxes on our end."

Without a reason to return in December, Lizzie had a feeling it would be a while before she saw her niece and nephew again. She had to get him to agree to visit regardless of the wedding. "Are those reservations confirmed?"

"Yes." He laughed and then sobered. "If you're worried there are too many differences between you and Lucky, like there were with Mom and Dad, don't be. I see how Lucky looks at you. That man would lasso the moon for you if you asked."

For her family, yes. For her? Not so much. The rodeo was too much of a lure for him, and she'd never leave the ranch. That thought was like a direct hit to her heart. "I'm glad you like him. He loves the Irwin family, especially Audrey and Zack."

"What's important is he loves our family for who we are, not what we own or represent." He leaned across the table. "I never understood what you saw in Jared."

She waited for those old feelings that always surfaced whenever she defended her ex in the past. Nothing. "Jared was charming when he wanted to be, but it didn't take long for him to show his true self to me."

For a long time, she thought she'd fallen in love with Jared, a man who showed one front to the world while only wanting what was best for him, but she hadn't. Time had finally helped put that relationship into perspective. She'd fallen for his smooth lines and his polished exterior until that fateful day when she discovered his true intent of using her as the means to a promotion that depended on her father's signature on a contract. He'd figured out the best way to get close to Dad was to cozy up to her. When she'd confronted him, he'd defended himself until he ran out of excuses and turned on her, calling her cold and stiff. He'd been a wolf in an expensive suit and cowboy boots. Lucky, though? He was the same inside and out, a true gentleman to the core.

She twisted the engagement ring on her finger, the adhesive tape a little looser. Some of it must have fallen off during the roundup. She'd best fix that when she arrived home. Then she realized if this was a real engagement, she wouldn't care what size of ring it was. It was the thought that counted.

"You've come a long way since then. I see it in the eyes of all the cowhands. They hold you in high esteem. So does Dad." He smiled. "So will you talk to Dad for me?"

Starting off with Jeff's news would put her father in a bad mood, and then she'd have to compound it with the status of her and Lucky's relationship. Still, it had to be done. Jeff put his finger on it. She was the barn manager and working heir to one of the largest ranches in southwest Colorado. Only by telling her father the whole truth could she then work on earning back the trust she'd lose when everything came to light.

With a nod, she agreed to Jeff's request.

WITH ONLY TWENTY-FOUR hours until Lucky had to head to Casper for the next rodeo, he'd tackle the deep-cleaning chores for the RV and trailer that he never had time for during the long traveling season. This late-morning sudden storm, perfect for this dreary Wednesday, prevented him from taking Butterscotch into the corral at the Silver Horseshoe and practicing ways to shave off milliseconds from the chute release. Besides, cleaning provided a perfect excuse for remaining at Will's ranch, an unexpected detour after the roundup. Will needed an extra cowhand for vaccinations, and Lucky was more than happy for an excuse to clear his head, something he couldn't do whenever Lizzie was around. Evening practice with Will and Ty provided a double win: an excuse to be at the Silver Horseshoe all day and night to prepare for the next rodeo.

He inserted a special attachment to his vacuum and began cleaning the RV's ceiling, taking care around the corners for the little cobwebs that had sprung up. A sudden loud noise caused him to turn off the vacuum. Someone was banging on his door, and it sounded like they meant business. Since the vacuum had given him away, Lucky had no choice but to open the door. For a second, Will stood on the step before sailing past Lucky, then he removed his raincoat and planted himself on the black leather couch opposite the kitchen sink.

"Make yourself comfortable," Lucky said in

a wry voice, gesturing with his arm for Will to come inside. He looked around for Sabrina but didn't see her outside the RV, so he closed the door before turning to Will, whose stony face reminded Lucky of what Will had looked like before he met Kelsea. Lucky kept his tone light. "Do you need a towel to dry off? Would you like something to drink? I can make some coffee—"

"When are you going to call off the engagement, Lucky?" Will didn't mince words and leaned his elbows on his knees. "Someone's going to get hurt the longer this goes on."

"Or we can just talk and make the both of us uncomfortable," Lucky muttered while pushing aside the vacuum.

Leaning against the refrigerator, Lucky kept his feet on the carpeted floor and his tongue in check. Lizzie's future depended on how this conversation played out. He wouldn't do anything that might cause her pain or embarrassment.

"Tell me you met Elizabeth before a few weeks ago, and that you love her. I'll apologize and we'll never speak of this conversation again." Will's gaze never left Lucky, concern radiating out of his dark brown eyes.

"Where's Sabrina?" Lucky looked away from Will, still expecting the third member of their trio to walk in any minute.

"She and Ty just left for the rodeo, along with Genie. She mentioned something in passing, and it confirmed my suspicion that you and Elizabeth met recently." Will stood and walked over to the basket of cleaning supplies. "I've never seen someone who's in love and about to endure a brief separation lose themselves in cleaning."

Lucky raised his eyebrows, doing mental cartwheels about how to get Will off his case. Nothing came to mind. "I'd expect Kelsea to bring this up, but you?"

"You're my best friend. I don't want to see you hurt." Will didn't even blink. Instead, he just shrugged and picked up the multipurpose cleaner. "Do you want some help or are you insisting on doing everything by yourself?"

Only the pitter-patter of raindrops on the trailer's roof broke the silence that extended for a few minutes.

"If you want to start on the sink and counter, I'll clean out the refrigerator." Lucky reached for the fresh box of baking soda next to the other supplies. "So people in love can't clean their houses? I'd think wanting to impress that special person would allow for some minor chores here and there."

"You've been at the Silver Horseshoe since the roundup." Will sprayed some cleaner on the countertop. "Either you had a fight, or you were never engaged. Since you've been walking around muttering goodbye to everything when you think no one is listening with an expression that portends doom, I'm guessing the latter."

Lucky plucked a new trash bag off the roll and snapped it open. "I'm not following your reasoning, Detective Sherlock. If I look as if doomsday was upon me, wouldn't that imply Lizzie and I had a fight?"

"It's more like you're taking in every motion as if your world was about to turn on its axis, like you were never going to see us again." Will reached for a sponge, then wiped the surfaces and let out a wry chuckle. "Now that I'm saying all of this out loud, it does seem absurd."

Lucky opened the refrigerator door and began ditching all the old takeout containers into a trash bag. "Almost as much as underestimating Lizzie." He stopped what he was doing and wiped his hands with a towel. "I won't do anything to hurt her."

Will sighed and made circular motions with the sponge. "You're the most admirable person I know, Lucky. Considering what you endured growing up, that's pretty darn amazing. You could have been bitter or distrustful of people, yet you give your heart to your friends. I'm just worried whatever you two are doing is going to leave your heart shattered, same as it did when that family blamed you for the son's underage drinking."

Will was one of the few people who knew about the alcohol incident and how Lucky ended up taking the blame. At first, he believed he'd land in another foster home, but instead he'd aged out of the system and then boarded the bus to Colorado.

"Lizzie's not like that. I respect her."

Will's brow furrowed. "That's what's confusing me. Elizabeth Irwin is the most efficient, dependable neighbor around. I can't believe she'd go along with anything like this."

Which was another reason Lucky had already made up his mind to stay on the road after the next rodeo. The good part about the height of the rodeo season was that there was always one happening somewhere. With this trailer, transportation wasn't a problem.

"Just because someone's efficient doesn't mean there's not a beating heart under the surface." There was so much more to Lizzie than she let on to most people.

Will studied him. Lucky didn't squirm or budge. Then Will threw the sponge in the sink. "There's no one else around. While I don't like keeping secrets from Kelsea, I'll have your back. What's the genuine story between you and Elizabeth?"

"I won't lie to you, and I won't do anything to get between you and Kelsea." Lucky had been in town the day Will met Kelsea. Lucky had arranged to meet Will at the Violet Ridge Inn for a drink so they could catch up on what was happening in their lives, but Will had spotted the sales representative who'd come to his ranch earlier that day sleeping in the hotel lobby. When she woke up with the two of them standing there, the sparks had been evident between her and Will, and Lucky had rescheduled a time for him and Will to talk. Over the next few months, Lucky had been privileged to witness the two of them fall in love in between his various rodeo stints. "So if that means keeping my cards close to my chest for now, so be it."

Will's gaze narrowed on something to the left of Lucky, and his friend reached out his arm. He plucked a piece of paper off the refrigerator, and Lucky groaned. He'd forgotten about the itinerary he'd created for himself late last night. "Colorado, Arizona, Wyoming, Texas, Nevada." Will scanned the list. "You'll be doing a lot of traveling to qualify for the year-end finals. When will you have time to return to Violet Ridge? Plan a wedding? Spend time with your fiancée?"

Staying busy, so busy he'd collapse on his bed every night, was the only way Lucky could think of to keep from having his heart shatter into a million pieces. "Gordon already arranged everything for the wedding, and Lizzie knows what the rodeo means to me." So far, so good. Everything he said was the truth. "People without obligations travel pretty fast."

Using the same and only magnet, Will pinned the itinerary back on the refrigerator. "I might be grasping at straws, but I'd hate to think you thought of our friendship as an obligation. You and Sabrina? We're more than friends. We're family." His voice cracked, and he stilled. Then he wiped something from the corner of his eye. "You kicked up too much dust in here."

"Your friendship kept me going too many times," Lucky admitted, that same dust also lodging in his throat.

"Would it help if Kelsea and I engineered a situation so that you two could call everything off? We can host a dinner tonight for you and Elizabeth to do just that."

Lucky appreciated the offer. This was why he'd miss Will, but he had no intention of putting Will in the middle of all of this any more than he'd ask Will to keep a secret from Kelsea. "Thanks, but Lizzie and I have this under control."

Will's gaze went to the refrigerator and the itinerary. "You're not coming back, are you? At least, not for a really long time. Till the dust settles and then some."

Will knew him too well. Next year, he'd find another rodeo, one that didn't take place in Violet Ridge, to kick off his season. A clean break was always for the best, and goodbyes ranked down there with pumping out his trailer. "When Cale took me in, I found hard work and decent meals did wonders for my sleep schedule."

"We have plenty of that here at the Silver Horseshoe, and I expect you home for the holidays after you make your first appearance at the year-end finals." Will moved his arm as if he was about to hug Lucky and then thought the better of it. "I'll save this hug for then."

For Lucky, this trailer was his home, but the full impact of Will's words hit him in the gut. "Thanks for believing I'll get that far."

"You and Butterscotch are fluid in motion in the arena. You make a good team." Will reached for his raincoat, donned it and headed for the door. "Sabrina, you and I make a good team, too. Whatever you need from us, all you have to do is ask."

Will opened the door and glanced behind him. Lucky nodded as rain pelted the ground outside the trailer, and Will departed. A slow ache spread across his chest at the thought of losing the best friend he'd ever had. While he'd like nothing more than to load Butterscotch and sneak away to the Casper rodeo, he had to make one more stop before he left town. He might not say goodbye to Will, but there was one person for whom he'd set aside his dislike for goodbyes.

Somehow, he'd find the courage to speak to Lizzie one last time.

CHAPTER TWELVE

WITH HIS RV SHIPSHAPE, Lucky ran out of reasons to stall any longer. It was time to say goodbye to Lizzie and head to Casper. He left his raincoat in the mudroom of the ranch house and dried his hair before he entered the kitchen. A sugary aroma warmed him to his toes. He found Tammy sliding cookies off an aluminum sheet with Zack and Audrey on the other side of her, licking their lips.

Zack reached for one, and Tammy batted away his hand. "They have to cool off first."

Then Audrey glanced toward Lucky and launched herself at him. "You're back. Where have you been? I missed you."

Her glasses dug into his hip, but he didn't mind much. "I was at my friend Will's ranch, practicing for the next rodeo. I have to keep in shape."

"Does that mean you can't try one of my special homemade Double I Ranch cowboy cookies?" Tammy waved one under his nose before placing it back with the others. "They're JR's favorites, with cranberries, dried cherries, coconut and almonds."

His mouth watered, and he rubbed his stomach. "I always make room for your cookies, Tammy. If they taste half as good as they smell, I can see why they're JR's favorites." He grinned, glad he had plenty of time for the drive before sunset. While he technically could wait until tomorrow to leave, he didn't want to draw out the goodbye.

While he didn't like leaving Lizzie to fend off the questions about their failed engagement alone, he was so close to making the year-end finals. What other choice did he have? His dream was within reach.

"You can each eat one cookie now," Tammy said, holding up her index finger to Zack and Audrey. Then she pulled Lucky aside while untying her apron and hanging it on a nearby hook. "Can you watch them while I finish making the chicken and dumplings for the cowhands? Nicole asked if I'd watch Audrey and Zack today while she and Jeff worked in Mr. Gordon's office. Lizzie and JR rode out to check on the cattle, and Grandma Eloise is having lunch in Violet Ridge with some of the local ladies."

Lucky glanced at Audrey, who was taking small nibbles of her cookie while Zack had obviously crammed the whole cookie in his mouth. "Say no more." He knew what it was like to be passed from adult to adult, and he wouldn't let them feel unwanted. "As long as you save some for me, that is."

"As if you even had to ask. Besides, seeing you will raise Lizzie's spirits, considering how she's been moping since you've been gone." She walked over to Audrey and Zack and ruffled their hair. "Do you want to spend time with Lucky?"

Zack pulled his video-game console from his pocket and flipped open the lid. "I don't need anyone to watch me. I can keep myself occupied."

Lucky recognized Zack's defensive posture. The boy was smart, and he'd obviously figured out what was happening. "It's raining, so we can't visit the duck pond, but I seem to remember a promise from the roundup to teach you and Audrey how to whittle."

Zack's eyes lit up. "Really? With a real knife and everything?"

"I want to make a unicorn." Audrey's head nodded faster than a bucking bronc.

"It might take a few lessons before you work your way up to that." Lucky thought of what he'd need. Everything was in his trailer, which he'd parked near the stable. "Safety instructions first."

Audrey tugged on Lucky's sleeve. "I'm going to name my unicorn Lucky."

Touched at the gesture, Lucky was about to speak when Zack started first. "I guess it might pass the time. I'll go so I can keep an eye on Audrey."

Despite his grudging tone, Lucky understood too well how Zack was on the verge of a big leap, no longer a young kid but not quite a tween. With caring support around him, Zack would adapt to the changes.

"Big brother looks good on you, Zack. Wait here while I okay this with Jeff." Lucky had barely pressed send on his text when Jeff provided his approval. He placed his phone back in his pocket. "We need to make a quick stop at my trailer, and then we'll find a good, dry place for whittling."

In the mudroom, they found a stand with a host of blue-and-brown golf umbrellas, all sporting the ranch logo. Lucky borrowed one while Audrey and Zack shared one.

He opened the back door only to find gray skies continuing their deluge of rain. Gusty breezes whipped the tops of the trees, and the three rushed along the path to Lucky's trailer. He hurriedly ushered them inside.

"Wow! All of this is yours?" Audrey's eyes, magnified by the thick lenses of her purple glasses dotted thick with rain droplets, grew as wide as a rodeo champion's belt buckle.

Lucky handed her a tissue so she could dry her glasses. She thanked him while Zack climbed the two steps to Lucky's bed. "This is so cool! You can go anywhere you want. I'd drive to the Grand Canyon and sleep under the stars."

"No, you wouldn't. You'd go off somewhere and play your video game all the time." Audrey joined him and started bouncing on the bed.

"Would not," Zack argued as he mimicked her actions.

"Would, too."

"Stop!" Lucky took a deep breath. "I have to sleep on that bed, thank you very much, and I have responsibilities, too. Tonight I'm leaving for the Casper rodeo."

Audrey frowned. "You're leaving?" Her face crumpled, and she sniffled. "I thought you were marrying Aunt Lizzie."

If Lizzie was here, they might have been able to clear up the misunderstanding, once and for all. Without Lizzie, though? He gulped. "I travel for my work, Audrey."

"It's like when Joey's dad goes on trips for his job. He always comes back, and Joey says his mom takes a long bath while he and his dad go out for fast food." Lucky hid a smile at Zack's matter-of-fact tone in teaching Audrey about how the world worked.

Audrey jumped off the bed and tugged at Lucky's damp flannel shirt. "Mommy and Daddy are taking us to the Summer Send-off before we go home. Are you taking Aunt Lizzie?"

Lucky had seen signs for the festival in town, but it didn't start until this weekend during the Casper rodeo. He'd love to go with this family.

Specifically, he'd love to see it through Lizzie's eyes. "I don't know."

"Dad says I can eat a corn dog. I've never had one before." Zack rubbed his stomach.

"And I've never been on a Ferris wheel before." Audrey made a circle with her index finger. "Will you be back from your rodeo in time to go with us? I won't be scared if you're on the Ferris wheel with me."

"Won't you want to go on it with your dad?" That seemed like a perfect father-daughter activity.

"I can go once with him, and once with you," Audrey pleaded, her hands clasped so tight her knuckles were turning white.

If he and Lizzie were engaged for real, he could see a little girl with Lizzie's serious expression and his curly hair, or a boy with her green eyes. They could even discuss the possibility of becoming foster parents. He dismissed the thought and contemplated Audrey's request. One return trip to Violet Ridge couldn't cause any additional permanent scarring to his heart, could it?

Zack's gaze burned into him. "We know you're busy." Zack's disappointment was clear.

Already, Zack had learned adults didn't always keep promises, a hard lesson for anyone but devastating for an eight-year-old. Lucky would already be letting down the Irwin family when they found out about him and Lizzie. He didn't want to let down Zack over this.

More time with Lizzie was a bonus. "I'll come back after the rodeo."

Audrey hugged Lucky's waist and then stepped back. "Promise?"

Lucky nodded. "Yep, and a cowboy promise is worth its weight in silver horseshoes." He glimpsed a hint of a smile on Zack's face. "And I promised to teach you how to whittle. Time's a wastin'."

The rain showed no sign of letting up, and Lucky bustled Audrey and Zack into the stable rather than getting mud all over the ranch house. Lizzie's office might be small, but that made it all the better for the first whittling lesson, as there'd be less chance of the two siblings wandering away and getting into trouble. They closed the umbrellas and said hello to the grooms.

Audrey peeked into a stall and turned toward Lucky. "What's her name?"

Lucky joined her and found the stable cat peering with one eye at them from her position of repose. "I don't know," Lucky admitted. "We'll ask Aunt Lizzie the next time we see her."

"She needs a good name." Audrey gave one nod, as if emphasizing her point.

They entered Lizzie's office and flicked on the light. Lucky placed the damp paper bag on Lizzie's desk before propping the door open with her boot scraper. A whiff of wildflowers hung in the air, and the small space seemed imprinted with traces of Lizzie: her day planner, a tube of ChapStick and a container of her preferred hand lotion. Lucky upended the bag, and the contents spilled out on the desk.

"What's with the potato peelers?" Zack grasped one and scowled. "I thought we were going to use real knives."

"In good time. Everyone starts somewhere." Cale had been patient with him when Lucky arrived on his ranch and coached him through everything step by step, and he'd do the same with Audrey and Zack. "And that somewhere is safety."

Zack looked bored, and Lucky saw Zack's hand moving toward his pocket, no doubt reaching for his ever-present video console. "Give me a chance before you reach for your game."

Zack rolled his eyes. "I thought you said this was gonna be fun."

"That depends on you." Lucky walked to the other side of the desk and sat in Lizzie's chair. "But it's no fun if you accidentally cut yourself."

Zack shrugged, but Lucky noticed he listened to the rules of how to handle a knife. "Remember, a dull knife is more dangerous than a sharp one." Then Lucky unwrapped the three bars of soap and handed one to Zack and one to Audrey. "We're just going to practice on this today. If you enjoy this hobby and if I have permission from your parents, I'll see if I can buy you beginner knives to keep here on the ranch for your visits."

Zack's eyes lit up, and then he sighed. "Mom will never go for that."

"That's why we're working with soap and then stripping bark from those three pieces of wood so you can prove you're ready for the responsibility. That, and being open and honest." Guilt at his failure to communicate the truth to the Irwin family, who'd taken him into their house over the past few weeks, gnawed at him.

"But soap? What can you do with soap?" Zack scoffed.

"Plenty." Lucky reached for his knife and one of the pristine bars of soap. In a few minutes, he carved a turtle. Zack relented once he saw the finished shape.

"Okay, maybe I'll try it." Zack strove for nonchalance, but the way he leaned forward gave everything away. He was hooked.

Lucky showed Audrey and Zack how to shave the soap with the vegetable peeler. In no time, Zack proved himself capable of handling a bigger challenge, and Lucky showed him how to strip bark from sticks.

"Nice job, Zack," Lucky praised him, and the joy on Zack's face was everything. "We have a little more time until lunch will be ready, so why don't you try my knife while I'm right here?"

"Really? Thanks. I remember everything you

said. Only use it with an adult present. Always sheath the knife when not in use." Zack recounted the rest of Lucky's lecture, and Lucky felt like a proud uncle.

Lucky waited while Zack donned the safety gloves, and then he demonstrated how to use the pocketknife under careful supervision. Zack made his first few cuts and then folded the knife. He placed it on the desk before he jumped to his feet. "Aunt Lizzie! Come look."

Lizzie stood in the doorway, her red hair damp and tousled from the rain. "What do we have here?"

Zack held up his stick. "I'm making a wand so I can be a wizard."

Audrey jumped from her chair and hugged her aunt before producing a mottled block of white soap. The little girl placed hers next to Lucky's turtle. "My turtle doesn't look as good. Guess it's 'cause I have a peeler and not a knife." She shrugged and smiled. "It's fun, but Grandma Eloise taught me how to cast with knitting needles. I like making a blanket for Teddy better."

Lizzie's eyebrows raised a fraction of an inch, and she wiggled her finger at Lucky. "Can I see you alone for a minute?"

Lucky pocketed his knife and nodded. "Sure thing." He winked at the kids. "Guess she's jealous and wants her own whittling lesson." He followed Lizzie, who stopped near the archway of the stable. "I'm supposed to be taking care of Audrey and Zack while Tammy makes chicken and dumplings, and their parents work."

"And how is treating them differently taking care of them? Did you hear Audrey?" Lizzie tapped her red cowboy boot against the straw floor. "I can't blame her for not enjoying your whittling lesson seeing as how she's using a vegetable peeler while Zack's using a knife."

"Wait a second." Lucky bristled at Lizzie's implication. "I'd never be so unkind as to make one of them feel inferior."

He'd had enough of that growing up with some of his foster parents showing preferential treatment to their biological children. Not all foster parents were like that. There were good people out there caring for the children who came into their home, and Lucky hoped someday to be one of the good ones.

Lizzie kept tapping her boot in time with the rhythm of the rain. "It looked like you were favoring Zack."

"What I was doing was taking their individual personalities into account. Audrey is younger and has some depth-perception issues." Lucky stayed calm and continued, "Her fine motor skills aren't as advanced as Zack's. If she likes knitting and sticks with it, that will help with her hand-eye coordination. She also fidgeted a lot during my safety talk. On the other hand, Zack listened and recited every rule back to me. He's a couple of years older than Audrey, and he finished his task faster, so I let him use my pocketknife once. That's all."

"Sorry. I should have listened first." Lizzie stared at him, the left corner of her lips scrunching upward in a half smile. "We just had our first fight."

Their gazes met, a plum opportunity for him to finish what hadn't even started, but he wanted more time with her. The mere thought of wanting to have something meaningful with Lizzie—a family, where they'd go through life together left him a little dizzy.

The clean lines of the luxurious stable came into view, a reminder they were from two different worlds. His life was on the road, and this was his big year on the circuit. And if he didn't make the finals this go-around, there was always next season, or the one after that. Have RV, will travel.

"A fight like that could lead to a broken engagement quite easily, but Tammy's making chicken and dumplings. You can't expect me to miss that, could you?" He kept his tone light.

"That would be too mean. After all, Tammy's chicken and dumplings are legendary and can't be missed." Her eyes started twinkling, and then she held out her hand. "Friends again?"

Friends. Could he deal with just that?

He slid his hand in hers, wanting more, specifically another kiss, so he could discover if his strong reaction to that first one was a fluke. As matters stood, he had no choice but to settle for this truce and her friendship. "It takes more than a little disagreement for me to break a friendship. I'm always there for my friends."

They heard the kids' voices before the pair appeared before them. "Aunt Lizzie, is it lunchtime?" Zack rubbed his tummy for emphasis. "I'm starving."

She laughed. "I'm sure Tammy's ready for us."

As they darted out of the stable under the umbrellas, Lucky caught sight of his RV through the misty rain. He should get in the trailer now and head for the next rodeo, and the next, and the next. Then, he remembered his promise to Audrey and Zack that he'd return from the rodeo for the Summer Send-off, and he groaned. Promises were forever, and this time at Violet Ridge was just temporary.

Lizzie glanced at him, and he longed to turn this friendship into a permanent relationship so he could share how beautiful she was with her hair wet from the rain, her cheeks kissed from the wind. He longed to take her aside and tell her how she made him feel inside—special and cared for and treasured. And yet he was a simple guy from upstate New York, a far cry from the man she deserved. So he only smiled and held the umbrella over Audrey.

"Last one to the chicken and dumplings is a wet blanket," he said while picking up the pace.

LIZZIE WALKED AN imaginary diagonal line along the pasture adjoining the stable. The ground was rather soft from yesterday's constant storms, but not so saturated as to cause trouble for any of the horses. While yesterday had been gray and dreary, today's dawn heralded blue skies, perfect for being on the range, checking on cattle and giving Andromeda free rein to gallop.

With the help of the youngest groom, Roy, she finished the morning chores and began turning out the horses. She paused at Butterscotch's stall. Should she allow Butterscotch some freedom in the pasture before the horse left for this weekend's rodeo? She pulled out her phone to text Lucky when a voice called out behind her.

"I saw the other horses going out to the pasture and realized it was time to load Butterscotch into the trailer. You made a good call yesterday asking me to stay for one more day because of the rain."

She swiveled and found Lucky there, wearing his old brown cowboy hat. "The flooding on the local interstate has cleared. Do you need some help putting him in his trailer?"

"Are you offering your services or Roy's?" His eyes held a hint of challenge.

"While Roy is most capable, I think you need

my personal touch." Then she blushed, as that could easily be misconstrued. "Um—"

He chuckled. "I know what you meant." Then he leaned against the side of the stable wall and grinned. "A wanderer like me could get spoiled by your personal touch."

A wanderer. Even after a couple of weeks on the finest ranch in Colorado, he still couldn't wait to hit the road while she cherished every minute on the ranch.

The stable cat investigated the source of the voices and wound her lithe body around Lucky's legs. He bent and lavished affection on her while the independent cat lapped up the attention. "You're spoiling her."

"What's her name? Audrey asked me yesterday, and I didn't know it." Lucky gave the cat a pat and stood straight again.

"Name?" Lizzie racked her brain.

"Everyone, even a stable cat, should have a name," he said.

"Let me think. I'm trying to remember what Sabrina called her when she had kittens last year. Will took one, and so did his uncle Barry for Regina's feed-and-seed in town. Good stable cats are snapped up around here." The cat came over to Lizzie and she petted her. "I don't think we've ever named her, and this sounds personal for you. I'm open to suggestions."

He approached Butterscotch and pulled an apple

slice from his pocket. "We should probably consult Audrey." Butterscotch nudged his shoulder as if asking for another slice. "She's really something. Last night when I told her and Zack goodbye for now, she reminded me about the Summer Send-off and showed me the app. She already knows what she wants to do, and she's only six. When I was her age…my mom took off. New York State couldn't track down my father, and so it began."

He'd been younger than Audrey when he entered the system, younger than she was when her mother died. He treated others with compassion, and her heart broke for the little boy who'd witnessed that.

The cat crossed back to him. Beyond the stable doors, Lizzie spotted a glimpse of Grandma Eloise, who'd come home yesterday from her lunch with a mouthful about how the town was still buzzing with news of hers and Lucky's engagement.

"How about Weezie? I think that's a nickname for Eloise."

"I like that." He scratched the cat behind her furry ear. "Congratulations, Weezie. May you live long and guard the stable well."

In no time, Lizzie helped Lucky load Butterscotch into the trailer. The gelding acted almost giddy at the thought of a ride, as if it was an adventure of a lifetime. Lucky's eyes seemed brighter than usual as well, also as if he couldn't wait to get on the open road. Who could blame him? He must have such an exciting life on the road, whereas Lizzie was always content knowing she belonged here on the ranch.

He dipped his hat in her direction, and his gaze lingered on her, almost as if he was wondering whether he should kiss her goodbye. She'd like nothing better.

Grandma Eloise approached them, her cane sinking into the softer ground. "Tammy sent me with something to tide you over until you return next week, a care package of food. I personally baked the apple pie yesterday, and JR thought you might like that book you two discussed on the roundup." She handed Lucky a tote bag. "I'll be here until Evie gets back from her honeymoon, so I expect to see you sooner rather than later."

He leaned over and kissed her cheek. "Thank you kindly." When he stepped back, Lizzie thought she saw his eyes misting. He'd probably never had anyone give him a care package before. "This is really something."

"Don't stop kissing your fiancée on my account." Grandma Eloise tapped her cane on the ground twice as if for extra emphasis, and then started back toward the ranch house.

Lizzie caught the older woman glancing back their way.

"I don't want to disappoint her." She closed her eyes and puckered.

When nothing happened, she opened her eyes and found Lucky leaning against the trailer, a few steps away, definitely too far away to kiss her. Why? Didn't he find her attractive?

"Yes, I do, and I want to kiss you." Lucky approached, and she gasped as she realized she'd asked her last question aloud. "But for the right reasons. Not for anyone else. Just you."

She shuffled her boots, suddenly self-conscious. "Oh."

She fidgeted with the engagement ring, and it slipped off her finger and plopped on the dirt. He reached down and brushed it off. "Wouldn't want you to lose this." He slid it back on her finger, and goose bumps dotted her arms. "If you want to have it resized while I'm gone, go ahead."

She made a note to add an extra layer of adhesive tape to the back of the ring as soon as Lucky left. "No. Anyway, I'll be giving it back to you soon, and it's not like this is a real ring, right?"

"Huh?" He leaned back against the trailer once more. "It's real."

She chuckled. "Of course it is, but the stones are fake, right? I mean who carries around a genuine diamond ring in a trailer?" Her chuckles faded in the wind, and her cheeks grew warm as the silence stretched out. The diamond caught the sunlight, and the warmth expanded to her neck and chest as well. "These are genuine diamonds?"

He nodded. "I thought Cherry was ready to get

married. She was, but to someone else. I'd been planning on asking Will to keep it in his safe, but I never did."

Butterscotch made his presence known, neighing and pawing the bottom of the trailer as if he wanted to get the show on the road.

"I'll wrap this again so I don't lose it." Her stomach was churning at his entrusting her with a valuable engagement ring.

He stepped toward her, taking her hands in his, sending shivers down her spine. Why did the worst person for her, a wanderer to her homebody self, elicit this type of reaction in her? "For the record, I wouldn't have bought you a diamond ring."

"You wouldn't?"

He shook his head. "I'd have bought you a ruby to match your hair and your fiery spirit. See you after the rodeo."

"Better yet, how about I kiss your cheek for luck? Just for us, and not for show."

She stood on her tiptoes, their hands still entwined. Her lips came in contact with the bristly stubble on his cheek, and his closeness erased everything but the happiness inside her.

He grinned, rubbing her kiss into his skin. "Now I'm sure to win."

She twisted the ring as he climbed into the front seat of the truck that hauled the trailer/RV unit and waved as he started up the engine. Rubies were her favorite, but she'd never told anyone else that.

Somehow, he knew her better than people who'd known her for her whole life. What would it be like to be with a special someone, sharing more roundups, more sunrise rides and, most of all, more magnetic kisses?

His trailer became a speck on the road and then disappeared altogether. Too bad the wanderer wasn't that special someone.

CHAPTER THIRTEEN

LIZZIE TAPPED HER ankle boots on the plush carpet in her father's office. This Sunday morning was almost over, and Jeff was still engrossed in his legal case, so much so he hadn't even noticed her approach. Or he wasn't acknowledging her. She held her composure together for Audrey and Zack, who'd been looking forward to the Summer Send-off all weekend. She was proud of how they'd completed all their chores yesterday and today in anticipation of the event. They were becoming real cowhands.

When her brother still didn't acknowledge her presence, she cleared her throat from the doorway. "Jeff? Audrey and Zack are ready and waiting."

He lowered his reading glasses and placed them next to his laptop. "For what? We aren't leaving for Boston until Friday."

"The Summer Send-off, remember? You promised to go with them, and I moved up the date since you said you had online appointments all day tomorrow. Are you always like this back home? They'll grow up before you know it and you'll have missed it." Lizzie couldn't believe her brother had already forgotten the Summer Send-off, if it ever was on his radar to begin with.

"We have an excellent nanny." Jeff picked up his glasses once more. "Nicole and I are putting in extra hours here since we're away from our paralegals and staff."

"Then next year we'll make arrangements to cover for that, but this year, it would be nice if you spent time with Zack and Audrey and made some memories." Her point clear, Lizzie left the room and then placed her back against the wall, purposefully bringing her head in contact with the solid surface.

Why could she confront her brother about his life and not her father about hers? She'd do just that once Dad returned from Hawaii. Hopefully, she'd changed enough, become strong enough for that. Immediately, she thought of Lucky and how forthright he'd been with her about everything and wished for some of it to have rubbed off on her.

At least she spoke her mind to Jeff. The rest was up to him. She hurried to the living room, where Zack and Audrey were waiting. She clapped her hands and pasted on a smile. "It's Aunt Lizzie's turn to spoil you. What are we waiting for?"

"Hopefully me?" Her breath escaped as she

recognized Lucky's voice from behind her. "I got your text about the day change and hurried back."

"Lucky!" Audrey ran to him and hugged him. "You won!"

Zack hurried over and gave an awkward shrug, although he looked like he really wanted to hug the rodeo cowboy. "Congratulations."

Lucky reached out his arm and included Zack in a quick group embrace before stepping back and showing everyone his new belt buckle. "I left the prize saddle in the trailer."

"I watched on television. You were amazing," Lizzie said, letting pride for his achievement wash over her.

Those blue eyes glinted, and he grinned. "It was your kiss that did it. You're my lucky charm."

Audrey tugged on his shirt. "Are you going with us to the Summer Send-off?" Then her eyes lit up behind her purple glasses. "Can I call you Uncle Lucky now?"

Lizzie reached for Audrey's hand at the same time Lucky did, and she backed away. She met Lucky's gaze, a misty film rising to the occasion. "How about you wait until after the wedding?" Lizzie asked.

Audrey seemed to take Lizzie's request in stride, but Lizzie saw an unfamiliar tic in Lucky's jaw as if she'd let him down. Being their uncle, anyone's uncle, was an honor Lucky would cherish.

THE AROMA OF grilled meat tempted Lucky's taste buds along with the sugary smell of funnel cakes. He waited outside the makeshift row of bathrooms for Audrey and Zack. Lizzie was a few yards away, lost in conversation with another rancher, something about the preferred method of branding cattle. She shook the rancher's hand and then strolled over to him, her head stuck in the paper map everyone received upon entrance. Her auburn hair was piled upon her head in a messy bun that complemented her summer outfit of a short-sleeve plaid shirt, jeans and ankle boots. She even made her casual clothes look smart.

Another reminder of how they were worlds apart.

When she reached his side, she didn't glance up from the pamphlet. "Where do you want to stage the breakup? At the Wild West show? On one of the rides?"

He placed his hand on the paper and lowered it until she met his gaze. "I appreciate the efficiency behind that statement, but look around you."

Crowds bustled about the fairgrounds on this beautiful Sunday afternoon. Vendors barked out their food options, and while the thought of trying fried jellybeans held an alluring appeal, what he really wanted was to get Lizzie alone and to himself.

"Exactly. Many people will witness our fight." Lizzie tapped her ankle boots on the cement sidewalk, a sure sign of how nervous she was. "It'll be the talk of Violet Ridge that our engagement is over."

"While it might be a sight more efficient to end this in public, I won't do it in front of Zack and Audrey." Many a night he'd heard adults fighting, sometimes over him, often over other issues in their lives.

"I didn't think of it like that. You're right, and thank you for thinking of them." She paused and then studied him closely. "You're speaking from experience, aren't you?"

He nodded. "There were nights when I'd lay awake after doors slammed."

"No child should have to go through that." She squeezed his arm. "You're an honorable man, Lucky. You're going to make someone a wonderful husband someday."

She leaned up and brushed his cheek with her soft lips. Sunshine glinted off the auburn highlights of her hair, and she seemed more relaxed. His promise to Audrey and Zack might have been the official reason he returned to Violet Ridge, but Lizzie held the real lasso encircling his heart. He was head over heels for her. While her family was a bonus, there were so many appealing qualities about her. Her polished exterior was part of her, as was her caring core. Everything she did was an act of love, from her tracking down a lost calf to being there for her niece and nephew.

He should have set forth for the next rodeo rather than detouring here, especially as she'd cautioned Audrey about calling him Uncle Lucky before the wedding. Perhaps it was a subtle hint not to get too attached to him. Yet he was already close, and he wanted more time by her side. More kisses, too.

Zack came out first, followed soon by Audrey, who wrinkled her nose. "I like inside bathrooms much better."

Lucky laughed and pushed her glasses back into place. "Pretend you're camping again."

Audrey perked up and smiled, the gap for her missing front tooth making her that much more adorable.

"What does everyone want to do first?" Lizzie held up the flier. "The merry-go-round? The Tilt-A-Whirl? The Ferris wheel?"

Lucky grinned, not surprised that she craved the thrill of the action. "So you like the rides?"

She blushed. "Who doesn't?"

He wouldn't know, as this was the first time he'd been to anything like this. He'd never had this sort of family outing with any of his foster parents, and once he started on the rodeo circuit, he'd been too busy learning the ropes or helping his new friends whenever Will mentioned this festival. "I'll take your word for it."

Her eyes widened. "It's your first time, isn't it?"

It was his turn for heat to spread across his face and down his neck. "I thought this would just be a small craft fair. The Summer Send-off is huge." He cricked his neck. "There are even hot-air balloons."

With scheduled shows, rides and food trucks, it would take the entire afternoon and evening to experience everything.

Audrey caught sight of something and pulled on Lucky's hand. "Ooh, there are games over there."

They walked in the direction of the carnival games, with the hawkers extolling the virtues of each. Lights flashed at the top of the brightly colored stalls, decked out with all sorts of prizes. Rows of stuffed animals decorated one booth while another featured various sports. Farther down the line, a row of rubber ducks in a plastic pool of water beckoned for preschoolers.

"Teddy wants a friend." Audrey dragged Lucky over to the booth with the ring toss. "So he won't forget this trip."

"You already have twenty stuffed animals back home. You don't need another one," Zack complained. "This is for kids."

"I'm a kid," Audrey protested.

Lucky extracted his wallet. "Memories are forever."

Lizzie scoffed. "No one ever wins at these." No sooner did those words escape her mouth than a man sank three basketballs and chose his prize.

She sighed and shrugged. "I'll prove myself wrong and give it a go."

Audrey's little chin jutted up. "I'm a big girl. I can do it myself."

"Yeah, right." Zack chuckled before her glare silenced him and sent his lips into a straight line.

Lucky plunked down enough money for Audrey to take several turns. The attendant accepted the bill, then handed Audrey three plastic rings and explained she needed to sink all of them around the glass milk jugs in order to win a prize.

Audrey scrunched her nose in concentration and tossed the first, encircling one of the jugs.

"You did it, Audrey! Just two more." Lizzie cheered for her niece and grasped Lucky's hand. He didn't want to ever let go. She kept her hand in place, smiling at him.

The next one also reached its target, and Lucky felt like he was back at his first rodeo, his nerves on full alert. Audrey grinned and pushed up her glasses, her face determined. The third ring fell short and clattered on the floor. Disappointment flickered for a second before she smiled. "I tried."

Her plucky spirit endeared her to him even more. Lucky stepped toward her and rolled up his flannel shirtsleeves. "It's my turn."

Zack shook his head and inserted himself between Lucky and his sister. "I want to win one for her." He glanced at Lucky. "I'm her big brother."

He couldn't be prouder of his own son. Lucky

smiled and nodded as the attendant placed three rings in front of the young boy. "Go for it."

Audrey hugged Zack, her eyes full of admiration. "I'll share if you win."

"Nah." Zack fingered a plastic ring and gauged the distance between him and the rings before he grinned back. "Just name him after me."

Lizzie gripped Lucky's hand, almost cutting off his circulation, but he wasn't about to complain or break Zack's concentration. One down, then two, and Lucky held his breath. The third flew across the distance and landed atop the others. Audrey selected a pink elk. "Meet Zacky."

Zack groaned. "I just had to say she could name it after me... I'll never live this down."

"A promise is a promise," Lucky said, laughing on the inside and the outside. Then he glanced at Lizzie and thought he glimpsed longing in those eyes. He released her hand and faced her. "Has anyone ever won a stuffed animal for you?"

She scuffed the ground with one of her ankle boots. "We're here for Zack and Audrey," she said.

He didn't miss her wistful glance at Audrey hugging her pink elk, though. Lucky rolled up his sleeves and dropped more money on the counter. He wanted Lizzie to have a permanent memento of this day. "I have all the time in the world."

"Glad to hear that." The attendant smiled as if rather confident of selling plenty of tickets to this group.

Lucky wasn't a calf-roping champion for nothing. The first landed around the milk jug, and his stomach clenched. He wanted this as much as he'd wanted his first belt buckle as a rodeo champion. The second also met its mark, and he let out the breath he didn't realize he'd been holding. Before he picked up the third ring, Lizzie tapped his arm. He faced her, and she leaned up to him on her tiptoes. She brushed his cheek with her lips. "For luck."

If anything, though, her kiss was distracting. She had no idea how beautiful she was or how much he wished their engagement was real. Women like her, though, didn't fall for cowboys who'd spent their childhood in and out of foster care. Yet when he was around her, she made him believe in hope.

He concentrated and tossed the ring. It bounced off a milk jug, and his shoulders slumped. Then the ring landed on the one behind it. He'd done it! Lizzie threw her arms around him.

"That was magnificent." She faced the attendant and picked out a fuzzy brown elk, hugging it to her side.

He captured the memory as his memento from this experience.

Lizzie whispered something to Audrey, who nodded and accepted Lizzie's stuffed animal, introducing the two elks to each other.

Lizzie reached into her purse and extracted

money from her wallet. She laid it on the counter. "Now it's my turn to win something for my nephew." "

She accepted the three rings from the attendant.

Then she faced Lucky and blew on her fingers. "I was the point guard on my high-school basketball team for a year when my father suggested I try something new, something that didn't involve the ranch."

She tossed the three rings with dexterity, all landing on their intended target. The attendant reached for another elk.

"Aunt Lizzie." Zack cleared his throat. "I'd like a baseball, not a stuffed animal."

The attendant placed it back on the shelf and handed Zack his prize. Then Lizzie plunked more money on the counter. "Three more rings, please."

What was she up to? Lucky didn't have to wait long to find out as once again, each ring landed around a different milk jug. She asked the attendant for the large tan-colored horse that resembled Butterscotch. After he used a long metal stick for the one Lizzie selected, she thanked him and then gave the stuffed animal to Lucky. "Everyone's first Summer Send-off needs something as special as they are."

Lucky felt like he could float higher than those hot-air balloons.

Zack tapped Lizzie's arm. "I'm hungry."

"Then it's time for food. We can all order something different and see what we like best." Lizzie ushered their group into the bustling crowd, her green eyes sparkling with happiness.

The four of them hustled away, but not before Lucky clutched the horse to his chest for a second, already a treasure he intended to keep. Today, he felt like this was his family, and any doubts he was falling for Lizzie were now gone. His feelings for the beautiful cowgirl were real. How would he ever get over her?

LIZZIE SAW COLORFUL hot-air balloons in the distance at the edge of the festival fairgrounds, which usually served as athletic fields. Violet Ridge prided itself on adding something new to each Summer Send-off, and this year was no different. From the middle of the makeshift picnic tables, she watched one soar into the sky, its orange and yellow colors bright and festive. That's how her heart felt whenever Lucky was around.

She snuck a glance at him. His thigh was pressed next to hers as they sat side by side on the bench across from Audrey and Zack. He dipped one end of his fried pickle into some sort of white sauce and then popped it in his mouth, contentment settling over his face.

Good. After his rodeo victory, he needed a day off, and she wanted to make it special. While he'd been competing in the rodeo, she'd taken time to think about the heartache and struggle he'd experienced while bouncing from one foster home to the next. Losing her mother at such an early age had weighed on her, but her father had loved her and her brothers as he'd coped with his grief and his broken marriage and the conflicting feelings about how it had ended so irrevocably. The ranch and stable provided plenty of room to explore and chores to keep her occupied.

Lucky had never had a place to call home.

Some might have grown jaded or aloof, but not Lucky. Instead, he was having the time of his life from the way he approached everything at the festival.

The balloon faded into the horizon, and guilt prickled at her about the whole situation. What had started as a way to not disappoint her father before his wedding was starting to cause anxiety. Somehow she'd started caring about Lucky, but she was putting him through too much by continuing this charade.

Lucky deserved more than a fleeting family. He deserved love.

Then she turned her attention to the remaining half of her barbecue beef sandwich and shoved the plate away from her. She wasn't hungry anymore.

She caught sight of Audrey's and Zack's faces, their cheeks stained with chocolate from the fried candy. Despite her heartache, she laughed and plucked two napkins from the pile.

"Audrey!" Lizzie exclaimed. "How did you get chocolate on your glasses?"

"I don't know." Her niece licked her lips. "I tried my best to get it all inside my tummy. That was so yummy. Mommy never lets us have anything like that."

That pronouncement made the barbecue sandwich sit even heavier in her stomach. Lizzie reached over the table and wiped Audrey's face. "You can tell your parents about Zack winning your new stuffed animal for you. I'll take full responsibility for the junk food."

Audrey faced Lucky, who was downing the last of his fried pickles. "You're sure Zacky is okay in the car?"

Lucky swallowed and then took a sip of his pop. "Zacky is sitting in your booster seat with a great view of the parking lot, watching everyone go home after a day of fun. He's also holding Zack's baseball so it doesn't get lost."

Hearing his tender and perceptive answers to Audrey's questions confirmed what Lizzie already knew. He had so much love inside him, waiting for a family of his own.

Zack wiped his hands on the bottom of his sky-blue T-shirt. "Can't you name it something else?" Zack wrinkled his nose.

"The elk will remind her that you cared enough to win it for her." Lizzie handed him a napkin. "What's next? The bumper cars?"

In the distance, another balloon, this one with alternating stripes of pink and red, soared beyond the horizon. Audrey pointed toward the field. "I'd like to go up in the sky."

"Junk food is one thing, but a hot-air-balloon ride? I can't do that without your parents' permission." There was no chance Lizzie would keep something like that from Jeff and Nicole, and she wasn't sure they'd say yes to this activity.

"I can text them. Can I borrow your phone, Aunt Lizzie?" Zack bounced in his seat. "That is probably so much fun."

Lucky already had his phone out and read his screen. "Sorry to disappoint you, but you have to be at least forty-eight inches to ride in one of them." He reached over and ruffled Audrey's hair. "You have a little more growing to do."

Audrey's lower lip quivered, and she glanced at Zack. "Do you want to go without me?"

Zack looked at the pink-and-red balloon with longing and then back at his sister. "Nah." Then his eyes grew round with mischief. "I'd rather see if you'd throw up if we rode the Tilt-A-Whirl."

Lucky held up his hand. "Hey, I found something. You can get a picture of you with your aunt Lizzie in one of the baskets."

Audrey's eyes lit up. She reached over and grasped Lizzie's arm. "Then next summer I'll be big enough to go up with you and Uncle Lucky."

Lizzie's head swirled. How was she going to explain the breakup to her niece and nephew?

She reached for her pamphlet. "What about those bumper cars instead? Audrey, you can ride with me. That sounds like a lot of fun."

Audrey shook her head. "I want a picture with you and Uncle Lucky. Then Mommy and Daddy will know I really want to do this next year because I'll sleep with the picture and Zacky every night."

Would Audrey be so excited to return when she and Lucky were no longer together, not that they were ever really together? Somehow, he'd become a fixture in her family, and it was her fault he wouldn't be here next summer. If Audrey found out the truth, Lizzie could lose the close bond with her she'd gained over the past month.

And she'd deserve that.

THE PHOTOGRAPHER GESTURED with his hands for the four of them to move closer together in the hot-air-balloon gondola. A wave of guilt swept over Lucky—he didn't think he should be in the picture. He moved away from Audrey, Zack and Lizzie. "You know what? This should be Aunt Lizzie with the two of you."

Audrey and Zack protested, and Lizzie implored him to stay. "This is your day, Lucky. I want you to be in the picture."

Her words struck him in the gut, and he moved

back into the frame. The photographer told some cheesy jokes to try to elicit smiles, but all Lucky had to do was turn toward Lizzie, her auburn hair free from its usual ponytail, her face light and happy with her hands on Zack's shoulders. There was something about her that always made him smile.

Within minutes, the pictures were ready. While Lizzie spoke with yet another rancher, the respect Lizzie commanded in the community on full display, Lucky purchased a set for him and one for Audrey, who hugged him. He stared at them for a long, hard minute. Anyone might mistake them for a real family, except they weren't.

More so, he'd have to keep these away from Will or Sabrina. They'd see the truth in a second, as Lucky hadn't been able to keep his eyes off Lizzie. It was written all over his too expressive face. He had been swept off his feet by the attractive cowgirl.

Then Audrey wrinkled her nose. "I look funny without my tooth."

Zack opened his mouth, but one glance from Lucky and Zack quickly clammed up. Lucky kneeled down until Audrey met his gaze. "I see a happy little girl in that picture, and the tooth will grow in so fast I won't even recognize you the next time I see you."

"Promise?" Her face lit up, and Lucky's insides clenched.

He prided himself on not making promises he knew he wouldn't keep.

He rose and gripped her hand. "I promise you're cute, with or without that tooth."

Lizzie finished her conversation and joined them. "Who's ready for some rides? It's not a Summer Send-off without a turn on the Tilt-A-Whirl and the Ferris wheel."

Zack's arm shot into the air, and Lucky laughed and joined Zack, shooting his arm upward.

THE TILT-A-WHIRL WAS as wonderful as Lizzie remembered, a rush with the cars going around a circular track, the centrifugal force causing a dizzying effect. She glanced at Lucky, his head slightly swaying as his feet claimed solid ground again. Her adrenaline burst from the ride was nothing compared to the swirl of feelings he created in her.

No sooner had they reached the main path than Audrey ran off in the distance.

"Audrey!" Lucky started rushing forward, as did Lizzie.

What was her niece thinking, running away from them in such a crowd?

Then Zack gasped and dashed after his sister, and Lizzie blew out a breath. How would she ever explain losing their children to Jeff and Nicole?

"Mom! Dad!" Lizzie heard Zack's shouts of joy over the noise of the crowd.

When she spotted her brother and sister-in-law heading toward her and Lucky, that knot in her stomach unraveled. Jeff scooped up Audrey, the joy clear on her expressive face while Nicole reached for Zack's hand, his body quivering with happiness.

Concern flitted through Lizzie. Had something happened at the ranch? Why else would they be here?

"Daddy, you should have seen Zack. He did something wonderful, and I can't wait for you to meet Zacky." Audrey grinned while Jeff seemed to hang on every word.

"Zacky?" Nicole blinked and shuddered. "It's not a goldfish or a pet pig or anything like that, right?"

"Zacky is an adorable pink elk," Lizzie said, and Nicole's eyes widened in alarm. "A stuffed pink elk."

Nicole exhaled before her gaze went to Zack's T-shirt. "What have you been eating?"

Jeff set Audrey back to a standing position and rested his arm around his wife's shoulder. "Nothing Lizzie wouldn't have eaten herself. We trusted them to her, and they're happy kids."

Trust. There was that word again. People trusted her, and she'd let everything with Lucky get out of control. As soon as her father was back, she'd clear the air and come clean about her pride over not having a plus-one for his wedding, which had escalated in no time.

"Thank you, both of you." Nicole brought Lizzie out of her reverie, and she found everyone looking at her.

"For what?" Lizzie didn't know what she'd missed.

"For reminding us they won't be this age forever." Jeff placed his free hand on Audrey's shoulder. "You and Lucky are off the hook. Enjoy the rest of the day, just the two of you."

In the blink of an eye, the foursome faded into the crowd, leaving Lizzie alone with Lucky. Without Zack and Audrey, she'd run out of reasons not to stage a scene to end this phony engagement once and for all. Just because she was starting to quiver whenever the lanky and attractive cowboy came into view didn't mean he felt the same way, and who could blame him, considering she'd acted before thinking too often in the past few weeks?

Her ankle boots became rooted to the sidewalk, and her mouth was drier than the ranch during a drought. The perfect opportunity was now upon them, but she was having so much fun. However, if they got everything into the open, this new friendship might develop into something deeper.

The sooner she acted, the sooner she'd know for sure. "This has been fun—"

"Lizzie, you won't deny me company on my

first Ferris wheel ride, will you?" He held up a handful of tickets.

Sitting with him in such a confined area? Where the sky was as blue as his eyes and the wind swayed the bucket enough for a thrill without worry of the world collapsing under her? She shivered with anticipation. "It would give us a chance to talk…"

He came over and put his finger on her lips. "About us, but not like that. Just talk about who we are on the inside. Get to know each other. I don't have to head to my next rodeo for a couple of days, so why don't we have some fun and ride that Ferris wheel?"

Sharing who she was on the inside with him was almost as scary as admitting her newfound feelings for him. Maybe more so as she'd lost loved ones in the past, first her mother and then Jared, since he'd wanted to be a part of the influential Irwin family rather than loving her for herself.

And yet the man in front of her whose face radiated joy at the Ferris wheel looming large in the center of the festival grounds had been through far more in his life and hadn't lost his optimism.

She couldn't resist his positive attitude, wrapped nicely with a ribbon of charm to pull him together. She only wished she were this handsome cowboy's lucky match. "You're impossible, do you know that?"

"I've been called worse." He grinned and held out the crook of his arm. "Are you game?"

She linked her arm through his and walked alongside him. One night of fun to cap off a perfect day seemed a little too good to be true—a lot like him, but she was more than willing to rise to the occasion.

UP CLOSE, the Ferris wheel loomed much larger than it looked from a distance. Lucky had no problem being in a closed arena with a two-hundred-and-fifty-pound calf, but this? This was a different story. At the front of the line, Lucky gulped as the attendant accepted two tickets.

"It's only fifty feet in the air." The attendant deposited the tickets while Lucky and Lizzie settled in the bucket seat. "It takes about eight minutes to reach the top with all the starts and stops. You picked the perfect time of day with sunset approaching."

The attendant closed the bar and moved the lever until they rose slightly to the next position. Lizzie reached over and patted his hand. "Are you okay? You're stark-white under your tan."

He didn't look down and instead practiced measured breathing. "Just dandy."

She rubbed his knuckles. "No, you're not. You're stressed, which is so unlike you."

It had taken one long bus ride to turn his life around and start afresh, and now one quick Ferris-wheel ride threatened to bring back his insecurities. "Cale taught me I can't control much, but I can control my feelings about how I approach my surroundings. He and his wife, Vivi, helped me learn how to survive on my own."

"They sound nice. It must have been a big change going from New York to Colorado." The Ferris wheel jerked into the next position, and their bucket swayed from the movement.

"It was nice being in control of where I went and when." He'd never admitted this to Will or Sabrina, even though he considered them his closest friends. "I guess I just like having the ground under my feet."

She chuckled before the smile left her lips. "Sorry. I wasn't laughing at your present predicament. It's ironic to me that you feel that way considering how often you ride a horse and how many times you've been in the air in the rodeo."

"Practice and training give me the confidence I need for the arena." He dared to peek over the edge and immediately moved back to the center. Instead of looking outward, he concentrated on Lizzie, cool and unflappable even with the evening breeze whipping through her hair. "Having Butterscotch in my corner this year helps."

Lizzie rubbed the back of his palm with her thumb, and suddenly he wanted the ride to go on forever. The warmth of her hand brought his racing pulse under control, and the engagement ring glinted in the rays of the setting sun. He wondered if a rough rodeo performer and a smooth ranch owner could make a success of a relationship. Cale had taught him nearly everything was possible with determination and hard work. And time spent with Lizzie was anything but hard. Taking this to the next level would have to wait until he finished this ride without having a panic attack.

"I know how you feel. When I'm riding Andromeda, it's like we're an unstoppable team."

Despite their differences, they had so much in common about what really mattered in life. That lifted his spirits.

"It's rare to find that kind of connection." Whether with an animal or a person, Lucky could attest to that. When something was right, could it be this effortless, this easy? His breathing steadied, and his usual calm flooded him and centered him in this moment.

She squeezed his hand. "Your resilience is inspiring."

"I learned from the best, Cale and Will." The Ferris wheel moved once more, and they were halfway to the top. "Cale told me something I believe with all my heart. Find a way to turn your biggest weakness into your biggest strength."

"You obviously succeeded. I admire how laid-back you are."

"Some of my foster families didn't see me that way." More than once, he'd been accused of being inattentive or uncaring. "It depends on your perspective."

Her green eyes glittered as brightly as the lights coming on around them. "From where I'm sitting, going with the flow and accepting others is a strength, and I think you feel more deeply than you let on. I understand that too well." She twisted the ring around her finger. "You must have loved her if you intended to propose to her. Remind me, what was her name?"

"Cherry." He shrugged and kept his focus on Lizzie so he wouldn't look down. "I thought I loved her, but she wanted someone different, someone more like her."

But whatever he'd felt for Cherry was nothing compared to the Tilt-A-Whirl of emotions he experienced whenever Lizzie was around, or even when she wasn't. He'd seen the beautiful cowgirl rise to her feet in the creek before they worked together and dislodged the calf's foot. Today, she'd proven she wouldn't judge him for his past, even going as far as winning him a stuffed horse. He'd keep that in his trailer, for sure.

"I thought I loved Jared until I found out he only wanted my father's signature on an important contract." Lizzie stared straight ahead. "It's hard when things don't work out as planned."

"But those are the times that mold us into who we are now." The Ferris wheel jerked in motion again, and they stopped one position away from the top.

"So you turned what you thought was a weakness into a strength. You accepted your resilience and used it to your advantage. How did you move on without looking backward?" Lizzie faced him, yearning in her eyes.

The evening breeze rustled her auburn hair, and her apple cheeks grew rosy pink, with a smattering of freckles obvious this close to her. Another memory for his permanent databank.

He stored it away and then considered her question. "It was that or stay bitter."

"I was rather bitter after I discovered Jared dated me so he could get close to my family. Afterward, I threw myself into the ranch. Somehow, I thrive best by staying in one place."

"I love seeing new places. That kept me going when Cherry broke up with me." His stomach clenched. He left Violet Ridge faster than a barrel racer when he'd seen Sabrina with Ty last Christmas, not that he'd felt anything for her beyond brotherly affection, but it was the impact of the family he'd formed with Will and Sabrina coming to an end that had overwhelmed him. He'd grasped the first excuse to leave so he wouldn't have to face harsh reality so close to the holidays.

Maybe he should thank Lizzie for everything that had transpired. He had intended on leaving, but she kept providing him with reasons to come back to Violet Ridge. All this time he thought he'd be able to walk away from everyone he cared about, even Will and Sabrina. That it would be easier to be the one who left rather than facing his fears of being left behind. Starting over was fine when he'd been eighteen. Now, though? Will and Sabrina were too important to him. They had made room for him, as had their respective spouses, Kelsea and Ty. He'd just been too afraid to accept their love. He wasn't afraid anymore.

It was nice having this town as a soft spot for landing amid the rough circumstances of life. New places were always on the horizon in his profession, but a home with someone there? He didn't realize until now how much he'd been missing having Lizzie to talk to, to hold her hand, to kiss.

The bucket lurched into the top position, and the breeze ruffled his hair. He'd never visit an amusement park without remembering this moment. From here, Violet Ridge seemed like a robin's egg nestled high in an oak tree. One thing was for certain— this moment was theirs and theirs alone with no outside influences dictating what they had to feel or do. Lizzie faced him, and that same knowledge gleamed in her eyes. He caressed her soft cheeks with his hands, and her lips met his in a kiss that sent him soaring even higher.

But it wasn't what was around them that made this moment so special, this kiss mesmerizing and real. It wasn't just a memory; he was living in the moment, seizing life by the horns. And he was kissing the most beautiful, action-oriented woman. Lizzie was so much more than the efficient facade she presented to the world, just as he was more than the laid-back rodeo cowboy. Her layers surprised and astounded him. He relished the moment—his first Ferris-wheel ride was both unforgettable and breathtaking.

The bucket jerked once more, and he broke the kiss, leaning his forehead on hers. He drank in the moment, heady for a kid who grew up never knowing where he'd be living from one week to the next.

"I'd say you made this day go from great to monumentally memorable," Lucky said.

"Hold on. The ride's about to get even better." She laced her hands through his and the wheel began to spin, gaining speed as it made its rotations, the world passing by in a blur.

Too soon, the attendant raised the bar that held them in the bucket, and he and Lizzie alit from the ride. He staggered for a second before regaining his equilibrium. And yet, he didn't want the dizziness he felt whenever she neared to end. He wanted to grasp this happiness with both hands and not let go. It might be time to take Cale's words to heart and change his biggest weakness into an undeniable strength. He didn't have any experience staying in one place, always moving on when the caseworker appeared or a friend called upon him. It was time to stop running when relationships took an unexpected turn. Growing up on the Double I, Lizzie was teaching him a thing or two about permanence, and he couldn't think of a better place than Violet Ridge for him to hang his lasso for good.

CHAPTER FOURTEEN

LIZZIE'S STABLE OFFICE was getting too crowded for her liking on this Wednesday. Over the past three days, she'd enjoyed Lucky's presence in the evenings after he spent the day with Ty and Will preparing for the next rodeo in Arizona, but he'd be leaving tomorrow night. Next Monday would herald his return, as well as that of the newly-weds. Would it also be the end of this friendship, or whatever it was that had been developing between her and Lucky?

She pushed that out of her mind as JR and Roy waited for her next move. A nervous gleam in his eye, Roy shifted in the doorway and switched the envelope from one hand to the other while her foreman frowned from his position in front of her desk. This past weekend at the Summer Send-off already seemed like it happened last year.

"JR…" Lizzie settled herself into her chair for the first time all morning. "You first."

"Our computers are down, and I can't access CattleMax." He referenced the program used for keeping track of the vaccinations and other records for the cattle. "I need another temporary cowhand to help with weighing the calves, except the bunkhouse is full."

"About that." Roy came forward and laid the envelope in front of Lizzie. "Maria and I set a date to get married. That there's my notice. In two weeks, I'll be working for her dad on their ranch."

Her headache was close to turning into a migraine. Lizzie kept from reaching for the bottle of ibuprofen in the bottom desk drawer. "We've enjoyed having you work here, Roy. We'll miss you. You're a hard worker." She made a note to include a bonus in his last paycheck, a wedding gift of sorts, while mentally rearranging the work schedule. "If I find a replacement before the two weeks are up, you can leave even earlier. Until then, those calves are our priority. After that, JR and I have to get started on winterizing."

Roy removed his hat and held it close to his chest. "I was sort of hoping you'd let me go early. Maria's dad is slowing down, and we need to bring in the hay."

Lizzie exhaled and nodded. The Vasquez family's ranch bordered hers and Will's, and Esteban was always gracious and accommodating. "Of course. I know him, and he's been a good neighbor to us." She faced JR. "At least that solves the issue about the bunkhouse."

It sure would help to have those new bunkhouses, each with updated kitchens and new beds, as a selling point for employment. Dad was due back soon, and she'd talk to him then. No use interrupting his honeymoon with news about their employment issues. Next week would be soon enough to discuss that and her plan to introduce Simmentals to the western pasture.

JR nodded. "I'll start putting out feelers."

"And I'll cut you your last check, Roy, at the ranch house." Lizzie reached for her red cowboy hat and donned it before escorting Roy to Dad's office. The ranch would be working with a skeletal staff until at least two new hires came on board.

In her father's office, she settled accounts with Roy, adding a bonus despite the lack of notice. It was the right thing to do, especially given that they'd be neighbors.

His eyes widened as he checked the amount. "There must be a mistake."

"No, you earned that. If you know anyone looking for work at competitive pay, send them to us." Besides, she should have seen Roy's departure coming, especially given how he and Maria had been sweet on each other for some time.

A commotion in the front of the house led to a quick goodbye, and Lizzie investigated the cause of the noise only to find Audrey hugging her grandpa Gordon while Zack was on the receiving end of an Evie embrace. Her dad appeared relaxed, with a rugged tan and a hint of a smile on his face. She'd never seen a Hawaiian shirt paired with a Stetson before, but it worked on him.

Jeff and Nicole emerged from the library, holding hands and appearing happier than ever. Jeff blinked. "I thought you were on your honeymoon until Monday."

"I couldn't keep him away any longer." Evie also seemed more relaxed and radiant.

"Good thing, too, as we ran into JR on the way inside." In the blink of an eye, Dad transformed from glowing newlywed back into the rancher everyone around here knew so well. "What's this about Roy?"

And just like that, she was back to square one in terms of ranch management. "I'm in charge of employment matters, especially the stable. I handled it and will continue to do so." She straightened her spine and took charge. "Once you and Evie get settled, I'll tell you about my plan to attract workers with a new perk."

Dad squeezed Audrey one more time before setting her near Jeff. "I'm settled now."

Evie reached for Audrey's and Zack's hands, one on each side of her. "How about we go see what good stuff Tammy baked while I was in Hawaii? Then later, before I lunch with Sabrina and my mother at Miss Tilly's Steak House, I'll see whether we brought back any souvenirs for you."

Her laugh was the answer, and Dad's gaze

didn't leave Evie until they disappeared from view. Lizzie pulled herself together and pointed to the living room. "Would it be easier if we were comfortable?"

"I've been sitting on an airplane too long, and I want to see my horse," Dad said. He opened the front door. "A long ride and a check of my cattle. That's my ideal afternoon."

Nicole kissed Jeff before squeezing his hand and heading in the direction of the kitchen. Something was going on between them. Had Violet Ridge's charms at the Summer Send-off finally entranced them into moving to the Double I? Lizzie wouldn't blame them one bit, especially given how Audrey and Zack had flourished over the past few weeks. No, she wouldn't be like her dad and presume otherwise. She trusted Jeff, and his family would be returning to their home.

Jeff gestured for Lizzie to exit first, and she hurried to catch up with her father, who was already halfway to the stable. "Hold on." She approached his side. "I know you love the trail on the other side of the stable, but it's the perfect place for a set of four new bunkhouses. Modern construction will help us attract and retain workers."

Wrinkles popped out on Gordon's forehead. "I built that trail myself."

This was one reason she'd been so hesitant to approach him. "I studied the plat maps and located another site for a riding trail, but I've consulted architects in town and placed our down payment. The current trail is the best and most economical choice for the construction. I've contracted renderings for the buildings, one of which will only house female cowhands."

They reached the stable, and Gordon's eyebrows raised. "You did all that without consulting me?"

She adjusted the cowboy hat on her head and met his stare. "Yes. You put me in charge of employment matters, and lodging and competitive salaries are part of that."

Gordon entered the stable and made a beeline for Margarita's stall. "Hmm, is she favoring her left leg? Is it swollen?"

"Not at all. Lucky took exceptional care of her during the roundup." He was a horse whisperer, and Margarita had connected with him. "And I walked her out to pasture at dawn and picked her hooves afterward."

"Lucky's a good man." That was high praise from her father, and the perfect opening as far as Lizzie was concerned.

"He is, but there's something you should know."

Gordon turned to her, his eyes discerning. "Springing the bunkhouses on me, the hour I return from my honeymoon, wasn't enough?"

She steeled herself as her father would have every right to be upset with her about her decision to spare his feelings on his wedding day by letting everyone believe something that wasn't real. Her pride aside, she'd have to accept whatever he decided about her future at the Double I. "This is much more important than the new construction."

"Thanks, Lizzie, but it's not fair for you to tell him what I should have been firm about all along." Jeff stepped forward. "I've been asking Lizzie to keep a secret until you returned from your honeymoon."

"Lizzie?" Gordon's throat bobbed. "I called you that before Heather died."

That was what he'd narrowed in on? Lizzie sighed. "I like it better than Elizabeth."

"Evie wants to travel more, let me trust the two of you with extra duties. So many changes." Gordon's mouth clamped into a straight line. "Still, your initiative with the bunkhouses is sound. What do you think, Jeff?"

Jeff shook his head and held up his hands. "I don't have a say in this. The ranch is yours and Lizzie's domain. Nicole and I aren't moving back. We're staying in Boston."

His jaw firm, Dad glanced at Lizzie. "And you knew about this? For how long?"

"Dad!" Jeff placed his hand on Dad's shoulder. "Don't blame Lizzie. I told you we weren't moving several times. This isn't where I belong. The roundup confirmed that. Nicole and I are happy in Boston. We want Zack and Audrey to spend summers here with you, Evie, Lizzie and Lucky. That family bond is important."

Dad scrubbed his chin and reached out for Margarita, who nickered and approached as if sensing something was wrong. He rubbed her muzzle and nodded. "Sometimes we see what we want to see and hear what we want to hear." He patted Margarita and moved away from the mare, placing his arm around Jeff. "That's a lot to digest in a short time. Evie has some commitments in New York over the winter. Would you be up to a visit from us if we make the jaunt to Boston afterward? Elizabeth, er, Lizzie and Lucky will no doubt be taking good care of Margarita and the ranch for me."

"How about we go see if Tammy has any of those cowboy cookies left?" Jeff headed for the exit, and Lizzie watched them leave.

So close and yet so far.

LUCKY THANKED THE clerk for ringing up the horse bit and left the saddlery. Downtown Violet Ridge sure was pretty, with the sun flooding its golden light on the pastel storefronts. Its glow didn't compare with the way Lizzie's hair shone in the dusk. Somehow, the two of them had to find a solution so they could spend time with each other free of the expectations everyone placed on them.

Since when did he care so much what others thought of him? He'd left everything familiar and headed for Steamboat Springs, all those years ago, without a second thought. But then he'd met Cale, who'd taken him under his wing and taught him about ranching and the rodeo. Eking out a living at what he loved was second to the friendships and connections he'd made along the way.

Until now, it was always easy to go from town to town with fresh faces to meet and new stories to hear. However, Cale had taught him a thing or two about facing up to what he'd started and being brave. Staying here and facing the aftermath once his engagement to Lizzie ended was the only courageous route out of this mess.

He ducked into the Blue Skies Coffee House. He ordered plain black coffee, a perfect pick-me-up on a Wednesday afternoon, and waited at the counter. The cowbell above the door jangled, and in walked Grandma Eloise, the thump of her cane pounding the hardwood floor, followed by Evie. If Evie was back in town earlier than expected, so was Gordon.

If he and Lizzie talked to Gordon together, the older rancher might accept his and Lizzie's need to figure out what they meant to each other before rushing into anything. Following behind them was Sabrina. Closing the door behind her, she squealed and made a beeline in his direction. "Congratulations. That was some ride last weekend."

"I could say the same about Ty." Sabrina's husband also finished first in his respective event. He removed his hat and nodded at the group. "Could I order for you while you take a seat? My treat."

Grandma Eloise perked up at his request. "I never refuse an offer from a handsome fellow."

Evie placed her packages on the hardwood floor next to an empty table. "That would be lovely. Then we can talk about tonight."

What was happening tonight?

After he memorized and placed their orders, Lucky waited at the counter while the three women settled at the table. When the barista called his name, he carried over their beverages and found Evie rubbing her mother's hand. "I just arrived back in Violet Ridge, and I already have to say goodbye." Evie's throat bobbed, and she sat straighter in her chair. "If you and Dad moved here, you'd be able to see Genie more often."

Grandma Eloise's eyes misted. "I'll keep that in mind in the future." Lucky had never heard her voice so husky. "For now, Bob needs to stay put in Texas, and it's time I go home. He needs me."

Love glistened from every pore of Grandma Eloise, and Lucky was in awe of the depth of her emotion. More than anything, he wanted that kind of relationship with Lizzie. As of now, their foundation was too shaky, a literal house of cards that threatened to topple over at any minute.

Evie gave another squeeze and then stared at Lucky. "Before I forget, Gordon and I are hosting a little get-together at Mama Rosa's tonight. Of course, you and Elizabeth are invited."

"My mother's idea of little and mine are worlds apart," Sabrina said, stifling a giggle.

Then this was definitely the night. With the Irwin family in full attendance, he and Lizzie had the perfect opportunity to clear the air that they wouldn't be getting married in December. If he made the finals, and after this weekend, that was more likely than ever, he could reimburse Gordon and Evie for the canceled contracts.

Who was he kidding? If nothing else, he could sell the engagement ring. That would more than cover his share of the expenses. Down the line, if he ever asked Lizzie to marry him, he'd buy her a ring of her own. Something with rubies to match her inner fire.

"As long as it's an early night for me since Butterscotch and I have to head to Arizona for the next rodeo at the crack of dawn." And there wasn't any reason to believe he wouldn't be asked to leave early after he and Lizzie talked to Gordon.

Evie smiled. "Well, that's between you and Elizabeth." Then her gaze fell on her mother, and her smile faded. "I'll miss you."

"There's no reason you can't come visit. Our door is open, and everyone at the assisted-living complex loves you." Grandma Eloise tapped her cane near Sabrina's foot. "And you bring Genie often. Bob loves seeing her. Ty's not so bad, either."

The implication was clear: Bob wasn't the only one who loved Genie. That sweet baby was a ray of sunshine, like Sabrina.

Tonight was the night to ask Lizzie if she could look past his rough childhood and care for him, even though she deserved someone who could offer her so much more. His troubled past was behind him. It was time to look forward.

Would it be a new beginning for him and Lizzie? Or the end?

EVEN THOUGH IT was only the last week of August, Lizzie grabbed a shawl for tonight's party. In the Colorado mountains, temperatures could take a tumble at a moment's notice. After a long Wednesday in the stable, she would have normally bowed out of a weeknight party, but she couldn't in this case. Goodbyes meant everything. They captured the moment and provided closure. She'd miss Grandma Eloise, and the older woman deserved to return to Texas after a family evening to share with her beloved Bob.

By the time she saw Zack and Audrey again, Audrey's adult tooth would have made its appearance. She'd miss her niece and nephew. Without a wedding in December, she wasn't sure whether Jeff and Nicole would make the trip to Violet Ridge even though they'd already purchased plane tickets.

The doorbell rang, and she found Lucky at

her doorstep, right on schedule. His gaze wandered over her, and his eyes widened. That made the extra effort and time with a hair dryer and the mascara wand well worth it. He held out a bouquet of pink and yellow snapdragons. "For you. The florist said they represent grace and strength."

She blinked, the sentiment not lost on her, and then placed her shawl on the entryway table next to her clutch. With both hands, she accepted the flowers. "Thank you. They're beautiful. I'll be right back." In no time, she returned with a lovely crystal vase that had belonged to her mother. "I'll just put these somewhere safe."

They looked more beautiful on her dresser next to the framed print of her and Lucky and the kids in the hot-air balloon gondola. In no time, she returned to the foyer.

Lucky removed his cowboy hat and placed it over his heart. "That dress almost does you justice."

"Thank you." She swirled around, and the flouncy asymmetrical skirt of her light pink lace dress swooshed above her knees.

Then she admired his appearance. He looked particularly handsome in that crisp blue denim shirt paired with black dress pants. She moved toward him and reached for his bolo tie. "May I?"

He nodded, and she straightened the thin pieces of the leather cord held together with a beautiful silver medallion with a daisy on it. "This is beautiful," she said, tracing the flower's petals.

"Cale gave it to me to celebrate my first rodeo win."

"That makes it more special." She reached for her shawl and small clutch. When she faced him once more, he was almost ashen under his deep tan. "Lucky, are you okay?"

He winced and leaned back against the wall. "So you told Gordon and Evie?"

"Told them what? I tried telling Dad about us earlier today, but Jeff interrupted me and said he and Nicole are staying in Boston. Another missed opportunity."

"You're not wearing the ring."

She checked her left ring finger, and it was, indeed, bare. Her heart thudded until she realized it must still be in the bathroom. "After a day in the stable, I reeked." She waved her hand under her nose. "I must have forgotten to put it back on after my shower. I'm still getting used to wearing it."

No sooner would she get used to the feeling of it on her finger than she'd be returning it to him. She hurried upstairs, and he followed, the sound of his boots loud against the dark cherry hardwood. Panic set in when she couldn't find the ring on the white quartz bathroom counter.

Her breathing became shallow spurts. She racked her brain but couldn't remember taking it off before her shower. When was the last time she'd seen it? She'd definitely worn it this morning at breakfast, but after that? It was a mystery about where or when it fell off. She laid the clutch and shawl on the counter and brought her hands to her face.

The only part of this engagement that had been real was that ring, and she'd lost it.

She faced him, tears forming in her eyes. "I'm sorry, Lucky. I should have been more careful with your ring."

"Hey, no tears. We'll find it. You might ruin your makeup, and you look beautiful." He approached her and gave her a hug. She inhaled his spicy aftershave and soap, his presence more than comforting. Beyond dependable, he calmed that need inside her to fill every waking moment with action. Even now, when she wanted to overturn the ranch house and stable, she stayed still in his arms, letting his solidity soothe her ruffled self. He stepped away and rubbed the side of one eye, moisture dotting his finger.

From inside her clutch, her phone buzzed, and she checked the incoming texts.

"Everyone is wondering where we are." She cleared her throat and reached for a tissue, dotting away the last of her tears. "Should I send our regrets? We can change and start looking in the stable for the ring."

"Tomorrow is soon enough to find it and talk to Gordon together. Too often, I never say goodbye." He wrapped her shawl around her shoulders. "I'd like to send Grandma Eloise, Zack and Audrey away with a hug and a parting word of friendship."

A poignant reminder of how he'd grown up. He was right. This night was going to be a special family occasion, and she wanted him by her side. He reached for her hand, and they made their way downstairs.

The problem was, she wanted him by her side for the long run. Would he take her losing his ring as a sign that she was careless about his feelings?

And his heart?

CHAPTER FIFTEEN

LUCKY ESCORTED LIZZIE to the front door of Mama Rosa's and halted. Lizzie looked at her bare finger and pursed her lips together, obviously devastated about losing the ring. It was just a possession. Everything except relationships could be replaced.

He approached her and fingered her silky shawl. "We'll find the ring tomorrow. I'm sure of it. It has to be somewhere at the ranch. How about we enjoy tonight?"

"You are a man beyond compare, Lucky Harper." In her three-inch heels, she leaned over and kissed his cheek. "How do you do it? How do you make everyone feel better about themselves when you're the one who has every right to be hurt by my care-less action?"

He savored the softness of her cheek with his fingers, the warm imprint from her skin linger-ing behind. "I had to learn how to be adaptable to survive, but that gave me an out, too. It was always easy to move on, to not make any emo-tional connections. I thought I didn't need them."

It turned out he needed them more than he'd known. Specifically, he wanted Lizzie in his life, but he needed more stability to become a part of her world.

Instead of leaving never to return, he now had an important reason to come back. Qualifying for the year-end finals would prove he belonged here in Lizzie's world.

Maybe if he made the finals, he'd also prove something to himself and be worthy of this magnificent woman. He wouldn't know, though, unless he gave it his all, something he couldn't do if he was distracted. And Lizzie was the biggest distraction to his head and his heart.

There was one other important factor in all of this. He had to prove to himself he could finish something he started.

More so, he could take the initiative with Sabrina. Instead of waiting for her to ask him for a position at her rodeo academy, he'd offer his services. A steady job in the area would give him a more constant base.

Lucky opened the door, and the maître d' nodded at them, coming around the tall reservation stand. "Please follow me. They're expecting you."

He and Lizzie entered the back room, and everyone yelled, "Surprise!"

A huge banner that read "Congratulations, Lizzie and Lucky!" was draped on the rear wall.

This wasn't a farewell party; it was an engagement party. For them.

Lucky's mouth dropped open, the shock invading his system. Gordon came forward, laughing. "Leave it to the engaged couple to show up half an hour late to their own party." He reached into his pocket and handed a handkerchief to Lucky with a discreet *ahem*. "You have Lizzie's lipstick on your cheek."

Friends came rushing toward them, expressing their best wishes, while Lucky rubbed his cheek with Gordon's handkerchief. He was still too numb to do anything else. Will approached with Kelsea, who hugged Lizzie. He raised his glass to Lucky. "Congratulations. Never happier to be wrong about something."

Music started playing over the speakers, and people milled about with flutes of champagne. Audrey rushed over and held up her own goblet containing a golden, fizzy liquid. "I love ginger ale. It's so yummy." She pushed her purple glasses higher. "And Mommy says I can stay up past my bedtime."

Evie approached with a crown for him and a tiara for Lizzie. "You had no idea how hard it was not to ruin the surprise of your engagement party this afternoon. I'm so happy for the both of you. You're perfect for each other."

Before he knew it, Lizzie was swept away to a different side of the room, and Gordon kept talking to him about his future plans after the year-end finals.

"I never think that far ahead," Lucky said.

Gordon seemed taken aback at that answer, and Lucky excused himself. Suddenly, the crowd seemed to part, and luminous light fell on Lizzie. He captured yet another internal photo of how she looked in this moment, her auburn hair cascading over her shoulders, her apple cheeks pink from the attention. While she preferred spending time with the animals on the ranch, there wasn't anything she wouldn't do for anyone in this room. Whether she was riding Andromeda or spurring others into action, Lizzie glowed from within.

He was hopelessly in love with Lizzie.

What was he going to do about it?

He gathered his wits, recalling the foster family he'd lost when the husband's best friend claimed Lucky had corrupted his underage son with alcohol. Others may have thought the worst of him, but he'd known the truth. Honesty was the way to move forward. That was how he lived with himself and could live up to being the type of man Lizzie deserved. He inhaled a deep breath and wondered where to start. He moved toward Lizzie, when Gordon clanged the side of his champagne flute with his fork.

The crowd silenced, and Gordon turned on the microphone. A loud, high-pitched squeal echoed through the room, and everyone winced. The echo ended, and Gordon began by thanking everyone for attending on short notice. Then he gestured for Lizzie and Lucky to join him. Lucky grabbed a flute of champagne from the nearby tray while reaching for Lizzie's hand. Her presence would help him through this.

Gordon smiled at them and then spoke into the microphone. "When I met Evie, I thought nothing could make me happier. Then I married the most captivating woman in the world, and I convinced myself that was the pinnacle." He winked at Evie, who winked right back at him. "But I was wrong. Seeing my daughter in love with the man who's captured her heart, the man who has made her smile and laugh, the man who encouraged her to reconnect with her inner Lizzie—that has raised the bar once again. To Lucky and Lizzie."

Everyone raised their glasses and drank. Lizzie moved to take the microphone. "There's something I need to say."

"There's more." Gordon kept the microphone and moved it close to his chest. "Evie and I talked about it. We're giving you and Lucky the cabin. Well, actually, Lucky, it's our gift to you. That way, you always have some place to stay when you're not heading to the next rodeo."

Lucky's fingers went numb. The flute of champagne slipped to the floor and broke into a myriad of shards, liquid spilling everywhere.

What had he done?

THE BUBBLES IN her ginger ale fizzed to the top, and Lizzie stared at the liquid. She limited herself to pop so her head would remain clear. There was still time to salvage this mess of a situation brought about by her pride and good, but misguided, intentions about Dad's wedding. She started counting the bubbles, anything to stop her from counting the consequences of her ill-fated decision. Tonight proved, once and for all, that she had to step up and face the music. It was no longer only about deposits that she could afford to repay; it was about trust.

If she'd earned Dad's trust with hard work, this prolonged engagement might have broken that tenuous thread. Dad might even demote her or, even worse, fire her. No matter what, though, she'd admit how it started when she claimed Lucky as her plus-one. Then she'd shore up her courage and tell Will and Sabrina that Lucky went along with her out of pity, or some other unfathomable reason.

And there wasn't anyone else who would have brought such joy to this entire experience. Lucky teased out a softer side of her, one that sought experiences with people rather than hiding in the stable. No one else had ever challenged her how he did with his calm yet practical manner. The handsome rodeo cowboy was special.

And his kisses?

Unforgettable and earth-shattering, the same

way he conducted himself in the arena, judging from the hour she'd watched this past weekend. The more hours she spent with him, the more that slow, radiant smile of his curled her toes. Many a time in the past few days she'd contrived excuses to see him and that grin. There was so much depth to him. He always provided her with a fresh perspective about one of the horses or something else on the ranch.

She glanced over the rim of the flute and observed Lucky, who looked forlorn. Anyone with eyes would sense there was something wrong between them. No one had yet commented on the fact she wasn't wearing his ring. After she cleared the air with her father, regardless of what happened with her job on the ranch, she'd head to the stable and comb through every stall and every inch of the place until she found the ring.

The servers were whisking away the dinner plates, and music began playing over the speakers. Couples moved to the makeshift dance floor, and Dad headed toward Lizzie while she saw Evie approaching Lucky.

"May I have this dance with the future bride?" Her father held out his arm, and Lizzie could hardly refuse such an offer, especially as she hadn't thanked him for the party.

Dad led her to the center of the floor, and they began their father-daughter dance. "Thank you for this, but…"

"I'm the one who should be thanking you. I reviewed the bunkhouse plans with Tammy and JR. They agree the updated living quarters are long overdue." He let out a blustery laugh. "This isn't a time for business. Evie's been a good influence on me. She's made me confront my life and my mistakes. I wanted to get you to myself because I owe you an apology. I wasn't a better father when you missed Heather, and I was dealing with how badly it ended between us. Audrey reminds me so much of you at that age, and I hope to be a better grandfather for her and Zack, and any other future grandchildren."

Never before had she seen his sentimental side. He claimed Evie was behind the change. She liked to think it was part Evie and part passage of time. She swallowed the big lump in her throat. "I never expected an apology. I understand the ranch is an enormous responsibility."

Slightly uncomfortable at the turn of events, she glanced at Lucky. His past gave her the wherewithal to confront her past. She didn't miss the longing look Lucky sent in her direction. For a split second, it almost seemed as though he wanted to dance with her and her alone, which was wishful thinking on her part. They weren't really a couple, and this was all staged for Dad's benefit.

Evie maneuvered herself and Lucky over to where she was dancing with Dad. "I believe I haven't danced with my husband yet." Her eyes sparkled as brightly as the sequins on her dress.

"The newlywed stage." Gordon's smile was as wide as his face. "There's nothing like it. You'll see later this year."

Lucky held out his arm, but he had to do so with everyone's gaze upon them. She relied on her instincts and rested her head near his cheek. They swayed in time to the sweet and slow love song.

The music came to an abrupt stop, and gasps echoed throughout the room. Lizzie wondered what was going on until goose bumps dotted her arm. She turned and found a solitary figure standing in the doorway, his uniform and regulation haircut bringing immediate recognition of her brother's arrival. She cheered and rushed over to him. "Ben!"

Lizzie reached her brother at the same time as the rest of her family. She waited her turn for her hug, and she grasped Ben's solid frame before stepping back and searching for Lucky. "You have to meet Lucky." She pulled Ben over to where the handsome rodeo cowboy was standing in the shadows, as if allowing the rest of her family to have a moment without him.

Didn't he know he was part of the family?

No, he didn't because none of this was supposed to be real, but somewhere over the past several weeks, reality blurred as Lucky reconnected her with feelings she'd repressed deep after the death of her mother. And the way he made her feel inside?

His calm optimism, despite all he'd endured, soothed and excited her at the same time. Her chest constricted as the truth slammed into her with more force than the Tilt-A-Whirl they had ridden at the Summer Send-off. He was a man beyond compare, and she was in love with Lucky Harper.

Now, what was she going to do to get them through this mess? She almost gasped, as the answer was so obvious. By herself, she couldn't do anything. With him by her side, though? Together, they made a formidable team.

However, it took two to make a team, and the crestfallen look on his face made it all too clear he didn't have the same feelings for her.

"I've heard so much about you." Ben's voice broke through Lizzie's thoughts, and she looked up in time to see Ben shake Lucky's hand. "No one else has ever made my sister look so happy."

How could someone look so happy on the outside and yet be so miserable on the inside?

Gordon came over and patted the backs of Ben and Lucky at the same time. "Will you be able to take time off at Christmas and return for their wedding?"

Ben laughed. "I haven't been back for five minutes and you're already asking when I'm coming home again. Guess you've finally noticed I haven't been around after all."

Gordon's chest fell and rose. "I deserve that. I hope we can take some time while you're home and resolve the issues between us."

Evie joined the group and hugged Ben. "You're here. I'm so happy to see you."

"The base is still talking about your concert. It's always a pleasure." Ben dipped his head in Evie's direction while Lucky kept backing away until he hit the wall.

At the sound of the thud, everyone turned in Lucky's direction. He blushed a deep red. "This is a family moment. I'll call it a night, especially since I have to leave tomorrow to head to the rodeo in Arizona."

"Any way you can stay the whole day?" Ben asked, removing his hat and placing it on a nearby table. "I'd like to spend some time getting to know my sister's fiancé."

Sabrina joined the group. "At last I get to meet my other stepbrother." She extended her hand and smiled. "I'm Sabrina Darling, Evie's daughter."

"You're the rodeo clown, and your husband's also in the rodeo. And you have a daughter, right?" Ben smiled but sounded like he was reciting information from an index card.

"Yes." Sabrina pulled out her phone and showed him a picture. "And I hope you get to meet Genie tomorrow. We'll be leaving early the day after next for the next rodeo."

Everyone's gaze fell on Lucky, and he shrugged. "Guess if Ty and Sabrina are staying, I can, too."

Evie grinned, and then she whispered something in Dad's ear. "Evie, you're absolutely right. I don't know why I didn't think of that sooner." His booming voice caused chills to cascade down Lizzie's spine.

Lizzie reached for Lucky's hand and spoke before Dad could make any more announcements. "Since we have all day tomorrow to catch up, Lucky and I are going to call it a night."

"What if tomorrow's your wedding day?" Gordon might have used the microphone as the guests in the room seemed to still and take note of his words. Then a buzz swept over the crowd, and everyone started clapping.

The metallic taste of fear coated her mouth, and sweat broke out on her forehead. This couldn't be happening. How had everything escalated so fast? Again. Her throat grew so dry she couldn't speak.

"We don't have a license." Lucky's calm tone was a match for his unruffled self.

Why wasn't he panicking along with her?

"There's no waiting period in Colorado, and you can get one tomorrow morning." Gordon waved away Lucky's concern. "Ben's here, and he just said he can't guarantee he'd be here at Christmas. It's obvious you and Lizzie are in love. You can get married and Lizzie can go with you to the rodeo. Then you can leave for your honeymoon from there."

Lizzie's breaths came fast and shallow. "No cake." Her voice came out more like a croak, and she found the strength to swallow. "And no dress."

Small details, and ones she didn't really care about, but she'd latch on to them if it postponed this wedding long enough for her and Lucky to end this once and for all.

Audrey wiggled her body into the middle of the circle. "Aunt Lizzie, you looked beautiful at Grandpa's wedding. That dress was so pretty."

Evie nodded. "You can wear your bridesmaid dress unless you want to try on my wedding gown for the something borrowed."

Zack joined her and pointed to the table in the corner. "And Tammy made that today. Isn't that a cake?"

Out of the mouths of babes. Lizzie entered full panic mode, and Ben reached over and rubbed her arm. "I missed Jeff's and Dad's weddings." Regret coated Ben's words. "I'd like to make it to one family event."

Gordon called out, "All of you are invited to our ranch tomorrow at three for the wedding. Plenty of time for morning ranch chores, followed by the afternoon ceremony."

Lizzie's cheeks went as numb as the rest of her, and she grasped at straws. "We don't have an officiant."

"I'm available." Zelda Baker stepped forward from the crowd. "I'm not only the former mayor, I'm also the justice of the peace."

How would she get herself and Lucky out of this mess? While everything was in place for an impromptu wedding, there was one thing missing: a groom in love with the bride. Somehow, they'd gone from having several months to end the engagement to less than eighteen hours. If Lucky didn't despise her before, he surely did now that she'd trapped them both in a situation that seemed destined to hurt too many people.

CHAPTER SIXTEEN

LATER THAT NIGHT, in the privacy of Will's stable, Lucky patted Butterscotch's muzzle and then reached into his coat pocket for an apple slice. "How did everything snowball so fast?"

One minute he was single and unattached, and the next he was single and attached. All this time, he thought he'd been craving time with Lizzie's family, when the truth was he'd fallen in love with her. Now she must loathe him. He could have put an end to this sooner, but belonging in Violet Ridge as part of the Irwin family had been like a dream come true.

Almost as much as his yearning to qualify for the finals. But even with that accomplishment close and within his grasp, victory would be hollow without Lizzie to share his joy.

Butterscotch whinnied as he could smell the apple Lucky still grasped. He held it out, and the gelding accepted it with gusto, the brush of his muzzle preceding the scratchy feel of the tongue against Lucky's callused hand. "We'll get through the breakup together, right? You and me?"

"Of course. Family sticks together." Will's firm voice came from behind, and Lucky's legs buckled as he realized what he'd muttered to his horse was loud enough for Will to overhear.

He waited for his breath to return as his friend emerged from the shadows. "You should have made yourself known earlier," Lucky said.

"Seems like that's my line," Will said. "Why don't you tell me the whole truth from the beginning?"

The moment he'd dreaded for so long was here. Once again, he was the kid piling his meager belongings into a trash bag with the caseworker standing by, waiting to take him to another temporary home. Leaving now would keep from putting Will in a bad spot when this fell apart. The Sullivan family had been ranching next to the Double I for some fifty years. More than neighbors, Will and Lizzie had grown up together, and Lucky had seen the interaction between the ranches over the past few weeks. Of course, Will would have to maintain good relations with his closest neighbor, leaving Lucky on the outside. What he intended to do all along was upon him, ripping his insides to shreds, and now it was irrevocable.

"You don't have to worry. The wedding's not going to happen, and this will all be over." In more ways than one, but it had been a good ride. Better than good. It had been nearly perfect.

That this was a fake engagement, where his heart became attached, kept it from being perfect. This time, he had no one to blame for what happened. He was an adult, and he was responsible for his actions.

"You don't get it, do you?" Will's gaze narrowed, and he moved closer. Out of nowhere, Will's dependable and trusty border collie, Rocket, circled him and Will until Lucky stood a few feet away from his friend.

"Get what?" Rocket and Will were working together, but Lucky didn't know their plan.

"You're family." Will's eyes showed the concern and care behind those simple words. "You, me and Sabrina. I will always be here for you."

Lucky considered his choices. When he began on the rodeo circuit, he hadn't had a family, and Will had taken him under his wing. Then Sabrina had joined their family when they had found themselves at the same bar one Saturday night. They'd bonded over comparing whose ride had been worse, Lucky's or Will's. Since Will had been nursing a broken nose, he'd won. Then there was the night when Will and Sabrina waited in the hospital ER room while he received stitches. He almost laughed at the memory of Will eating a bucket of edible cookie dough while Sabrina applied their facial masks on her birthday.

Lucky stopped strolling down memory lane, especially with Will's direct gaze shooting lasers at him. "We had some pretty good times, but everything comes to an end."

"Kelsea's taught me a thing or two about beginnings. Why is this the end and not the beginning?"

Lucky gulped and told Will everything.

"Why didn't you tell me the truth sooner?" Will folded his arms and leaned against the unpainted wood of the nearest stall. "You used to trust me."

"At first it was because of the Irwins. They made me feel like I was part of their family, and you know why I couldn't resist that. But it's because of Lizzie." The mental picture of her atop the Ferris wheel with the wind mussing her auburn hair flashed in front of him. "I meant it when I said I wouldn't embarrass her. She's special, and original, and, well…" Lucky rolled his neck and sighed.

Will reached up to the wall behind him and handed Lucky a currycomb before taking one for himself and tending to his stallion, Domino. "Sabrina and I will always have your back, same as you've always had ours."

He had found his family after all. That should have meant everything, yet without Lizzie? It was bittersweet indeed.

Together they cared for the horses, falling into the same familiar pattern as the past couple of years whenever Lucky visited the Silver Horseshoe. The rhythmic strokes of combing Butterscotch soothed him, but try as he might, he still couldn't come up with answers to his problems. There wasn't an easy way out that wouldn't hurt Lizzie.

"How did you keep it together when Kelsea left the ranch?" Lucky's throat clogged as he had to figure out how he'd find the strength to hit the road for the next rodeo tomorrow, alone, like always. He wanted to stay and comfort Lizzie rather than just walk away, but her family would be there for her.

The sound of the stable door sliding open gave Lucky time to pull himself together. Kelsea entered the stable with a plate of sandwiches and cookies. "You should have asked for a better bachelor party. Even though dinner was delicious and filling, I thought you could use some nourishment." She set the dish on a stool and glanced at Lucky, then Will. "I'll tend to the goats before I call it a night."

She hugged Lucky and kissed Will before taking her leave. Will reached for the top sandwich. "I didn't keep it together. My uncle Barry told me I was a bear before I booked my flight to Atlanta."

Will and Kelsea had gone through a rough patch after they met. While it had been obvious to everyone around them they were in love, a forced separation had finally caused them to confront their feelings.

It would be nice if he knew the same outcome was waiting for him and Lizzie. Better than nice, but a happy ending depended on two people feeling the same way.

"I can't guarantee I'll take it that well."

Will swallowed the bite of his sandwich. "You're the calmest, steadiest person I've ever met, but sometimes you have to take action and fight for what's right." Then his smile faded as he kept his gaze on Lucky. "You're in love with her."

It wasn't a question, but a statement. He owed Will, and himself, the truth about this. "Yeah."

"If you don't cancel the wedding before she walks down the aisle, I'll object," Will said.

That was one reason Lucky cared so much about Will and Sabrina. Either would do anything for him.

Even though Will had Kelsea and Sabrina had Ty, they still had his back and always would.

No matter how hard the next few days would be, he had to stand up and do the right thing.

"Thank you, but Lizzie and I got ourselves into this, and we have to get ourselves out of it." Before the wedding, though, Lucky had to do something important, something he should have done a long time ago. He glanced at his watch. He still had fifteen hours until the wedding. More than enough time for something too important to wait any longer. "Can I borrow your truck?"

Will reached into his pocket and threw Lucky a set of keys. "Return it with a full tank of gas."

Lucky caught them and raised his eyebrows. "No questions asked?"

"For the record, I don't let my uncle Barry borrow it." Will grinned. "But I trust you, Lucky."

It was time he trusted himself. Lucky reached for a couple of sandwiches and added a cookie the size of his hand for good measure. "See you at the wedding."

WITH ONLY THE faint ray of morning light on the horizon that heralded her wedding day, a ceremony she had to stop, Lizzie steered the UTV around the pothole. JR grasped the sides of his passenger seat, and Lizzie lifted her foot ever so slightly off the gas. Arriving at the field in one piece took priority over speed, same as the animals took priority over solving her dilemma without Lucky. Moose barked from the rear, a reassuring sound that he'd find any stragglers who might have wandered away from the herd. They approached the field where the cowhand waited for them with the plaintive sound of lowing cows growing louder.

Lizzie parked the UTV. JR and Moose hurried toward Sweeney, the reliable night cowhand who notified them a mere forty-five minutes ago at the first signs of bloat, a potentially serious issue this time of year for cattle. She grabbed the medical kit from the rear of the UTV and joined them.

Sweeney had already treated the worst case, and the cow was now recovering. In no time, she and JR checked the rest of the herd and found five more displaying the classic signs of bloat. With their stomachs protruding and lack of movement, there was no time to lose. The three of them worked in tandem and alleviated the symptoms of the cow who appeared to have the worst case.

"Should we call the vet?" Sweeney asked.

"Go ahead, while JR and I keep treating the cows." Lizzie reached for her bag and assembled the tube for the procedure to fight the bloat. "I don't think any of them are at the surgical stage, but it's wise to have her here in case any of them worsen."

The third cow had her full attention when a stethoscope came into view, followed by the person attached to it. She'd been so busy she hadn't even heard the vet pull up in another of the ranch's UTVs. She looked over, and to her surprise, her father emerged as well.

"Didn't expect to find you here," Dad said. "Not with the wedding later today."

She concentrated on the task before her. An animal was in distress, and she couldn't let that go without doing something about it, even if it was supposed to be her wedding day.

Not that she had any intention of going through with the ceremony.

It wasn't that she didn't want to marry Lucky.

She did. However, he deserved a wedding and a marriage with love and respect and honesty, and so did she. The cowboy who'd stolen her heart didn't realize everything he did to make others happy, especially her. While she wanted nothing more than to see his smile every day, she couldn't go through with the ceremony like this. Not with a lie between them and the community she loved.

And not without him knowing she loved him.

The cow bleated, and she focused her energy on the animal. Sweat poured down her face, the heat of late summer coming on full force. The brightness of noonday flooded the field, bathing the clumps of wildflowers in a golden glow. Finally, the cow gave a slight bellow, her relief evident, and Lizzie stepped back. Her stomach grumbled, and JR handed her a protein bar. "Thanks."

She ate the energy bar, and another case confronted them. They continued treating the affected cattle. Finally, the vet snapped her bag closed. "I'll consider this a happy ending, since they all survived without surgery."

They listened to the vet as she gave tips about symptoms and treatment. JR pointed to some forage in the distance. "That patch of sweet clover over there. It's most likely the cause of their distress. I'll take care of it now."

Lizzie nodded while JR headed to the UTV for the tools he'd need for that task. While clover didn't usually result in bloat, certain cattle were more susceptible and the wet conditions of the past few days would have exacerbated the likelihood of that being the culprit.

Would her plan for adding Simmentals to the ranch with their leaner bodies be something that would mean they could avoid this morning's near calamity in the future? Perhaps not, but she'd still need to address this addition with her father. With a half-hour ride back to the ranch, there was no better time for a long-overdue conversation, starting with the cattle and ending with the truth about the fake engagement. Even if he fired her on the spot, the ranch would benefit from her changes.

The vet stayed with JR, leaving her alone with her father. This wouldn't be easy, but she wasn't the same Elizabeth she was when Lucky dropped that fated peppermint in the straw. She could do this.

Her father yielding the driver seat to her came as the latest surprise today. While her brothers had been driving the UTVs as long as she could remember, her father had always assumed he'd drive in her presence. Lizzie took the wheel and eased the UTV onto the dirt path.

"I texted Evie—"

"About today—"

Silence came over them and lasted a moment too long. "You first," she said, keeping her gaze on the road.

"Evie texted the guests and pushed everything

to five tonight, not that you've mentioned the wedding once today." Then he sniffed the air. "What's that odor?"

She glanced at the jeans and flannel shirt she had thrown on while it was still dark outside, and they now featured dirt mixed with grass stains. Two showers might start making a dent in the strong stench coming off her. "Me." She took a deep breath and then coughed. "What would you think of introducing Simmentals to the ranch?"

"That you were avoiding the subject of your wedding."

He wasn't wrong, but she had to know one thing before she confided in him the wedding wasn't happening today. "What if Jeff or Ben had brought up the subject of introducing another breed of cattle to the ranch?"

"I don't know if Jeff could distinguish between an Angus and a Holstein anymore." Dad laughed with a blustery huff. "And Ben? Takes after your mom's side of the family. Military life suits him, just like ranch life suits you."

This didn't make sense to her. "Then why have you treated me different all these years?"

"Huh?" A quick look at her father showed his consternation. "How have I done that?"

"You've always acted one way with Jeff and Ben and another way with me, like you kept forgetting I grew up."

"You're six years younger than Ben and ten

years younger than Jeff. Even on a ranch, that's significant." Dad's lack of hesitation cemented his answer. "All three of you are unique, but you're the one I trust running the ranch."

I was taking their individual personalities into account. Audrey is younger than Zack. Lucky's response to her accusation of treating the siblings differently echoed in her mind. All this time she'd thought Dad had been giving preferential treatment to her brothers and while he'd treated her differently, it was out of deference to her younger age, affording her more respect and responsibility as she grew older. She should have seen it for herself, but she'd been too close to look objectively at the whole situation, a lesson she needed if she'd run the ranch someday.

This newfound knowledge gave her added strength. "I stand by the changes I'm proposing as far as the bunkhouses and the Simmentals."

"And that's why I'm glad you found Lucky. Just like Evie keeps me grounded, he's perfect for you. He's the restful calm to your energetic initiative."

Her heart ached at the mention of Lucky's name. This weekend, he'd head to the rodeo, and then there'd be the one after that, his RV/horse trailer combination the only home he'd ever really had. A home on wheels, it took him anywhere he wanted to be, and why would he want to be with her when he could go anyplace at a minute's notice?

The truth came to her in a flash.

She didn't need to pour out her heart to Dad.

She needed to pour out her heart to Lucky.

She stepped on the gas, this newfound realization too important to hold in any longer. Out of the corner of her eye, she saw her father grip the seat, his knuckles turning white. "Speaking of Evie, I'd like to get back to her in one piece."

"I need to talk to Lucky."

"Slow down, and you'll have your whole life to talk to him."

She eased her foot off the pedal as the offensive odor surrounding her almost made her gag. "Maybe I should take a shower first?"

"Only if you want to talk to him in the same room." Dad laughed at his joke as the stable came into view.

She parked the UTV and headed for the guesthouse, where her dress was waiting. There was no time to lose before guests would arrive, and a shower wasn't a luxury but a necessity. After she didn't smell like cattle, she'd share her heart with Lucas Harper.

What they decided to do from there was up to them.

SHORTLY AFTER TWO in the afternoon, Lucky shut the door of Will's truck at the same time Cale Padilla did. Cale let out a long, low whistle. "That's some ranch house."

Lucky agreed with Cale's assessment of the

Double I. Not that he had expected Cale to drop everything at the Cattle Crown Ranch and drive to Violet Ridge with him, but he had.

After Lucky had arrived at Cale's ranch, it was like no time had elapsed, although there were more crow's-feet wrinkles near Cale's brown eyes and a few streaks of silver in his black hair. His mentor was still robust, his heart as big as ever. He and Vivi had listened to Lucky for five minutes before hugging him and sending him to their guest room to sleep for a few hours, but not before admonishing him he shouldn't have waited so long to visit.

When he awakened, a large breakfast awaited him, as did two sets of eyes eager for an explanation. Lucky started with a long overdue apology for staying away so many years.

Lucky had been so certain there was no more room in Vivi's and Cale's hearts for him, so he'd pretty much kept his distance once he'd joined the rodeo. They'd been hurt at his absence, but they understood he needed time to make a life for himself and work things out on his own. They just hadn't expected him to take quite so long.

The four-hour trip to Violet Ridge had given Lucky and Cale more time to finish clearing the air and updating each other on their lives, including details about their respective families, with Lucky telling Cale about the changes in Will's life and Sabrina's.

But now came the biggest risk of his life. He had to lay everything on the line with Lizzie. While he was willing to marry her today, pledge his heart to her for everyone to see, they had to do what was right for them so they could move forward with no false pretenses. She was worth the wait.

And if she didn't love him? Well, last night with Will and today with Cale proved he'd been wrong about how others felt about him in the past. Sometimes the truth hurt, but it was better to be honest and hurt than live with a guilty conscience.

As they approached the front door of the ranch house, Lucky found time for one more apology to Cale. "This might be a wild goose chase. There's no guarantee I'm getting married today," Lucky warned in a tone low enough only for Cale to hear.

"There are no guarantees in life, period." Cale removed his battered brown cowboy hat and placed it against his chest. "But Vivi and I have missed you. Before we left, she told me to tell you she's sorry for missing your big day. Her mare is due any hour now, and she wants to be there to see the new foal. But it took you too long to come back. You're like a son to us, Lucky. We're here for you, no matter what happens today."

Lucky expected the house to be a beehive of activity, considering the wedding was set to start in less than an hour, but no one answered the front door. Cale's gaze almost burned a hole in the back of his head, and Lucky turned with a shrug.

"They must be at the meadow already." He reached into his pocket and checked for any messages from Lizzie, but there were none. "I'll let Lizzie know I'm back."

He shot off a quick text with an urgent plea to talk to her as soon as possible. Only by talking to each other could they determine the path for the rest of their lives.

Then he placed his phone in his jeans, and Cale looked at him. "It is a casual wedding, right?"

"You're my guest, so you're fine," Lucky said, while plucking his own flannel shirt, the worse for wear since he'd driven half the night and quite a while today. "But I've looked better after my dead-last rodeo finishes. I'll take you to the kitchen first and see if I can rummage up a snack for you while I shower and change into something more appropriate for the groom." While his brown cowboy hat and jeans were like a second skin to him, he'd left Ben's tuxedo in one of the guest rooms.

Lucky led Cale past the mudroom into the kitchen.

"Seems as though you know your way around here," Cale said.

Tammy was nowhere to be found, confirming Lucky's guess everyone was already at the meadow. He glanced at his watch. "I'll have to take the fastest shower in the history of showers to make it there by three. You can wait in the living room. If anyone asks, just tell them you're a guest of the groom."

Lucky settled Cale in the formal living room in time to see Gordon's office door open and shut. *Perfect.* He'd just give Gordon a heads-up he had to talk to Lizzie before the wedding and that if they were late to stall everyone.

It was up to Lizzie how long everyone would be waiting, or if they'd explain there'd be no wedding, either today or any other day.

He hurried to the office door and rapped on it a few times before hearing the command to enter. Gordon stood behind the desk, looking through drawers, his gray hair damp. To his surprise, Gordon wore jeans and a plaid shirt, not the attire he expected of the father of the bride.

His breath whooshed out of him. Lizzie must have leveled with him. Lucky didn't know whether to be thankful or devastated. If she loved him, he'd have gone through with the wedding in a heartbeat.

"So you know." Lucky sagged, relieved that Gordon had finally learned what really happened. He only hoped there were no hard feelings since Lizzie had had her father's state of mind at heart when this all started.

"I can't say I really approve at this point. Time will tell whether Lizzie is right. I'm used to calling the shots, but she's all grown up. She's right that I have to give her the same freedom that I afford Jeff and Ben." Gordon gave up his search and stared at Lucky.

That look told Lucky everything. He knew all about the fake engagement. A weight lifted from Lucky's shoulders.

"Then you'll want these back." Lucky pulled out his key ring and extracted the cabin keys, placing them on Gordon's desk. "Who knew a peppermint could cause so much trouble? You're not mad with Lizzie about this engagement farce, are you? I'm as much to blame as she is."

Equal culpability. It was nice to shoulder the blame with her. Even though Lizzie wasn't by his side, he knew she was in this with him. With that in mind, he steeled himself for whatever Gordon had to say.

"Care for a drink?" Gordon reached behind him and placed two rock glasses on the desk, pushing one in Lucky's direction. He produced a decanter and poured a splash of an amber liquid, presumably Scotch, into each. "Why don't you back up and begin at the beginning?"

Lucky accepted the drink and swished it around the cup. "If you've already heard Lizzie's side of the story, why hear the same thing twice?"

"Humor me." Gordon smiled and sat in the plush leather executive chair before he sipped his drink.

Lucky settled across from him and placed his

crystal glass next to the keys. "Growing up in foster care, it was nice to be a part of your family for a while. And Lizzie? She went along with all of this so you'd have a happy wedding. That's just who she is. She'd do anything for you, sir." He launched into the story, making sure to paint Lizzie in the best possible light, as she tended to be hard on herself.

Gordon poured another drink and downed it before he stared at Lucky. "Do you love my daughter?"

"Yes, sir."

"And Cale is here?" Gordon tapped his fingers together as if he was forming a steeple. "In my living room?"

"I had to make that right before the ceremony, same as Lizzie, and I knew you had to know the truth." It was the day of reckoning, but he could hold his head high, and did exactly that while he headed for the door. "Thank you for listening to my side of the story."

"You keep talking like the wedding's off." Gordon's words made him pause at the door. "No one's told me any differently."

Lucky faced him, the older rancher's face like stone, not giving away any expression. "It's on as scheduled?"

"As far as I know. Evie's the one in charge." Gordon frowned. "With everything that's happened, I haven't seen her in the past few hours.

My gear's at the guest house. I'd better change and then find Evie and Lizzie. See you later."

With a light step, Lucky hurried upstairs and was ready in record time. Even the bow tie, thanks to Will's previous lesson, cooperated. At last, the tide seemed to be turning in his favor.

He and Cale proceeded to the meadow, and what a pair they made with Lucky in Ben's tailored tuxedo and Cale in his boots and jeans. But this was a working ranch, and Lizzie would understand, once he explained Cale's sudden appearance.

Rodeo calves danced in his stomach. This was it. His wedding day. He fidgeted with his tuxedo lapel and thought about changing his clothes into something more comfortable. He decided against it, wanting to look his best for Lizzie, and for himself. There were times as a little boy he asked himself if he was worthy of love and a family. He'd cobbled together the best family, and he wanted Lizzie to be his wife. But before anything else happened, he had to talk to her and find out how she felt about her dad's reaction. That was only part of it. He wanted to scream from the top of the Ferris wheel he loved her and hoped she'd be willing to do the same. Love was within his grasp, and he wanted to claim it, along with their future.

He found Tammy with her arms full, muttering to herself. "First, it was happening in December, then it was happening at three, then it wasn't happening at three."

"Tammy?" Lucky approached the cook carefully, as she was balancing a long sheet cake. "Did I hear you right? The wedding's not at three?"

"Why do you think I'm taking the cake back to the house? The chocolate will melt out here." Tammy swept past him and loaded the cake into the van.

Lucky wobbled, the ground shaking under his feet. He would have preferred hearing the news from Lizzie, not Tammy, but it was true. The wedding was canceled.

Cale rushed over and supported Lucky's elbow. "I heard. I'm sorry, Lucky. Vivi and I would love to have you stay with us for a while."

The rodeo was where he belonged. "I have to be in Williams, Arizona, tomorrow morning." His legs steadied, and he found his phone. "Hold on a minute."

He texted Lizzie regarding the current status of the wedding. Cale stayed silent while Lucky waited. No reply. It was over.

"I'm calling Vivi. See if she can round up the neighbors to help for a few days while I go with you to the rodeo." Cale whipped out his phone and walked over to the front row of seats.

Lucky called Lizzie, and it went to voice mail. He needed more than fifteen seconds to say everything, but this would have to suffice. He poured out his heart. "I've worked my whole life for a chance at the finals, and I'm going to give it my all this weekend, but I'm coming back to Violet Ridge for you, for us." He swallowed and loosened his collar. "I understand why you called off the wedding, considering you told your dad and he listened to my side of it, but I sure would appreciate the honor of taking you out on a date Monday night. Just the two of us. Because I'm in love with you, and I'd like to court you the right way."

The new engagement and wedding ring he'd purchased in Denver earlier today on the drive with Cale weighed heavily in his pocket. He gave a long lingering glance at the arch of flowers with strands of small twinkle lights wound around the arbor and along the framework over the rows of seats. For a second, he saw what could have been the scene later today. Lizzie, looking beautiful in wedding dress with her auburn hair cascading over her shoulders. While her family would have been a bonus, and they were the reason he and Lizzie had even talked in the first place, they were no longer his driving motivation behind wanting to see Lizzie smile or hold her hand through the disappointments.

It was Lizzie herself, a strong and vibrant woman who worked as hard, if not harder, than anyone on this ranch. Being with her boosted his confidence and made him feel like he could conquer the world, or, at the very least, earn a spot at the year-end finals.

She made him feel worthy of her, regardless of his past.

His relationship with Lizzie might be hanging on by the thread of a rope, but it wasn't over, and neither was his shot at the finals. Even if the wedding wasn't happening today, the rodeo would still go on, and he'd give nothing less than his best.

LIZZIE LOOKED AT herself in the guesthouse mirror. Audrey was right. Her bridesmaid dress was the perfect wedding dress. The dusty pink set off her auburn hair, and the delicate embroidered flowers were exactly what she'd have picked out under different circumstances. Who'd have believed that the cowhand covered with dirt and smelling like cattle could transform into someone this beautiful who smelled like a rose garden in the space of two hours?

She turned and faced her sister-in-law and Evie, the women responsible for taking her in hand and delivering someone she hardly recognized in the mirror. "You two are amazing. Thank you."

Evie twisted the mascara wand into its case before embracing Lizzie. "And you, my darling stepdaughter, are also a natural wonder. What's more, you're family. I'd do anything for you or Jeff or

Ben." Then Evie reached out and hugged Nicole. "And you and yours."

Nicole plucked out a couple of tissues from the box and approached Lizzie, puckering her lips as a signal for her to blot her lipstick. Lizzie did as directed, and Nicole smiled. "Perfect." She faced Evie, her face blushing a rosy red. "It's still astonishing that my father-in-law married Evalynne."

"He married Evie." Lizzie shook her head. "Evalynne's a bonus."

She smiled at her stepmother, and everything clicked into place. Her family supported and loved her. That was what had drawn Lucky toward accepting her plus-one invitation after the fact. Unlike Jared, who'd been impressed with the Irwin family name and status, Lucky didn't stand on pretense. He'd stood in the creek with her until the calf was free. They'd been drenched and covered with mud, but his relief had been as clear as hers. He didn't brush off Zack and Audrey, but spent time with them, going so far as teaching them how to whittle. He was as happy with a stuffed animal from a carnival stall as he'd been when presented the keys to a luxurious mountain cabin.

Her family had taken in Lucky and, in doing so, given the two of them time and opportunity to find each other and fall in love. That moment on the Ferris wheel had changed everything. Lizzie drew in a deep breath and smoothed the pale pink dress.

"I have to find Lucky. There's something I have to say to him before the wedding."

While that had been her intent all day, the time was finally right. "See you soon."

A light knock at the door caused everyone to look in that direction. Gordon ducked his head into the room. "Is this a good time?"

Lizzie shook her head and gathered her skirt in her hands. "I have to find Lucky first. It can't wait."

Gordon entered the room, his tuxedo perfectly paired with his cowboy hat. He removed his hat and placed it on the dresser. "This can't, either. Can I have a minute with Elizabeth?"

"I'd best check on my family." Nicole brushed past him, and Evie kissed Gordon before leaving the room.

Lizzie tapped her foot, the tip of her cowboy boot coming into contact with the hardwood floor. The order of these conversations was out of whack. She had to talk to Lucky first. Afterward, they'd talk to her father together. From there? Who knew whether the wedding would occur even though she already knew she'd like nothing more than to marry the rodeo cowboy.

"Dad, this really—"

"I had an interesting conversation with Lucky an hour ago," Dad said. "He's a fine man."

One look at her father told her everything. "You know, then?" She gulped. "That I lied."

"I know Lucky's side of it. I'd like to hear yours."

She sank onto the bed, an icy chill running through her, while Dad sat next to her. "He did it for me." She squared her shoulders and told him everything, fully accepting her part in the charade. "I expect you're disappointed in me. If you want my resignation since I lied to you, I understand."

"That's a bit extreme, don't you think? The ranch will survive, and you're the right Irwin to make sure it does." He reached for her hand and held it in his own. "Lucky told me you didn't want to ruin my wedding. He was rather adamant I understand you went along with this so you wouldn't ruin my day."

"Actually, my pride started all of it. I didn't want everyone to think I couldn't get a date." Getting this off her chest felt like a boulder had lifted off her. "Then it snowballed."

Someone knocked, and Sabrina entered. "Have you seen Lucky?"

That was her entire goal for the day, and the one thing she hadn't accomplished. "No."

Dad stood and headed toward Sabrina. "I talked to him less than an hour ago. He was going to show his guest, Cale, around the ranch while I changed into my tuxedo."

"I thought I saw Lucky's trailer on the highway, heading south." Sabrina frowned and then smiled. "Ty told me I must be mistaken, and I obviously was."

That chill returned, and Lizzie shivered. Lucky's horse trailer/RV was too distinctive. "So he talked to you before you changed?" Dad nodded while Lizzie started putting the pieces together. "Did anyone tell Lucky we pushed the wedding back to five?"

"Evie notified the guests. Let me check with her." Dad rose and left the room. He returned with a grim expression. "Evie thought you told Lucky."

Lizzie entered the bathroom and searched for her phone. It wasn't there. First, the ring. Now her phone. She was losing things left and right, and now she might have lost the most important part of her life. *Lucky.*

Her jacket pocket. She'd left it in the tack room, the odor of the offending outerwear quite pronounced upon their return from the cattle meadow. Wasting no time, she excused herself and hurried to the stable, relieved she'd chosen boots for her wedding rather than heels. She found her phone and gasped at the number of texts and voice mails she missed. Quite a few of them were from Lucky.

Without further ado, she started listening to his voice mail, tuning him out as soon as he said he told her father everything. While she'd taken a shower, he'd discovered the wedding was off. Of course he headed to the next rodeo. He was gone. Without her.

There was only one person for whom she'd have left the Double I.

Lucky.

But he didn't ask her to go with him.

"He told me the same thing," Dad said.

She started at the sound of his voice. She turned around and found him there. "He told you what?" Her voice came out in a whisper. "That he was leaving and returning to the rodeo by himself."

"That he's in love with you." Dad stared at her with thoughtful deliberation. "You only heard the first part, didn't you? Play the message again."

Hadn't she learned anything over these past few weeks but to listen and gather all the facts before jumping to conclusions? She did as her father requested, and joy started spreading through her. "He loves me."

A goofy smile came over her, and she'd never felt this light. Chords of wedding music reached her ears, and her grin faded. It was time to face everyone.

"I'll make the announcement." Dad started for the stable doors.

Lizzie ran and caught up with him. "I got myself into this. I'll say something." She reached up and kissed her father's cheek. "But thanks for offering."

Guests were being seated, and Lizzie steeled herself as she approached the musicians. She whispered to them, and they stopped playing before she proceeded to the front. In the back, she saw her brothers and the rest of the family looking her way. When Jeff and his family arrived for Dad's wedding, she'd hidden in the stable. Now they were all here for her, and she loved them for the support.

Somehow, though, she had to tread carefully as she intended for Lucky to become a part of her family permanently.

"Hello." She stopped talking when a sea of faces looked at her. For a second, she wished she was saying this to Andromeda, but she could, and would, do this. There would be consequences because of the past few weeks, and she'd face them head-on.

"There's been a slight hitch in the proceedings. You see, I thought a date to my father's wedding would get my brother off my case, but instead, that led to a series of misunderstandings that created a false impression that Lucky and I were engaged. We weren't then, but that's not to say we might not become engaged and get married down the road. However, what we decide to do will be between us and it'll be for the right reasons. Today was the right outcome for the wrong reasons, so there won't be a wedding, but rest assured, this is only the beginning, not the end. Thank you."

She hurried into her father's arms, and her family surrounded her in an embrace of love. Her father released her, his eyes full of pride. "You handled that well."

She knew what else she had to do. "Dad, we're short-staffed without Roy, but I need to go talk to Lucky."

"I know." He smiled and nodded. "We'll manage for the weekend."

Audrey tugged on Lizzie's dress, tears in her eyes. "Does this mean I can't call him Uncle Lucky? I want to say goodbye."

"I was going to give this to him for your wedding present," Zack said as he reached into his pocket and pulled out a piece of wood that Lizzie thought sort of resembled an elephant.

Zack handed it to her, and her heart almost burst with how much Zack had grown since he'd arrived. "It's beautiful."

"I've always wanted to see a rodeo," Nicole said, putting her hand on her sister-in-law's arm. "We're supposed to leave tomorrow night, but we can go home on Sunday instead. I hear there's a rodeo this weekend in Arizona we should attend. Show our support for a certain contestant."

Tears formed in Lizzie's eyes at Nicole's unexpected request. While a formidable lawyer, and more than a match for her brother, Nicole had always seemed distant. Once Lizzie got to know her better, she understood her sister-in-law's fear that she didn't belong here. With time, she was learning everyone accepted her, and she was more at ease. The important thing was how much she loved Jeff, her kids and her career. She and Nicole had a lot in common, and Lizzie could see them building a friendship on that foundation.

Lizzie squeezed the elephant and caught sight of her bare ring finger. As much as she'd like nothing better than to leave for the rodeo and Lucky's side immediately, she needed to do something important first, and enlisted her family's help to get it done.

CHAPTER SEVENTEEN

THE NEXT DAY, Lucky opened Butterscotch's grooming kit at the stall assigned to his American quarter horse at the rodeo fairgrounds. With extra care, considering he was running on little, if any, sleep, he cleaned the horse's hooves and then selected the currycomb from the leather kit. Next, he loosened the dirt and dust from the trailer ride to Arizona. The chore was rhythmic and soothing, something he needed since Lizzie hadn't returned his voice mail. He should have found her and confronted her with his feelings right there rather than relying on Gordon's and Tammy's statements.

The hardest part about leaving early was competing tonight. Being distracted in a rodeo arena with an energetic calf was never a good idea.

Should he forfeit his event and head back to the ranch a day early, rather than risk injury in the ring, since his mind wasn't in the best place? He needed the points if he had any chance of making the finals, but there was always next year. A relationship with Lizzie? That was once in a lifetime.

Taking special care of Butterscotch's sensitive shoulders, he dislodged the dirt from the flank and combed in the direction of the hair growth.

The tan horse swished his tail, and Lucky finished his task. He swapped out the comb for a soft body brush. "This will make you shine tonight." His gelding gave a soft snuff, as if setting Lucky to rights about his ability to captivate the crowd no matter how he looked. "Humor me."

"Anytime."

"That settles it, Butterscotch." Lucky reeled and rested his head against his gelding's flank. "I'm going to pull out. I'm hearing her voice."

Something brushed his shoulder, and he almost fell backward. He turned and found Lizzie there, a vision in her red cowboy hat and boots. "Now you're seeing me, too, but I assure you I'm quite real."

His mouth dropped. She was a long way from her beloved Double I. Could it be that, after all these years, someone didn't want to wait another day to see him? Tell him she loved him? While he loved Cale and Vivi, Will and Sabrina, all members of his adopted family, no one had ever dropped everything just for him. Instead, they'd patiently waited for him to realize he wanted them in their lives. Sometimes, though, it was nice to be asked.

Lizzie held out her hand, and the diamond engagement ring sat nestled in her palm. His heart sank. "You found it."

She didn't drive all this way for a big revelation or to join him on the tour. She'd come to return the ring.

Once he accepted it, it would be official. Their fake engagement would come to its fitting end.

"I would have arrived last night, only a few hours behind you, but I wanted—no, needed—to find this and return it to you." She pushed her hand in his direction.

"It's yours." He curled her fingers around the ring. It wasn't his, and in a way, it never had been. "Where was it?"

"We scoured the stable. I was about to give up when I remember I refilled the feed buckets that day. I moved the trough, and it was lodged between the bin and the wall," Lizzie said with a smile. "I left a mess to clean up on Monday."

So much for their date. "You could have left the ring with Will rather than coming all this way to tell me you're busy in person."

"I came all this way to attend a rodeo. You see, the man I love is going to win his event, and I've never even seen him compete in person. He's coming home to Violet Ridge, and on Monday night, we'll talk about every minute of the rodeo on our date." She wiggled the ring onto the fourth finger of her right hand.

Wait! Did she just say she loved him? He almost swooned. "Did it take canceling our wedding to make you realize you love me?"

"I didn't cancel our wedding. I'm hoping it was only postponed." Lizzie stopped talking when other rodeo contestants entered the stable and started grooming their horses. Her gaze darted around as if she was seeing where she was for the first time. "Is there somewhere else we can talk? Don't get me wrong, I love Butterscotch and any stable is like a second home, but we need some privacy. Besides, I have something important to show you."

Curiosity over what that could be compelled him to pick up his grooming kit. He followed her outside the stable, only to find the Irwin family waiting for him.

Audrey launched herself at him. "I couldn't go back to Boston without giving you a hug."

Zack hugged Lucky and presented him with a small wood carving. "It's an elephant. They say elephants don't forget, so I wanted to make you something so you wouldn't forget me."

His throat constricted at the gesture, and he soaked in everyone's presence, making another forever memory. Grandma Eloise's eyes sparkled, Jeff and Nicole nodded his way, and Evie smiled. He didn't know Ben well enough to read his expression, but he looked forward to making his acquaintance. Lizzie hugged his arm close to his side. "Dad is taking over stable duties today."

"And loving every minute." Evie's reassuring tone matched her demeanor, and she reached out her hand to him, keys transferring from her grip to his. "Gordon and I agreed you should have these. The cabin is yours whenever you visit Lizzie. Or even if you're spending time with Sabrina and Ty, or Will and Kelsea."

His heart swelled. "All of you came for me? Even after I lied? Even after the wedding didn't go on as planned?"

Jeff stepped forward and patted him on the back. "Once you save an Irwin, you're part of the family. Lizzie didn't tell you that?"

She hadn't told him many things yet, but Lucky planned on listening to her every day for the rest of his life. That, and ride horses with her, and kiss her. Often.

Somehow, she and her family had made room in their hearts for him, and that sent him clear near over the moon.

"Lizzie and I have a lot to talk about. Why don't you all make yourselves comfortable in my trailer? Especially you, Grandma Eloise."

The older woman smiled and tapped her cane in the dirt. "Evie arranged for a private flight back to Texas tomorrow. I'll be in the stands for your competition tonight, but it was a long drive and I don't mind resting a bit." She fluffed up her hair. "That way, Bob will see me at my best."

Lucky leaned forward and kissed her leathery,

wrinkled cheek. "I have a feeling that Bob always sees the best of you."

"You flatterer, you." She hugged Lizzie first before embracing him. "You take good care of my step-granddaughter."

Lucky ushered everyone to his trailer and didn't try to hide the stuffed horse Lizzie won for him from its position of honor at his dinette table. As a matter of fact, there were more signs of his personal life around the trailer now than a few weeks ago: the book JR had lent him, his whittling knife on the nightstand and a framed picture of him and Lizzie from Gordon and Evie's wedding. Sometime in the past few weeks, he'd allowed himself the privilege of attaching sentimental value to objects, ones he'd keep and display, knowing he wouldn't have to shove everything in a garbage bag at a moment's notice. Audrey and Zack were busy bouncing on his bed when he escaped outside with Lizzie. Having her family's support was everything, but there was one person's support he valued above theirs, and he was holding her hand.

THE FAIRGROUNDS BUSTLED with the activity that preceded the start of the rodeo. Lizzie walked alongside Lucky to a trail where silver aspens provided plenty of shade, their leafy branches extending overhead. Black-eyed Susans and marigolds lined the side of the trail, their sweet fragrance a perfect counterpart to the coolness of this last day of August.

She stopped and grasped his hand. "Why did you tell Butterscotch you're going to forfeit? I know how much this means to you."

"There are other rodeos, but only one you."

His words, so simple, carried love in every syllable, and she would make sure he felt that same love and support as long as she had breath in her lungs.

"You'd have driven back to Violet Ridge for me?" She released him and twisted the ring on her right finger. One look at him revealed the answer.

"I love you, Elizabeth Irwin. You'll always be Lizzie to me."

He bent toward her, his hand reaching up and cupping her chin, his callused fingers soft against her skin. He kissed her and the part of her that was anxious, always seeking action on the ranch, settled into a peaceful calm. Somewhere along the line, their relationship had changed from nothing to everything. She let go of the past and embraced the future, the sweetness of this kiss flooding her with him. Lucky loved her, and she'd make sure he knew every day how much love was in his life.

After a few minutes, she touched her forehead to his. "I love you, Lucas Harper, and I'm looking forward to our first date on Monday night."

He laughed, that slow, deep chuckle she wanted to hear often, the one that made her feel all warm and shivery inside. "It seems as though we did this backward. Fell in love and then started dating."

She leaned her head on his shoulder. "You should know I'm not much for half measures."

He tilted his head until it touched hers. "That's what makes you undeniably you."

While she could stay like this for quite a while, she faced him. "I'm staying to watch you compete, of course. We all are."

"Butterscotch and I would be honored." His cheeks reddened as though he wasn't used to people coming out for him.

"The Irwin family is here in force. Audrey and Zack talked Jeff and Nicole into attending before they head back to Boston, and Grandma Eloise will tell her husband all about your performance. Ben hasn't been to a rodeo in years. I think he misses Violet Ridge."

His lips met hers, and she knew without any doubt that someday soon Lucky would be an official part of the Irwin family. But that was the tip of the saddle. Best of all, he loved her for herself. This was the real thing, and she reveled in the joy of his kiss.

EPILOGUE

Eight months later

LUCKY HAD NEVER seen the Silver Horseshoe look so festive as it did on this spring evening. Will and Kelsea were welcoming the new season with a festive celebration. He and Lizzie also suspected there'd be an announcement from the couple about a future addition to their family.

The weather was acting in true Colorado fashion, as he learned to expect from his adopted state. Last week, a blanket of snow greeted him as he and Lizzie walked from the guesthouse to the stable. Today, sunshine had flooded the paddock with warm weather, causing him to shed his jacket before noon.

Fairy lights lit up the barn, which had been transformed into a party space. Half of Violet Ridge mingled inside and outside the barn, as people everywhere enjoyed a bowl of chili or huckleberry cobbler. He accepted two drinks, a beer for himself and a ginger ale for his wife of two months.

Even in a crowd this size, he had no trouble spotting Lizzie, radiant in her red cowboy hat and jeans. This morning, they'd waited together for five minutes until the pregnancy test confirmed they were expecting. He didn't care whether it was a boy or a girl, just as long as the little one was healthy. He'd waited a long time for a family, before he realized he'd had one all along. Now he cherished both of his families, his honorary one of his best friends and the one who possessed his heart.

Sabrina came over and eyed the drinks. "Lizzie's drinking ginger ale?" She glanced Lizzie's way with a grin. "This might be presumptuous, but is Genie gaining another cousin? Are Evie and Gordon going to be grandparents again?"

He and Will and Sabrina were closer than siblings, and together for the long haul. "Stay tuned. Tonight's Will and Kelsea's night, though."

Will headed their way, a goofy smile on his face, and Lucky met Sabrina's gaze. They both laughed, and Will's grin was replaced with a glare that was anything but menacing.

"Are you two planning something?" Will asked, grinning.

"Why, Will." Sabrina crooked her arm through his. "Whatever gave you that idea?"

"That gleam in your eye, my dear Sabrina."
Will arched an eyebrow.

"We're just wondering whether you and Kelsea
are going to make the announcement about the
baby before Snow and Flake break loose of the
pen and disrupt the festivities." Sabrina laughed
while talking about Will's infamous pair of goats,
who loved Kelsea but gave Will a rough time.

"Ha, ha." Will pretended to laugh and then
stilled. "Wait. How did you know she's pregnant?
We just got off the phone with Kelsea's father and
sister a few minutes before the party started."

Lucky leaned against the barn post and smiled.
"You know how they say expectant women glow?"
He couldn't help but sneak a glance at Lizzie, who
was positively radiant, before facing Will. "You're
glowing, Will."

"Expectant fathers don't glow." His friend
glowered at them and then wiped his face. "That's
just sweat."

Will's uncle Barry approached the trio and
threw himself at Will in a huge embrace. "I knew
it. I knew Kelsea was pregnant. Rocket's been
guarding her at all costs. I'm going to be a great-
uncle. This is big, really, really big. Snow and
Flake are going to be guardian goats." His eyes
lit up, and he rubbed his hands together. "That's
it. At last I have my million-dollar idea. Guardian goats. I can see it now."

Barry's wife, Regina, came over, shaking her

head, her eyes twinkling. "Come with me, my darling husband, and tell me all about it." She shepherded him away, but not before turning her head and whispering that she'd dissuade him before the night ended.

As soon as the pair was out of listening distance, Lucky burst out laughing with his friends, taking care not to spill the drinks.

Will shook his head and then sighed. "Oh, well. If Uncle Barry hadn't had a big idea, the three of us wouldn't be here now."

Lucky nodded, knowing too well that Barry Sullivan was the real reason Kelsea had arrived at the Silver Horseshoe. Then Sabrina had arrived at the ranch, seeking a job so she could support her unborn child. Will had arranged for an interview at the Double I, where Sabrina had worked as the barn manager until Ty reappeared in her life. And now, the Double I was his home base, where he and Lizzie had taken up residence in the guesthouse and where they'd bring home their little pardner in approximately seven and a half months. Making his life complete was the offer Ty and Sabrina extended to become a full partner in their rodeo academy. He'd called Lizzie on the spot and accepted the job without a second thought.

"I don't know about that." Sabrina tugged at one of her long brown braids. "You two are family, so we'd still be together. It's just everyone else wouldn't be here tonight."

She grinned, and Lucky laughed. The three of them were family, through thick and thin, and he loved they'd be alongside him and Lizzie when the time was right for their announcement. If they'd learned anything since their fake engagement, it was communicating with each other and their friends.

The twang of country music came out of the speakers, and guests started tapping their boots along with the rhythm. Ty came over and winked at Sabrina. "While Evie and Gordon have Genie for the evening, may I have this dance with my beautiful wife?"

"Thought you'd never ask. I do love a good dance with my husband." Sabrina kissed Ty and then waved at Will and Lucky.

Will laughed until Kelsea sidled up to him and nudged him. "One dance, and then I'll make sure Snow and Flake are properly penned for the evening and can't get out."

Will tipped his hat, as if he had to give careful consideration to his reputation as a gruff cowboy, but he wasn't fooling Lucky or Kelsea. "Deal."

The two ambled away, Kelsea's sunshine the perfect balance to Will's rougher edges. Lucky tightened his grip on the drinks, but didn't have a long way to walk as Lizzie met him in the middle.

"I thought I'd have to send a search party for

you." She accepted her ginger ale with a smile, lifting her glass for good measure.

Lucky sipped his beer and then placed his half-full glass on the closest tray table. "Never. I know a good thing when I see it." Lucky held out his arm. "And you are the best."

She smiled and then situated her empty glass next to his. Her ruby engagement ring with a cluster of diamonds surrounding the oval gem gleamed in the glow of the fairy lights. "Dance with me?"

"I'd be delighted to have this dance. Lizzie, you always keep me on my toes."

They glided to the makeshift dance area. She fit perfectly in his arms and nestled her head against his shoulder while the slow song played. He'd waited his life for a family, and now he had two. Besides, Lizzie was worth the wait, and so was the newest member they'd greet later this year.

Life didn't get any better than this moment with the woman he loved in his arms. He was a lucky man, indeed.

* * * * *